DESPERATE MEASURES

BOOKS BY STUART WOODS

FICTION

Desperate Measures[†] • Turbulence[†] • Shoot First[†] • Unbound[†]
Quick & Dirty[†] • Indecent Exposure[†] • Fast & Loose[†] • Below the Belt[†]
Sex, Lies & Serious Money[†] • Dishonorable Intentions[†]
Family Jewels[†] • Scandalous Behavior[†] • Foreign Affairs[†]
Naked Greed[†] • Hot Pursuit[†] • Insatiable Appetites[†] • Paris Match[†]
Cut and Thrust[†] • Carnal Curiosity[†] • Standup Guy[†]
Doing Hard Time[†] • Unintended Consequences[†]
Collateral Damage[†] • Severe Clear[†] • Unnatural Acts[†] • D.C. Dead[†]
Son of Stone[†] • Bel-Air Dead[†] • Strategic Moves[†]
Santa Fe Edge[§] • Lucid Intervals[†] • Kisser[†] • Hothouse Orchid[*]
Loitering with Intent[†] • Mounting Fears[‡] • Hot Mahogany[†]
Santa Fe Dead[§] • Beverly Hills Dead • Shoot Him If He Runs[†]
Fresh Disasters[†] • Short Straw[§] • Dark Harbor[†] • Iron Orchid[*]
Two-Dollar Bill[†] • The Prince of Beverly Hills • Reckless Abandon[†]
Capital Crimes[‡] • Dirty Work[†] • Blood Orchid[*] • The Short Forever[†]
Orchid Blues[*] • Cold Paradise[†] • L.A. Dead[†] • The Run[‡]
Worst Fears Realized[†] • Orchid Beach[*] • Swimming to Catalina[†]
Dead in the Water[†] • Dirt[†] • Choke • Imperfect Strangers
Heat • Dead Eyes • L.A. Times • Santa Fe Rules[§]
New York Dead[†] • Palindrome • Grass Roots[‡] • White Cargo
Deep Lie[‡] • Under the Lake • Run Before the Wind[‡] • Chiefs[‡]

COAUTHORED BOOKS

The Money Shot[**] (with Parnell Hall)
Barely Legal[††] (with Parnell Hall)
Smooth Operator[**] (with Parnell Hall)

TRAVEL

A Romantic's Guide to the Country Inns of Britain and Ireland (1979)

MEMOIR

Blue Water, Green Skipper

[*]A Holly Barker Novel
[†]A Stone Barrington Novel
[‡]A Will Lee Novel
[§]An Ed Eagle Novel
[**]A Teddy Fay Novel
[††]A Herbie Fisher Novel

DESPERATE MEASURES

STUART WOODS

G. P. Putnam's Sons | New York

PUTNAM

G. P. PUTNAM'S SONS
Publishers Since 1838
An imprint of Penguin Random House LLC
375 Hudson Street
New York, New York 10014

Library of Congress Cataloging-in-Publication Data

Names: Woods, Stuart, author.
Title: Desperate measures / Stuart Woods.
Description: New York : G. P. Putnam's Sons, 2018. | Series: A Stone
    Barrington novel
Identifiers: LCCN 2018022152 (print) | LCCN 2018022724 (ebook) | ISBN
    9780735219229 (Hardcover) | ISBN 9780735219243 (ePub) | ISBN
Subjects: | GSAFD: Mystery fiction. | Suspense fiction.
Classification: LCC PS3573.O642 (ebook) | LCC PS3573.O642 D47 2018 (print) |
    DDC 813/.54—dc23
LC record available at https://lccn.loc.gov/2018022152
p.   cm.

Printed in the United States of America
10 9 8 7 6 5 4 3 2 1

BOOK DESIGN BY KATY RIEGEL

DESPERATE MEASURES

1

THE EARLY-MORNING CONVERSATION had taken place in bed in London, after drinking brandy with guests until the wee hours. So if Stone had once remembered what was said, he had now forgotten it.

He struggled to put it together in his mind during their flight from his house, Windward Hall, in England, back to Teterboro, but he had failed. There wasn't much conversation on the airplane, but he put that down to Kelly's hangover, which must have been as monumental as his, since she had matched him drink for drink. Once they were back at his house in New York, they had dinner and went to bed early.

He woke at seven the following morning, a preordered breakfast on a tray resting on his belly. There were empty dishes on her side of the bed and sounds of packing from her dressing room. His eggs were cold, but he ate them anyway, to settle his stomach.

Kelly came out of the dressing room naked, with predictable results. When they were spent, she stood up.

"I told you yesterday that I'd gotten a chopper ride back to Langley today, didn't I?"

Of course she had, he could remember that much. "Surely, not at this hour," he said.

"I'm to be there at nine-forty-five sharp for a ten o'clock departure, and I can't miss it. Fred can drive me to the heliport."

"No," he said, getting up. "I'll drive you myself."

"Thank you," she said, then went back into the dressing room.

HE SURVEYED HIS FACE in the bathroom mirror and was surprised to find that he didn't look like a man with a hangover. What was more, he didn't *feel* like a man with a hangover. He felt perfectly normal, except that he still couldn't remember their conversation in London. He shaved, showered, dressed, and called down to Fred, his factotum. "I won't need you this morning," he said. "I'll drive myself."

"As you wish, Mr. Barrington," Fred replied.

IN THE CAR KELLY SAID, "Fred is going to collect my other luggage at the hotel and send it to me." She had a suite in a residential hotel not far from his house.

"Plenty of room at my house," Stone replied.

"Stone," she said, "do you remember our conversation in London?"

"Of course," Stone lied.

"Because you're not behaving like a man who's being abandoned."

That rocked him. "'Abandoned'?"

"Do you remember my telling you that I'm returning to the Agency—and that they want me to live down there in a place they've found for me?"

"Yes," he lied again, "and I'm very sad about it." That last part wasn't a lie; he suddenly felt overwhelmingly sad.

"It's sweet of you to say so, but I think you'll have forgotten me before long."

Stone knew a cue when he heard one. "I'll never forget you," he said.

"Oh, shut up!" Kelly cried, beginning to weep. "Did you expect me to pass up a promotion and give up a career I've put fourteen years into?"

"I'm not sure what I expected," he said. And that wasn't a lie, either.

He drove to the East Side Heliport, was admitted to the ramp, and stopped beside the experimental Sikorsky X-2 helicopter the Central Intelligence Agency was testing for the builder. The pilot stowed Kelly's luggage, assisted her to a rear seat, and handed her a headset.

"Well," she said to Stone. "I could never say it wasn't fun."

"Neither could I," Stone said. He kissed her, then closed and locked the door. The rotors began to turn, and he backed away as the machine lifted off and pointed itself to the south.

He was still backing up when he bumped into someone, hard. He turned to find a miniature airline pilot standing behind him. "I'm so sorry," he said.

"You shouldn't walk backward at a heliport," she replied. She was, in fact, not a miniature at all, but a small woman in an airline captain's uniform.

"What can I do to make it up to you?" he asked, for she was quite beautiful, too.

"If you have a car, you can give me a lift," she replied.

"I do, and I'd be delighted. Where to: Westchester? New Jersey? Los Angeles?"

"Lexington Avenue will do," she said.

He took her single bag and walked her to the Bentley.

"I hope this is not a joke car," she said.

"It's a perfectly serious car," he replied, stowing her bag in the trunk and opening the front passenger door for her.

"Are you a chauffeur?" she asked.

"Only for you," he replied, getting into the driver's seat. He held out a hand. "I'm Stone Barrington."

She took the hand. "I'm Faith Barnacle," she said.

"Faith?"

"It's better than Hope or Charity, isn't it? I'm the victim of a pious Catholic mother."

"It's certainly the best of the three. I'm trying to think of a barnacle joke, but I can't remember one."

"That's all right, I would have heard it in high school, anyway."

Stone got the car started and moving. "Where on Lex?"

"East Forty-seventh Street," she replied. "It's one of those seedy hostelries where they store airline employees when they're not being used."

"For whom do you fly?"

"Pan American Airlines," she said.

"Didn't they go out of business a couple of decades ago?"

"I just wanted to see if you were paying attention. I fly for Trans-Continent, a charter airline. We've only got three airplanes, and I fly them all."

"How many pilots do they employ?"

"Somewhere between a dozen and a dozen and a half, depending on the season and the day of the week."

Stone pulled up in front of the hotel and popped the trunk, so the doorman could take her bag.

"How does the week ahead look?" he asked.

"I'm here for three nights."

"Will you have dinner with me tonight?"

"Thank you, yes. It's either you or *Jeopardy!*, and I hate *Jeopardy!*"

He gave her his card. "I'm just a few blocks downtown. Come for a drink at my house, and we'll go out from there."

"At what hour?"

"Six-thirty?"

"Fine. How shall I dress?"

"Nicely."

"What are you wearing?"

"A necktie."

"This is going to be interesting," she said, getting out and waving goodbye.

Driving back to his house, Stone suddenly recalled, in great detail, his conversation with Kelly in London. It made him sad again.

2

STONE PULLED THE CAR into the garage and went into his office. Bob, his Labrador retriever, and Joan Robertson, his secretary, greeted him with equal enthusiasm.

"I perceive that you are alone," Joan said.

"You are very perceptive. Bob doesn't seem to mind." Bob was offering him his favorite toy, a red dragon. "Nobody wants that dreadful toy," Stone said, scratching his ears.

"He wasn't going to give it to you," Joan said. "He just wants you to know he has it."

"Do I have anything to do?" Stone asked.

"No, I've done it all," she replied.

"Then I'll find something else to do," he said, slipping into his chair. He picked up the phone and dialed.

"Bacchetti."

"How do?" Stone asked.

"I do pretty good," Dino replied. They had been partners

many years before on the NYPD; now Dino was the police commissioner for New York City.

"Come for a drink at six-thirty, then let's have dinner."

"I take it you're back on the right side of the Atlantic."

"If I'm not, I will be by cocktail time."

"Are you bringing what's-her-name?"

"No. What's-her-name has taken flight from my existence; Lance Cabot has lured her back to her nest." Lance was the director of the Central Intelligence Agency.

"Smart girl," Dino said. "I'll check with Viv. If I don't call you back, we'll see you at six-thirty."

"Done," Stone said, then hung up and buzzed Joan.

"Yes, boss?"

"You must have something for me to do," he said.

"Do you do windows?" she asked.

"I do not."

"Then there's no hope for you. Go watch those political programs you love so much."

Stone hung up, yawned, and turned on the TV.

FAITH WAS PUNCTUAL. He met her at the door and walked her through the living room to his study. "Another couple is joining us shortly," he said. "Let's get a head start on them. What would you like?"

"A bourbon on the rocks," she said. "Knob Creek, if you have it."

"I have it in abundance," Stone said, pouring them each one. They sat down before the fire.

"This is a very nice room," she said.

"Thank you."

"And the living room was very nice, too, as is the house and the neighborhood."

"On behalf of the neighbors, I thank you."

"How do you live so well?"

"Well, I got the house cheap: I inherited it from a great-aunt. My father, who was a cabinetmaker and furniture designer, made all the paneling, shelves, and did the woodwork."

"I see," she said, "sort of. Did you get the Bentley cheap?"

"I got a pretty good deal on it."

"What do you do?"

"I'm a partner in a law firm, Woodman & Weld."

"Never heard of it."

"There's no reason you should have, unless you're suing or being sued or want an estate managed or a will written."

"None of the above," she said.

"How long have you been flying?" Stone asked.

"Since I was sixteen," she said. "I went to high school in the town where I was born—Delano, Georgia—then graduated from the aviation university, Embry Riddle, in Florida, with a diploma and an ATP license. I flew packages and freight, was first officer on a Lear, then got in a lot of single-pilot jet time in Citations. I flew for an airline, right seat for eight or nine years, then I joined Trans-Continent and made captain as soon as they needed one."

"Total time?"

"A little over fifteen thousand hours. You sound like a pilot."

"I am. I fly a CJ3-Plus."

"Nice. I flew one for a charter service for two years. Total time?"

"About four thousand hours, half of it in Citations. Lately, I've been flying a borrowed Citation Latitude."

"That's a great airplane. My charter service ordered three of them and sent me to Flight Safety for a type rating. Then, the day I got my rating, the charter service went bust. They reneged on their order for the three Latitudes, and I had to buy my own ticket home."

"That's a sad story, but at least you got the type rating."

The doorbell rang, but Stone kept his seat. "They'll let themselves in," he said. "Their names are Dino and Viv Bacchetti." He spelled the name for her.

The Bacchettis spilled into the room and demanded liquor. Stone introduced them to Faith, then did the pouring of Dino's scotch and Viv's martini.

"So, how did you two meet?" Viv asked.

"She body-blocked me at the heliport today," Stone said.

"He was walking backward and nearly knocked me down," Faith explained.

"Why were you both at the heliport?" Dino asked.

"Stone was seeing a friend off, and I had hitched a ride into the city from JFK on a chopper," Faith said. "The pilot's a friend."

"Sounds like fate at work," Viv said.

THEY FINISHED THEIR DRINKS, then left the house and got into Dino's car. "Patroon," he said.

"What's Patroon?" Faith asked.

"A very good restaurant," Stone replied.

"Dino," she asked, "why does your car have a blue light on top?"

"It's a police car," Dino replied.

"In a manner of speaking," Stone said. "Not every police officer has this ride, but Dino, for reasons I've never understood, is the police commissioner for the City of New York."

"I've never felt so safe," Faith said.

THEY ARRIVED AT THE RESTAURANT, were greeted and seated by the owner, Ken Aretsky, and ordered drinks. When they had been delivered, Dino took a deep breath. "Faith, this is not a good time to feel safe."

"What are you talking about, Dino?" Stone asked.

"While you were swanning around London, we had two homicides on the Upper East Side."

"Only two?" Stone asked. "Why is that remarkable?"

"Because both were small, blond, and beautiful," Dino said. "Like you, Faith."

3

S TONE AND DINO had worked homicide together, so Stone thought about this the way a cop would. "Anything else in common?"

"The manner of their deaths," Dino said.

"Which was?"

"I don't want to talk about it."

Stone frowned. Dino never didn't want to talk about anything at all. Stone took a breath to ask another question, but Dino gave him the slightest shake of his head, and he didn't ask it.

"Come on, Dino." This was Faith talking, and she looked as though she was going to get an answer.

"I haven't had enough to drink to tell you about that," Dino replied.

Faith was going to persist, but Stone said, "Drop it. He's serious."

"Well, I have a license to carry," Faith said, "so I will."

"A New York City license?" Dino asked.

"New York, Florida, and California," Faith replied. "It's an option for airline pilots. I have to shoot twice a month, requalify once a month, and pay for my own gun and ammunition, but it makes me feel better. I fly charters, and sometimes the groups get rowdy. I've had them banging on the cockpit door."

"Have you ever had to draw your weapon?" Dino asked.

"Only once. I didn't point it at anybody, and there wasn't one in the chamber. Still, its presence had a calming effect on the two-hundred-and-fifty-pound guy who wanted to fly the airplane."

"Good for you," Dino said. "That shows judgment and restraint. Would you like to be a police officer? I'll give you a good assignment right out of the Academy."

"Do you have an assignment available that involves flying an airplane?"

"How about a helicopter?"

Faith shook her head. "They scare me shitless."

"Me, too," Dino said, "and that's just riding in them."

"Well, this is a first," Stone said. "Dino has never offered my date a job."

"I'm serious," Dino said.

"I know," Stone replied.

"Thanks, Dino," Faith said. "I'm flattered, but I like wings on my aircraft, and I enjoy travel."

"You should hire her, Stone," Viv said. "You've been flying the Latitude with pro pilots."

"Only because it's illegal for me to fly it alone. Anyway, it's not my airplane; it belongs to your boss." Viv worked for Mike Freeman, at Strategic Services, the world's second-largest security company. Viv was also a retired NYPD detective. Stone had recently swapped airplanes with Mike—on a temporary basis—when he had wanted to fly to London, and he would have to give back the Latitude soon.

Dinner came, and they enjoyed it.

DINO'S CAR DROPPED them off after dinner. "Nightcap?" Stone asked Faith.

"Sure."

They went into the study.

"You haven't seen the master suite, have you?"

"No," she replied, "but I have the distinct feeling I'm about to."

He poured them each a drink. "Right this way," he said.

They took the elevator to the top floor, and Stone showed Faith into the master suite. Shortly after that, he gave her a tour of the bed.

"Well," she said afterward, toying with the bed's remote control until it sat her up. "When my day started in Miami this morning I didn't expect to finish it in your bed."

"I'm glad to be of service," Stone said.

"You serve well," she replied. "There's something I have to explain to you, though."

"You don't have to explain anything to me, unless you have an angry husband tucked away somewhere."

"I have an angry *ex*-husband," she said, "but he's well out of the picture, in Chicago, and I hardly ever fly there. But he's not the problem."

"All right, what do you need to explain?"

"I'm a three-time girl," she said.

Stone shook his head. "I'm not following."

"I'm not interested in getting married," she said, "not even interested in having a regular boyfriend."

"Okay," Stone said.

"Maybe not," she replied. "The way I keep either of those things from happening is, I never fuck any man more than three times." She sighed. "Not that I don't *love* sex."

"How did you happen to select the number three?" Stone asked.

"Three times is a turning point: either I'm sick of a man by then or I want to continue to fuck him. The way I keep from continuing is by stopping at three times."

"We'll see," Stone replied.

"I'm not kidding," she said.

"It's too early to make that decision," Stone pointed out.

"You're right, of course; we've got two more times to go."

Stone reached for her. "Let's use number two now," he said.

"Good idea," she replied. "We can save ourselves for number three."

He pulled her on top of him and slipped inside of her.

She smiled. "No lubrication required," she said.

They moved together. "This is awfully good," Stone said. "Seems like a shame to limit it to three times, when we're just learning about each other."

"Oh, don't worry," she said, moving faster, "by the time we've done it three times, we'll know all there is to know about each other."

He rolled over on top of her without losing his place. "I think you're the smallest woman I've ever made love to," he said.

"Do you like that about me?"

"There isn't anything I don't like about you, except the three-strikes-and-you're-out thing."

"This isn't a strike," she said, "but it's a ball."

"Well put," Stone said, sensing that she was about to come and moving faster.

Faith began to make the right noises, and in a moment, they came together.

WHEN THEY RECOVERED THEMSELVES, Faith produced an iPhone from the purse at her bedside and began to tap it.

"Checking your e-mail?" Stone asked.

"That and the *New York Times* online," she said. "Oh, Jesus."

"What's wrong?"

"I just found out why Dino didn't want to tell me how those two girls died."

4

S TONE GOT READY to go down to his office while Faith was still in bed, reading the print edition of the *Times*.

"Are you going to tell me how those girls died?" he asked.

"No."

"Why not?"

"Because, like Dino, I don't care to discuss it."

"I can read the paper, too, you know."

"Then read it, but that subject is not going to pass my lips."

"As you wish," Stone said. "I've got to go downstairs and at least pretend to work. Can you amuse yourself?"

She smiled. "That won't be necessary," she said, "you've already amused me."

"You've got two more nights in town, right?"

"And you know how to count!"

"I do. What would you like to do with them?"

"Well, I think it's best if I go back to my hotel room and watch *Jeopardy!* tonight, but we can have dinner tomorrow night."

"Why not both nights?"

"Because we have only one fuck left, and I'd rather it be departure sex, so I'll have something to think about on my Saturday flight."

"You're determined to stick to that rule, then?"

"Unalterably."

"As you wish," Stone replied and headed for the door.

"Stone," she called, stopping him in his tracks. "I absolutely *love* fucking you. Doesn't that count for something?"

"Sure, but it would count more if you weren't counting."

"When I've finished the *Times* I'll shower and let myself out," she said.

"Do you do the crossword?"

"No."

Stone separated the Arts section from the paper and gave her the rest. "Six-thirty here, tomorrow evening? I'll have Fred drive you to the airport Saturday morning."

"I don't have to be there until noon," she said.

"See you tomorrow evening." He ran down the stairs for exercise and went to his desk.

Joan came in with the mail. "Have you read the *Times*, yet?"

"Sort of, Faith commandeered it."

"Terrible what's happening to those girls on the East Side, isn't it?"

"That's what I hear, but neither Dino nor Faith would tell me about it. Will you?"

"It's just as well you don't know," Joan replied. "You'd toss your breakfast."

"I've got a strong stomach," Stone said. "I don't know why nobody believes that."

"It's not as strong as you think," Joan said, then went back to her office.

STONE HAD JUST FINISHED the *Times* crossword when Joan buzzed him. "Mike Freeman on one," she said.

Stone picked up the phone. "Mike?"

"Good morning and welcome back."

"Thank you, good to be back."

"Did you enjoy the Citation Latitude?"

"I did. It's a lovely airplane, and I enjoyed all the space. I actually got some sleep on the transatlantic."

"How would you like to make our swap deal permanent?" Mike asked.

"Are you serious?"

"Well, not permanent without some money changing hands."

"Why would you want to swap?"

"Because I've discovered that we're using your CJ3-Plus a lot more than we were using the Latitude. It has just the right range and capacity to meet more than ninety percent of our needs. On the other hand, you have lots of longer flights: Key West, Santa Fe, L.A. We've put only about two hundred hours on the Latitude, not counting your transatlantic, and we've got the Gulfstreams for longer flights."

"How much money are we talking about?"

Mike mentioned a number.

Stone mentioned a smaller number.

"Let's split the difference," Mike said. "Remember, you get to expense one hundred percent of the depreciation; that almost pays for the difference in price. And you'll continue to enjoy the privileges of our hangar space. If you want to keep your tail number, our shop can do that for you."

Stone thought about that. "All right, done."

"I'll send you a sales contract before the day's out," Mike said.

"I'll look forward to receiving it." Stone hung up and thought for another minute, then he picked up the phone and buzzed the master suite.

"Yes?" Faith said. "You looking for me?"

"I am," Stone said. "How would you like to fly a Citation Latitude today?"

"Goody, yes!"

"Get dressed and get down here." He hung up and buzzed Joan. "Please call the Strategic Services hangar and ask them to refuel the Latitude and have it on the ramp in an hour, and ask Fred to drive me to Teterboro and wait for me for a couple of hours."

"Will do."

STONE AND FAITH did the preflight together. "You've never flown the actual airplane, have you? Just the simulator."

"Right."

"Then you're flying left seat today," he said.

"Where are we going?"

"Nowhere special."

FAITH SEEMED RIGHT at home setting up the avionics and completing the checklist. "Have you filed an instrument flight plan?" she asked.

"No, we'll go VFR," Stone replied. "Ask departure for direct Carmel." He explained the autothrottles to her.

She called ground for permission to taxi. Five minutes later they were headed north toward the CMK VOR beacon. They leveled at fifteen thousand feet, and Stone asked her to do some turns and stalls, then he pretty much ran her through the checklist for a checkride. She handled everything perfectly.

"Okay," he said, "let's go back. Ask for the ILS 6." She contacted New York Approach, asked for the instrument approach, and got it.

Back at the hangar she shut down the engines. "That felt like a checkride," she said.

"It wasn't a checkride," Stone replied. "It was an audition."

5

THE FOLLOWING EVENING Faith arrived on time, and they had a drink in Stone's study.

"How much money did you make last year?" Stone asked her.

"A hundred and six thousand dollars," she said. "Probably about the same this year."

"I've bought the Latitude," Stone said. "Signed the contract today."

"Really?"

"Really."

"Does this have something to do with the offer I can't refuse?"

"It does. I'll pay you a hundred and fifty thousand dollars a year to be my full-time pilot."

"Are you . . ." she began.

He cut her off. "Wait, you haven't heard the whole deal. You'll get free medical insurance; when we're traveling you'll get five hundred dollars a day, per diem, to cover a hotel, meals, and transportation. If we're where I have a house, you can use a guest room and keep the money. You won't just be my chief pilot; you'll be my flight department. You'll keep the maintenance logs up to date, make sure we don't miss any inspections, and order any necessary repairs and approve the work. Whatever is to do with the airplane is your job. Got it?"

"Got it."

"Also, you'll maintain a list of another few pilots who are qualified, should you fall ill or be otherwise unavailable. I expect you know about Pat Frank's service?"

"I do."

"She'll be a good source for pilots. Anytime we fly transatlantic I'll want two pilots aboard, so I can get some sleep. You'll also be in charge of arranging catering, when we need it, and of hiring a flight attendant for some flights."

He opened a leather folder on the coffee table and handed her a sheaf of papers. "Here's your contract. Read it carefully and tell me if you have any questions."

It took her only a few minutes to read it. "What's this about annual training?" she asked.

"Are you a certified flight instructor?"

"Yes."

"Then you'll be in charge of training me. I insure myself, so I don't have to go to flight school, though I do have to take a checkride every year, just like you, and keep my medical current. In fact, you can conduct the training while we're flying, and once in a while we'll do turns and stalls. You'll do a three-day refresher at Flight Safety every year, and so will your backup pilot."

"I can do that." She signed the document and handed it back to him. He signed a copy and gave it to her. "Welcome aboard," he said. "Do you have a New York apartment?"

"No, I'll have to find a place."

He handed her a key and pointed to a door off the living room. "Go through there, then through another door, and take the elevator to the fifth floor. I own the building next door, and my staff lives there. Fred and Helene moved in together, so there's an empty on the top floor. Go look at it; I'll wait."

She took the key and disappeared. Fifteen minutes later she returned. "It's perfect," she said.

"There's a Mercedes station wagon in the garage; Fred uses it for shopping. It's yours whenever you need it; just check with Fred first."

"Do you want me to be in uniform when we fly?"

"Yes, but you won't need the jacket and cap; just bars on your shoulders to let people know you're crew; same with any backup pilot: that helps when dealing with ground personnel at strange airports and, especially, overseas."

"Oh, by the way," she said, "I'm qualified for London City Airport."

"Good, but you won't need that often. I have a seven-thousand-foot runway on my property in the south of England."

"I'm qualified for Aspen, too."

"Okay. I've never flown in there, but you never can tell. Any other questions?"

"Nope."

"Then let's go up to P. J. Clarke's and have some dinner."

————

THEIR TABLE WASN'T READY, so they sat down at the bar to wait. A bartender Stone didn't know came over; he was staring at Faith.

"Patty?" he said, as in disbelief. "Patty Jorgensen?"

Faith shook her head. "No, that's not my name."

He took their drink order and went to fill it.

"What was that about?" Stone asked.

"You heard him. He thought I was Patty Jorgensen."

"Who's Patty Jorgensen?"

"She's the latest murder victim. Her picture was in yesterday's *New York Times*. I was struck by the resemblance, too. We could have been sisters."

"I'm glad we're getting you out of that hotel," Stone said.

"Me, too. I'll move into my new apartment tomorrow."

Stone still didn't know how those girls died and nobody would tell him. He made a mental note to find out.

"Why don't you move into your new apartment tonight?" Stone asked.

"Okay. I have another small bag to pack back at the hotel."

FRED DROVE THEM BACK to her hotel, and they waited for her to pack the rest of her things. Fifteen minutes passed, and Stone began to worry. He got out of the car and walked into the hotel lobby, which was deserted; not even a night clerk. A mop bucket on wheels stood in the middle of the floor, unmanned, the mop standing up in the bucket. A few wet swipes on the floor were drying. The guy must have gone to the john, he thought.

He went behind the desk and looked up her room number, then dialed it on the house phone: no answer. The elevator was the old-fashioned kind: no operator. Stone got on and tried the control lever: no joy. He pressed buttons, but nothing happened.

Suddenly, a man in a greasy uniform appeared. "Help you, mister?"

"Yes, tenth floor, get moving."

"Right," the man said. He took a key from his pocket, inserted it into a slot, and turned it, then pressed the control lever. The elevator began to move, but it was a slow one. Stone stood, tapping his foot.

"Tenth floor," the man said, opening the doors.

"Wait here," Stone said.

"Can't do that, mister."

Stone reached out, turned the key and put it in his pocket. "Wait here," he said and strode down the hallway. Her door stood ajar, a key in the lock; an eerie glow came from the room, some sort of night-light. He opened the door with a detective's caution and walked into the room, ready for anything, staying close to the walls. The bathroom door was closed; he hammered on it twice, then flung it open. Nothing. Nothing behind the shower curtain or in a utility closet. He went back into the room and looked around. No luggage, no forgotten cosmetics, nothing.

He ran back to the elevator and tossed the operator his key. "The lobby," he said. The trip down seemed little faster. He gave the man a twenty and strode across the lobby. A desk clerk was on duty, and a man was, once more, swabbing the floor.

On the street he looked carefully up and down and saw no one who looked out of place. He opened the car's rear door—a search was better done on wheels.

"Where have *you* been?" Faith asked.

"Looking for you," he replied. "I went upstairs. How'd you get down here?"

"I used the back elevator that opens onto the side street. Larry, the elevator operator, wasn't answering, which isn't unusual."

"The lobby was completely empty," Stone said.

"There's a game. They would all have been watching in the assistant manager's office."

"Home, Fred," Stone said, taking a deep breath.

"You look funny," Faith said.

"I feel funny," he replied. "And I'm glad to get you out of this neighborhood."

BACK AT THE HOUSE, Fred collected her luggage, and Stone gave her a kiss. "Good night."

"Don't you want that last roll in the hay?" she asked. "It's always the best one."

"Let's bank it," Stone said, then went upstairs, undressed, and fell into bed, still shaking a little.

6

STONE WAS AT HIS DESK as usual when Joan came in. "Do you remember that you have a Centurion board meeting in Los Angeles the day after tomorrow?" she asked.

"I remembered the moment you mentioned it," Stone replied. Centurion Studios was the Hollywood film company where Stone's son, Peter, and Dino's son, Ben, were based. Ben was, in addition to being Peter's partner, head of production at the studio, and Stone served on its board of directors.

"They want to know if you're attending."

"Tell them yes, then call Peter for me and ask if he and Ben and their wives would like to join me at the Arrington Hotel for dinner tomorrow evening."

"Certainly."

"Then tell Faith about the trip and ask her to get everything ready with the airplane. She's my new pilot."

"So I heard on the household grapevine," Joan said. "It's not like you were going to tell me."

"Her contract is somewhere on your crowded desktop," Stone said. "Put her on the payroll and the health insurance policy. She's also the new head of my flight department, so you will be relieved of all those tasks. You might bring her up-to-date."

"Anything else?"

"Anything you can think of," Stone said. He called Dino.

"Bacchetti."

"I heard a rumor you're batching it," Stone said.

"Yeah, Viv is in L.A."

"Dinner tonight at Rotisserie Georgette? Seven?"

"Why not? Are you bringing Faith?"

"No, I bought the Latitude from Mike Freeman, and Faith is now an employee—my chief pilot and the head of my flight department. I don't screw around with employees."

"I didn't know you had a flight department."

"Joan was it, until now."

"See you tonight." They both hung up.

STONE MET DINO AT GEORGETTE, one of their favorite restaurants. They ordered drinks and a roast chicken, specialty of the house.

"So," Dino said, "you got tired of Faith, so you hired her so you wouldn't have to sleep with her?"

"Nope. Faith has a three-fuck policy."

"What is a 'three-fuck policy'?"

"She doesn't want a husband or a regular boyfriend, so she limits sex to three times, then dumps them. She figures the fourth time is when she starts to get into trouble."

"Well, that's a new wrinkle," Dino said. "I sort of admire her logic."

"If she doesn't want what she doesn't want, then her policy is a sane one, I guess."

"So, you used up your three times at bat?"

"Only two. I discovered that I resented the limitation, so I decided to limit it myself instead."

"So the two of you won't be joining the mile-high club on your new airplane? Does the FAA have a regulation barring sex at altitude?"

"There's not a specific no-screw regulation that I'm aware of, but they have lots of loosely worded rules that could cover a multitude of sins."

"Conduct unbecoming a licensed pilot?" Dino asked.

"Something like that. Also, there's a regulation about being in control of the airplane at all times, so I guess if the pilots are screwing there could be control issues."

"Especially on takeoff and landing?"

Stone laughed. "Especially."

"I was going to join Viv for a couple of days in L.A.," Dino said. "Mind if I tag along?"

"Be glad to have your company. Be at Teterboro at nine AM. You and Viv stay with me at the Arrington." Stone had led a group who had begun building new hotels, the first on land in Bel-Air that had belonged to Arrington's first husband, the film actor Vance Calder, and the original contract entitled him to build a house on the property.

"Thank you. We'll take you up on that."

"I've invited Peter and Ben and their wives to dinner tomorrow night."

"Good, saves me the trouble."

"Dino," Stone said, "I want details on the murders of those girls on the East Side."

"Yeah, I knew you'd insist, but you won't like it."

"I don't expect to like it. I just want to know what's going on. I had a scare last night with Faith at that seedy hotel on Lexington, where the charter airlines put their crews."

"Yeah, that place is on the downtown edge of the area where the murders are happening."

"Come on, cough it up."

"Okay, here's what the medical examiner is telling us: the girls are rendered unconscious, maybe chemically, then taken somewhere and stripped by the perpetrators."

"More than one perp?"

"So they say. They're then awakened, beaten, and sexually assaulted. The corpses are covered in bruises and welts."

"Any DNA traces?"

"None. The girls are strangled or suffocated, then bathed to clean away incriminating DNA, then they're redressed, taped into garbage bags, and left in public wastebaskets on the street in the middle of the night."

"That's meticulous," Stone said.

"It gets more meticulous: they're made up and given manicures and pedicures, too, so that there are no traces of another person if they scratch or kick them, and their hair is washed and styled and their clothes are washed before they're redressed and put out for collection. We've notified every trash crew working the East Side to be on the alert for bodies."

"Why the makeup and the hairdressing?" Stone asked.

"The ME says it's a guilt thing on the part of the perps.

They want them to look nice when they're found. They use the girls' own makeup, so they're not buying cosmetics in the neighborhood."

"These people are going to be very hard to catch," Stone said.

"You're right, pal. They're going to have to be caught in the act—the act of murder or the act of disposal—and waiting for that to happen could take years."

"They've got to have a base," Stone said. "An apartment or a room where they take their victims; someplace they won't be seen or overheard."

"We're on that," Dino said. "We're on all of it. I've tripled patrols on the East Side."

"I wish I could think of something to suggest," Stone said.

"I wish you could, too, pal."

7

STONE SAT IN THE RIGHT seat and watched closely as Faith ran through her checklist, then got a clearance from ATC, and taxied to the runway. She began her takeoff run, then rotated; Stone handled the gear lever and the flaps for her, and the airplane climbed to its preset altitude of 1,500 feet. They had a departure procedure to fly, and Stone was surprised that Faith hand-flew it instead of just switching on the autopilot, as he would have done in her place. Stone regarded the autopilot as a better operator than he, as many pilots did.

"Do you hand-fly a lot?" he asked Faith as she got an altitude change and a vector to the west from ATC.

"No, I just wanted you to know I could do it. I don't want you to be wondering if I can handle the airplane."

"I'm impressed," Stone said. They were cleared to flight level 045, or 45,000 feet, and when they had leveled off, Stone unbuckled. "I'm going to sit with Dino," he said. "There's nothing here you can't handle, but let me know if you need somebody in the right seat."

He grabbed the *New York Times* from the cabinet top behind him and walked aft, standing almost erect in the six-foot headroom of the cabin. He settled into the seat opposite Dino and put on a headset, in case Faith needed anything. She came on almost immediately.

"Dino has had a text message to call his office," she said.

Stone passed the message on to Dino and pointed out where the satphone was. "Call home base," he said.

Dino picked up the phone, dialed the number, and spoke to someone for a couple of minutes, then returned the phone to its snap-in cradle.

"Anything urgent?" Stone asked, taking off his headset.

"Urgent, but everything is being done," he said. "A garbage truck from the East Side took its cargo back to the dump, and found a dead girl among the trash. They missed it when loading. According to the ME, she was killed while you and I were dining on roast chicken last night."

"I didn't need to know that," Stone said.

"Listen, you always want to know everything, so I'm not going to edit the news for you."

"Was everything in line with the previous killings?"

"Everything," Dino said. "She even had a purse, with the strap over her arm. The killers thoughtfully supplied her wallet and driver's license, so we didn't have to go to the trouble of identifying her."

"They're getting pretty confident, aren't they?"

"Smug, I'd say. In every other respect, this killing matches the others. Everything is being done that has to be done, and my office is making the announcement over my signature, so I'm not needed back there."

"There are times, aren't there, when it's great not to be needed?"

Dino snorted. "I think my chief of staff enjoys rubbing it in."

Stone handed Dino the first section of the *Times.* "Here, distract yourself."

Dino took the paper but folded it in his lap and stared out the window.

Since the anti-airport fanatics on the Santa Monica city council had made a deal with the FAA to shorten SMO's single runway to 3,500 feet, in order to keep out jet traffic, they landed at Burbank, where a Bentley from the Arrington met them and transported them to the hotel. It was a longer drive than from SMO.

THE BUTLER SITUATED STONE and Dino in their respective rooms and took Faith to the guesthouse. Stone had given Faith an invitation to join them for dinner.

Stone and Dino got into bathing suits and robes and headed for the pool, where the thoughtful butler brought drinks and snacks on floating trays. Viv arrived shortly after and joined them in the pool.

"Dino told me about Faith's three-fuck policy," she said to Stone, amused. "Are you finding that hard to live with?"

"No, that's a choice she gets to make for herself, and I'm not going to try to hustle her into changing it."

"Good policy. That will keep your name out of the papers."

"Sex is fun only when it's freely given," Stone said.

"Good point," Viv said, "though I've known men who preferred to try to take it more roughly."

"How'd that work out for them?" Stone asked.

"On one occasion, a broken wrist," Viv replied, "on another, a fat ear; and on yet another, a rearranged nose, requiring bandaging for several days and steak on both eyes."

"Did they know you were a cop?" Stone asked.

"Not at first, but later. One of them swore he'd bring charges against me, but fortunately for him, he thought it over."

THE BOYS AND THEIR WIVES arrived in time for cocktails, and Stone had a moment to sit down alone with Peter and Ben.

"There's something on the board meeting agenda I should warn you about," Ben said. "There's a move afoot among some of the shareholders—the more recent ones—to sell off our back lot and turn it into condo heaven."

"Do they have anything like the support they need?" Stone asked.

"It's closer than we would like," Peter said. "I think Ben is going to have to make a do-or-die speech to the shareholders to hang on to it. God, I love the back lot; we can do so much with the standing sets to make them into anything at all, from ancient Rome to 1920s New York."

"Not to mention the money we save by not needing to go on location so much," Ben said. "I've come up with a number on our costs over the past five years that should impress the board."

"Who are these stockholders who want to develop the land?" Stone asked.

"Newer directors and production companies who somehow think that, if we sell it off, they'll get a chunk of cash."

"Will they?" Stone asked.

"My plan is to fix things so they won't, and when that incentive disappears, they'll come around, and then they'll go to dinner parties and tell their friends how they saved the back lot."

"What is it," Stone asked, "forty acres?"

"Closer to sixty," Ben replied. "Of course, there are parts we don't use much anymore, like the Mississippi riverboat. I've arranged for the board to have lunch aboard the boat, which is in beautiful condition, and I think they'll want to keep it."

"Good idea," Stone said. "We'll have our shares to vote, and Ed Eagle will be on our side with his shares. Have you heard if he's coming?"

"He's already here," Ben said. "He's bought an apartment that overlooks the back lot, and I don't think he'll want to spoil his view."

8

STONE LOOKED OUT ACROSS the Mississippi River, toward downtown Los Angeles, and listened to a Dixieland band while saloon girls served the board and stockholders drinks and lunch, and a riverboat gambler and a man in a black suit fought a gunfight on the stern of the riverboat.

When everyone was suitably oiled, and the agenda had been ticked off, Ben Bacchetti rose. "What do you think of Old Man River?" he asked, getting a rousing round of applause. He had some sheets of paper passed out to those present and took them through the income and the production savings made from the rental and use of the back lot, and while the iron was hot, he got a vote that saved the property.

As the sun began to wane, the riverboat docked at Natchez and dumped the happy group onto the dock and into horse-drawn carriages that took them back to the parking lot. Stone took his party—which included Ed Eagle and Dino, as well as Viv and Faith, who were there as guests—up to the top deck, where they had a bottle of champagne and watched the sun go down on a fairly smog-free city.

"A good day's work," Stone said to Ben.

"I'm proud of you," Dino said to his son.

"We'll have to fight them again next year, but I have plans to make it harder for them. It always amazes me that a group of stockholders would want to fuck up a well-oiled company so they can make a few extra bucks. It's not as though they need the money: the studio police counted a dozen Bentleys, two dozen Mercedes, and a large assortment of Ferraris, Aston Martins, and Lamborghinis in the guest parking lot. Oh, there was one Prius, for the green-minded, I guess."

They were quiet for a moment, then Viv shaded her eyes from the setting sun and pointed aft, where a pink blob floated in the river. "What's that?" she asked.

Everybody gazed lazily aft, then Dino got to his feet and shaded his eyes. "Get me some binoculars," he said to a crewman. The man vanished and came back with the instrument. Dino focused. "It's one of two things," he said. "It's either a life-size doll or a dead body. I think we should find out which."

Two crew members ran down to the dock, got an outboard motor started, and puttered out to where the pink lump floated. The commander of the studio police came out onto the deck and joined them, radio in hand. The instrument squawked, and there was an exchange of information. "It's the body of a woman," he said.

Dino spoke up. "Then you'd better call somebody you know on the LAPD and ask for homicide detectives, the ME, a crime scene team, and an ambulance."

The man made the call, and the two crewmen began ferrying the body back to the dock.

"I think we'd better have a look at this," Dino said.

Stone followed him ashore and down to the dock. "Leave her in the boat," Dino said to them. He and Stone got in and had a close look at the body.

"Was she serving drinks?" Dino asked.

"I honestly don't know," Stone said. He turned to the captain, who had followed them down. "Do you know her?"

"No," the man said.

"I think you'd better conduct a roll call and see who's missing," Stone said. "That'll give the police a head start when they get here."

The captain left and returned with a clipboard. "I've checked the whole list," he said, "and nobody's missing."

Ben stepped up. "I've given instructions for every department to count heads and report anyone who's missing from their offices."

The LAPD arrived and were greeted by the commander of the studio police, who brought them to the dock.

An older detective said, "My God, is that Dino Bacchetti?"

The two pumped hands and Dino introduced everybody. "This is Lieutenant Molder Carson, known to one and all as 'Moldy.'"

"What've we got here?" Carson asked, walking over to the boat.

"What you specialize in?" Dino said.

"Has anybody fucked with the body?"

"Only to get her out of the water and into the boat," Dino said. "I watched them, and they did it well."

The medical examiner arrived with the ambulance and made a quick examination of the body. "She's badly bruised pretty much all over, but I can't find a fatal wound. I need to get her back to the morgue, and on a table, before I can tell you more."

The corpse was placed in a body bag and driven away.

Stone and Dino walked slowly to their waiting carriage, followed by the others.

"Notice anything familiar about her?" Dino asked.

"No, I don't know her."

"Well, she's not much more than five feet tall, a hundred pounds, and blond."

Faith, who was walking beside Stone, stopped, then turned aside and vomited.

9

THEY ALL HAD dinner at the table by the pool. While the others chatted, Stone and Dino managed a more private conversation.

"It's a coincidence," Stone said.

"You think everything is a coincidence," Dino replied. "You say so all the time."

"No, I don't. What I say all the time is that our lives are made up of strings of coincidences, that if you take any important, life-changing event in your history and trace it back far enough, you'll find that some slim coincidence changed everything. And if you string enough of those coincidences together, what you get is fate."

"That's just so much horseshit," Dino said evenly. "I don't believe in coincidences, especially where homicides are concerned."

"Oh, come on, Dino."

"You think it's any kind of coincidence at all that a body

turns up in L.A., where you and I are, and the crime closely matches three, four others in New York?"

"Well . . ."

"These homicides are not only connected," Dino said, "they're perpetrated by the same person or persons."

"Well," Stone said, "if the ME's estimate of time of death is correct, then that couldn't be the case because this murder and the last one in New York were committed at roughly the same time, two days ago—while we were dining on roast chicken at Rotisserie Georgette—so it can't be the same guy."

"There's a connection, believe me," Dino said. "And on top of it all, they're fucking with you and me, just for fun."

"They're not fucking with me," Stone said. "You're the cop. If they're fucking with anybody, it's you. Don't you feel fucked with?"

"Of course, I do," Dino said, "but the connection in all this is Faith."

"Let me get this straight," Stone said. "You think they're picking victims who look like Faith, just to drive me crazy?"

"Aren't they driving you crazy?' Dino asked.

"Well, a little, I guess."

"Then whatever they're doing is working."

"They're driving you crazy, too," Stone pointed out.

"Thank God the victims don't look like Viv, or I would already be crazy."

"Do you think Faith is safe out here?" Stone asked. Faith was tucked up in bed in the guesthouse with a cup of broth to settle her stomach.

"How the hell should I know?" Dino asked. "She was within

fifty yards of our floater half a dozen times this afternoon. The perps could have snatched her, if they'd felt like it."

The butler approached. "The medical examiner is on the phone for Commissioner Bacchetti," he said. He led Dino to a lounge chair a few feet away and handed him a phone.

Dino put his feet up and chatted for a couple of minutes, then he put down the phone and returned to the table. "Okay," he said, "the ME confirms his first estimate of time of death. The girl had a tiny purse tucked into her vagina, just big enough to hold her driver's license, a credit card, and a few bucks. Her name is Elizabeth Sweeney."

"Where does she live?"

"Santa Monica."

Viv came over and sat with them.

"We're going to stop talking about this now. We're going to all behave as if we've had a pleasant day in the California sunshine, riding down the L.A. branch of the Mississippi River," Dino said.

"All that is true," Viv said.

"And we're enjoying a good dinner under the stars, and the ME didn't call."

"The ME called?" Viv asked. "What did he say?"

"You see why I'm going crazy here?" he asked Stone.

"She died in L.A. while Dino and I were having dinner in New York," Stone said. "Her name is Elizabeth Sweeney, and she lives in Santa Monica."

"And Dino thinks the killings are related."

"It was his idea," Dino replied, pointing at Stone.

"Don't point that thing at me," Stone said. "You had the same idea at the same time."

"This is why I'm going crazy," Dino said. "I've already ruled out the killings as a subject of dinner table conversation, so that we can enjoy our dinner and the evening, but you people just won't leave it alone."

Viv kissed him on the forehead. "I'm sorry, darling, of course we'll stop talking about it, won't we, Stone?"

"Absolutely," Stone replied.

"How did they identify her?" Viv asked.

Dino picked up his dinner plate and carried it to the other end of the pool, where he collapsed on a chaise longue and tried to eat.

"Oops," Viv said.

10

THE FOLLOWING MORNING after breakfast Dino convened a meeting around Stone's dining room table. Present were himself, Stone, and Viv, plus the two LAPD detectives assigned to the case and their captain.

Dino picked up a phone and dialed a number. "Get them on the speaker phone," he said.

"We're here, Commish," a man's voice said.

"Okay," Dino said, "what we've got present here is a bi-coastal team to investigate a series of homicides apparently occurring on both coasts, fairly simultaneously. I've already assigned a team to the East Coast killings, and present is the West Coast team. I propose that we have a daily conference call to share what each group has. We also have the relevant ME at each end. Everybody on board?"

There was a positive chorus of noises from both coasts.

"Also, I've asked two other people with homicide experience to join us. Both are retired NYPD detectives, both outstanding ones: Stone Barrington, who is an attorney in New York, a former detective, and my NYPD partner for many years; and my wife, Vivian Bacchetti—who likes to be called Viv—who is very experienced in these things as she also was an NYPD detective, and is now chief operating officer of Strategic Services, a worldwide security company. Anybody object to them helping out?"

There was a positive rumble at both ends.

"There's a stenographer in New York who is transcribing our conversation and will issue notes on our discussions from time to time, so we won't forget anything. Since the killings started in New York, I'll ask Lieutenant Greg Martin to give us a summary of what has been learned there, then we'll hear from the LAPD team. Greg?"

"Thanks, Commissioner," Greg said. "We've had four homicides on the Upper East Side of New York, all fitting a pattern: the victims were all young women of small stature and slim build, with blond hair, all very pretty. They appear to have been taken from their neighborhoods to what the killers believe is a secure location, stripped, beaten severely, and raped. They were then killed by suffocation or strangulation, and their bodies were bathed, their bodily cavities irrigated, and their personal makeup applied to their faces. Their clothing was laundered. Then they were dressed again, placed in a large plastic garbage bag, and dumped in municipal trash bins. All were discovered on garbage trucks, except for one, who was found when her body was dumped at a municipal facility. In some cases, identification was found on the bodies, in others they were identified by fingerprints, DNA testing, or photo ID means. No evidence of any kind relating to their killers was found on them. That's all we've got."

"Thanks, Greg," Dino said. "Moldy? Give us your rundown."

Moldy read from notes. "The subject was found on the back lot of a movie studio, where Commissioner Bacchetti, Mr. Barrington, and Mrs. Bacchetti were attending a social event in connection with a board and stockholder meeting of Centurion Studios. She had been dumped in a lake that's shaped to resemble a river, a lake on studio property, where two other bodies have been found in the past five years. There's fairly easy access from a road. Her appearance was similar to the New York victims: small, pretty, and slight of build, with blond hair. And her corpse had been treated in much the same way as the New York victims. No DNA, traces of fibers, or other evidence of the killers were found on her body. She was identified from her driver's license, found in a small purse, tucked into her vagina. She had a Third Street address, in Santa Monica, and she was killed on the same night as the fourth victim in New York. That's it."

"All right," Dino said. "I believe we can say without contradiction that there is more than one killer involved, on more than one coast, and that they are working in league with each other. Their motives are unknown, unless we believe it possible that the killers may have a motive to embarrass Stone Barrington or me, or both, which seems unlikely in the extreme. Am I missing anything?"

Moldy spoke up, directing his voice toward the phone. "Greg, what have you learned about the employment of your victims?"

"One was a copilot for a charter airline, new to the job, two were secretaries or office workers, the last was an actress, working mostly in TV commercials. There appears to be no employment connection among them. How about yours?"

"She is an actress who may have visited Centurion Studios in pursuit of her career, but we have not been able to ascertain who, if anyone, she saw here. She had no appointments at the studio."

"Greg," Dino said, "what steps are you proposing?"

"Commissioner," Greg replied, "we have identified two NYPD officers, one a detective, who resemble the victims in a general way in size and hair color, both very pretty. We are considering making one of them a presence on the Upper East Side over a period of days, under the strictest surveillance at all times, to see if she attracts the attention of the killers. In addition to surveillance, she will be equipped with an electronic means of signaling distress, to help keep her safe. Our detective is also extremely skilled in personal protection techniques. This plan will require a large commitment of personnel and equipment and will require your personal approval before beginning. Our supervisor and the chief of detectives have already approved the plan."

"Then you may consider the plan approved," Dino said. "Be very careful, but don't waste any time. Moldy?"

"Commissioner, we continue to investigate by every means at our disposal."

"All right," Dino said. "Does anyone have anything else to contribute?"

"Commissioner," Greg said, "we do not place any credence in your theory that the killers' motive is to embarrass you.

Mr. Barrington, maybe. If he's being watched, we might identify the watcher, and if we did, that would constitute a major break in the case."

"Stone," Dino said. "Do you mind being surveilled in connection with this case?"

"Yes, I do, most emphatically," Stone replied, "and I doubt very much if it would produce any leads."

"Greg, you and your team are authorized to surveil Mr. Barrington, whether he likes it or not, starting when he lands at Teterboro on his return to New York."

"Yes, Commissioner, when will that be?"

"Stone?" Dino asked.

"Six o'clock tomorrow evening at Jet Aviation, Teterboro," Stone said, "but I think it's a waste of time and manpower."

"Objection noted," Dino said, "and ignored."

11

S TONE FLEW HIS NEW airplane home, with Faith in the right seat. He had never flown an airplane coast-to-coast, nonstop, because he had never owned one with that much range. He landed with plenty of fuel still aboard.

As he shut down the engines at Teterboro, Fred pulled the Bentley up to the door and supervised the unloading and re-loading of Stone's and Faith's luggage, while Dino's people loaded his and Viv's luggage aboard his police vehicle. They were the first to drive away, but another black SUV lurked on the sidelines.

"Mr. Barrington," Fred said, "the policemen in that car have told me that they have orders to never let you out of their sight, except when you're at home. What shall I tell them?"

"I'd like you to tell them to go fuck themselves," Stone said, "but that wouldn't help. I'm not in any danger, but Faith may very well be." He called Faith over. "I want both of you to understand this," he said. "You two are not to be out of sight of each other except when in your living quarters. Fred, at all other times, I want you armed and ready to intervene should anyone—and I mean *anyone*—approach Faith."

"Yes, sir," Fred replied.

"Faith?" Stone said. "Are you on board?"

"I can take care of myself," she said. "I'll go armed."

"Not good enough," Stone replied. "We have five young women who look like you, all dead, because they thought they could take care of themselves. Your only other choice is to quit your job and go on the run, and that might very well not work."

"Oh, all right," she said, exasperated. "How long do I have to put up with this?"

"Until these crimes are solved and the perpetrators jailed. And I don't think you'll find Fred hard to put up with. He's an ex–Royal Marine commando with many skills, and also a crack shot. If there's any shooting to be done, try to let him do it."

"I'm sorry, Fred," she said to him, "I didn't intend to disparage your help. I'm grateful for it."

"Thank you, miss," Fred said. "Shall we depart for the city?"

They all got into the Bentley and were soon headed for the tunnel into the city. "I should tell you, Faith," Stone said, "this car is armored and will repel gunfire and most bombs. Forget about the Mercedes; if you want to go anywhere, go in this."

"Right," she said.

At the house, Fred pulled all the way into the garage before closing the door behind them, then he asked them to wait a moment while he had a look around the garage. He produced a small but powerful flashlight and illuminated every dark corner and anteroom in the basement, then Stone and Faith disembarked. "If I get scared," Faith asked, "can I come and sleep with you?"

"If you get scared," Stone said, "call Fred. You'll be much safer with him than with me." He went upstairs to the master suite, and she went to her own apartment.

THE FOLLOWING MORNING Stone was at his desk when Faith came in carrying a nylon carryall. "I'd like to get the logbooks in order and schedule some maintenance," she said to Stone. "Is there someplace I can work?"

Stone buzzed Joan, and she came in. "Please put Faith in the little office next to yours, and let her make it her own. It is now the Flight Department. Direct any and all calls about the aircraft to her."

"Yes, sir," Joan said.

"And Joan, you should know that Faith is under the protection of the NYPD, and they are surveilling me, as well. Faith, Joan is armed and so am I, and I assume you are, too."

She nodded.

"I think the most important thing we can all do to get through this, if trouble comes, is try not to shoot each other."

"I'll give that my best efforts," Joan said. Faith nodded.

Shortly afterward, both women were settled and at work in their offices.

Stone called Dino.

"Bacchetti."

"Good morning, sleep well?"

"As well as I can sleep while worrying," Dino said

"Please don't worry about us. We're battened down here, and everybody is armed."

"You think you and your ménage are all I have to worry about?" Dino demanded. "We had two homicides in the city last night."

"Any of them connected to the East Side?"

"No, both of the victims were men—a gay couple in Chelsea."

"I'm glad it wasn't one of ours."

"Every garbage truck in the city is on the lookout for fresh corpses," Dino said. "If there's another one out there, they'll find it."

"Is Viv continuing on to London today?"

"She is."

"Then why don't you come over here this evening and have dinner with Faith and me. I don't think we should be swanning around restaurants, in these circumstances."

"Neither do I. I've got a late meeting—I'll try to be there by seven-thirty."

"We'll save you some scotch," Stone said, then hung up.

AROUND SEVEN, Faith called down from her apartment. "I don't really feel well enough for a jolly dinner with you and Dino," she said. "Helene will bring me something on a tray."

"Now, don't go and get all depressed on me," Stone said. "We'll get through this."

"There's nothing to do but watch TV," she said.

"My library is at your disposal," Stone said, "and you can go anywhere you like, as long as you and Fred are joined at the hip."

"I'd rather be joined with you," she said. "Did you get tired of fucking me?"

"Listen, sweetheart, I'm playing by *your* rules, remember? I have nothing but the most pleasant memories of sex with you, but I'd rather fast than be rationed."

"Oh, all right, then. I'll come down to dinner. What time?"

"Seven-thirty is good," he said.

"How are we dressing?"

"In street clothing—no nightgowns or pajamas, you might get Dino all riled."

"Now there's a thought," she said, then hung up.

12

DINO ARRIVED, and they all sat down before the fire in Stone's study.

"I don't think I've ever seen you look so tired," Stone said to Dino.

"I don't think I've ever *been* so tired," Dino replied, taking a gulp of his drink. "I'm taking the Scottish remedy for fatigue. It'll start to work soon."

"Any news at all?"

"Not a whiff," Dino said. "It's like these people were going full steam ahead, then slammed on the brakes."

"Are you disappointed?" Faith asked.

"No, I'm relieved, but I know more is coming. I just don't know when."

"Dino," Stone said, "I know you've probably investigated it, but I think you should have another close look at the Keystone Hotel, on Lex."

"You're right. We've already looked at it. What makes you think it needs further attention?"

"A few nights ago, I dropped Faith off there to pick up her belongings, and she took so long, I got worried and went looking for her. The lobby was completely deserted, and that's odd for a hotel."

"Who should have been there?" Dino asked.

"A janitor mopping the floor—only his bucket and mop were there—the elevator operator, and the desk clerk. I tried to take myself up in the elevator, but it was locked. The operator finally showed up and took me upstairs, but Faith wasn't there. When I came downstairs again, the janitor and the desk clerk had reemerged, and everything seemed normal."

"Where was Faith?"

"In the car, waiting," she said. "When the elevator operator didn't answer my ring, I took the automatic elevator in the rear of the building and walked around the corner to where Fred was waiting in the car. I told Stone there was a ball game on TV, and they were probably watching it in the assistant manager's office."

"How long do you think the lobby was empty?" Dino asked.

"There's no way to tell," Stone replied.

"All three of them were there when I went into the building," Faith said. "Between then and when Stone came back to the car again, maybe ten, fifteen minutes. I had some packing to do."

"Is the lobby often deserted?" Dino asked.

"Yes. The only guests these days are airline people, who are on a contract. I think they've stopped taking other reservations."

"Why is that?"

"I've heard that the hotel is scheduled for gutting and a complete renovation as a high-end hotel/condo combination. That's what the desk clerk told me."

"I don't know what to make of that story," Dino said.

"Neither do I," Stone replied. "The whole business just struck me as creepy. Can you think of an excuse to have a look around the place, especially the lower levels?"

"Of course I can," Dino replied, "and if I can't, I've got a few hundred detectives who could come up with probable cause for a search warrant on the fly. I just don't think I can spare the manpower while we're in the middle of this murder spree to look again into something so ordinary and plausible."

"Have you had the FBI in on this?" Stone asked.

"Why would I want those fuckers involved?" Dino asked. "I avoid them like the plague, unless I really need them for something, which isn't often."

"You don't have any profilers on the force, do you? The FBI specializes in profiling prospective murder perps."

"Yeah, and half the time it's a lot of horseshit."

"And what about the other half of the time?" Stone asked. "I think I'd use anything that had a fifty percent probability of producing some real leads."

"Do I look that desperate?" Dino asked.

"You certainly do," Stone replied.

Dino tossed down the rest of his drink and handed Stone his glass. "You still tending bar?"

"Sure." Stone got up and poured the drink.

"All right," Dino said.

"All right, what?"

"All right, I'll call somebody over at Fedville tomorrow morning and get one of their readers of tea leaves sent over."

"Good idea," Stone said. "I wish I'd thought of it."

"Mark my words," Dino said. "They're going to send me some little jerk fresh out of Quantico, who'll gaze at the ceiling and spout a lot of crap."

"Well, if he has only one good idea, it might be worth it."

"Why don't you have profilers in the NYPD?" Faith asked.

"We sent some people down to Quantico to do a course with those people, and they kept dozing off in the classes. When they got back, they were worse cops and more of a pain in the ass than before we sent them down there."

"That sounds like a lot of grouch to me," Faith said.

"Dino is mostly grouch," Stone put in.

"I'm good at grouch," Dino said. "Grouch has always worked very well for me. It keeps people on their toes."

"I never knew *grouch* was a motivator," Faith said.

"It also keeps their ideas on point and their sentences short," Dino said. "You wouldn't believe how much time grouch saves me."

"Right," Stone said. "Nobody wants to argue with somebody they know will bite their head off, if they say the wrong thing or don't say it fast enough."

"That's what I want to avoid," Dino said. "Them saying the wrong thing. I only give them time to say the right thing."

"This is beginning to sound like one of those business management things," Faith said. "'Grouch your way to the top.' That sort of thing."

"Dino," Stone said, "you could make a fortune giving classes to business leaders on grouch and its uses."

"You mean, like Trump University?"

"Well, you'd need less content and more fraud for that," Stone said. "Maybe you should just write the book. Faith has already given you the title. Start taking notes."

"I could just leave a tape recorder running in my office," Dino said, getting into the swing of things, "and have my secretary transcribe the good stuff at the end of the day."

"Good idea," Faith said. "Maybe you should attach one of those GoPro cameras to your head, so you can pick up the reactions of your victims."

"'Victims'?" Dino asked. "What victims?"

"Sorry, colleagues and staffers. Their reactions would be good to use in the television commercials."

"Television commercials?"

"For the book. You'll need a hot-and-heavy ad campaign to move sales."

Fred came into the room with a sizzling porterhouse steak on a platter.

"Saved by the beef," Stone said.

13

THE FOLLOWING LATE AFTERNOON, Stone opened his briefcase, and one end of the handle came off in his hand. Upon examination, it was found to be missing a tiny screw, the sort of part that is available only at expensive luggage stores.

He checked on Joan and Faith, who were both working away like beavers, then emptied his briefcase, tucked it under his arm, and left the house, headed uptown, walking. He finished up at a fancy luggage shop at Park and Fifty-sixth Street, went inside, and had a brief conversation with their repair artist, who eventually admitted he could supply and fit the screw. Stone sat down and picked up a magazine from a table to while away the time. Shortly, a woman fell into his lap.

This was more than a metaphor. She was missing a shoe, the shoe was missing a heel, and when he stood her upright, she rested all her weight on the other foot.

"I'm so terribly sorry," she said.

Stone was not so sorry. She was tall, slim, had auburn hair, was beautifully dressed in an Armani suit, and she had managed the fall without getting so much as a hair out of place. He sat her down in the chair and retrieved the shoe and the heel.

"I'm afraid you're not walking anywhere on this," he said, then looked at her foot, which was beginning to swell. "Nor on that," he said, pointing at her ankle.

"Oh, swell," she said.

A salesman appeared belatedly and made all the right noises, for which Stone was grateful.

"You sold me three cases, a matched set, last summer," she said. "I need one more case, like that." She pointed at a grouping on a high shelf. "The smaller one, second from the right."

While the salesman looked for a ladder, Stone made haste. "May I ask where you're headed?" he said.

"To the Carlyle Hotel," she said.

"While you conclude your purchase, I'll arrange some transport for you."

"That would be very kind," she said.

Stone got Fred on the phone and instructed him, then returned to her side. She was signing a credit card receipt, and the salesman took the case away to have it wrapped. "I'm afraid your ankle is taking on cantaloupe proportions," he said. "Does it hurt?"

She thought about that. "Yes," she said, "but not as much as it's going to hurt when I try to walk on it. I think I'd better go to an emergency room."

"That's not going to be as much fun as it sounds," Stone

said. "You'll be there until midnight waiting for everybody with chest pains to be looked at. Ankles are not high on the emergency list of a New York hospital."

"What do you suggest?" she said.

Stone, from the corner of his eye, saw the Bentley glide to a halt outside. "Put this in your purse," he said, handing her the broken shoe and heel. She tucked it into her Birkin bag, a commodious purse more expensive that many luxury cars. "Let's get you back to the Carlyle. I know a doctor who makes house calls, and we'll get him to look at that. My car is outside."

He got her standing on her good foot, while she rested a hand on his shoulder and tried hopping. It didn't work very well. "There's always the fireman's carry," Stone said. "I learned that as a Boy Scout."

"Not on Park Avenue," she said. "Why don't we try the old over-the-threshold carry, beloved of so many newlyweds. I won't tell anybody we're not married, if you won't."

"Good idea," Stone said. He scooped her up into his arms and strode out of the shop and across the sidewalk, while the salesman tried to keep up with her package.

Fred saw them coming, got a rear door open, and assisted Stone with tucking her into the backseat, while the salesman put her case on the front passenger seat and handed Stone his briefcase. "No charge, Mr. Barrington," he said.

Stone thanked him, then got into the other rear seat and handed Fred the briefcase. "The Carlyle, Fred."

"'Barrington'?" she asked. "Is that your name?"

"It is, first name is Stone."

"I'm Cilla Scott," she replied. "Priscilla, really, but I dropped the *Pris* at puberty."

"One moment," Stone said, whipping out his cell phone, calling the Carlyle, and asking for the concierge. "Good afternoon, George, this is Stone Barrington. Fine, thanks. I'm bringing you a wounded guest, and we need a wheelchair at the East Seventy-sixth Street entrance in five minutes. Thank you."

"Good thinking," she said.

"As dainty as you are, I don't think I could carry you all the way to your room. Excuse me, one more call to make." He pressed the button. "Kevin, Stone Barrington. I have a patient requiring a house call, and bring that portable X-ray thing of yours. Carlyle Hotel . . ." He looked at her, and she gave him the room number. "Twenty-eighth floor. Name of Ms. Scott. Possible broken ankle. Bring painkillers." He thanked the man and hung up. "Half an hour," he said.

"Well," Cilla said. "You are blindingly efficient. I don't think you've forgotten a thing."

They arrived at the side door to the Carlyle and were greeted by a doorman with a wheelchair. "Mr. Barrington? I'm Eddie. We're all ready for Ms. Scott." They got her into the wheelchair. Moments later, they were shooting skyward. She handed Stone her key—the Carlyle still used actual keys—and Stone let them into a large, south-facing suite with a spectacular skyline view. Stone gave Eddie a fifty and thanked him.

"There's a bar over there," she said. "Would you fix me some sort of whiskey on the rocks and make something for yourself?"

"That skill lies within my repertoire," Stone said. He found half a bottle of Knob Creek and poured them each a drink. "Try that," he said, handing it to her.

She took a swig. "Perfect," she said, "what is it?"

"Knob Creek bourbon. Knob Creek is in Kentucky, where Abraham Lincoln once lived. You can't get any more patriotic than that."

"You're making that up," she said.

"I am reciting American history. Google it."

She took another swig. "It seems to be finding its way to all the right places."

"It will do that," Stone replied. He looked at his watch. "Dr. Kevin should be here shortly, and we'll soon know if he has to amputate."

"Sit down," she said, patting the chair beside her.

He dragged over an ottoman, placed her wounded foot on it, and then sat down.

"Tell me about yourself," she said.

"I don't give recitations, but I do answer questions," Stone replied. So she began to question him.

14

THE DOCTOR ARRIVED and was shown his patient. "This is Dr. Kevin O'Connor," Stone said. "Kevin, Ms. Scott." The doctor dragged up a chair and examined her ankle, pressing here and there, while she winced.

"I don't think it's broken," he said, "but we'll get a picture." He set up a contraption on the footstool and looked at the resulting X-ray on his laptop. "It's not broken," he said, "just badly sprained, and not for the first time. There's quite a lot of scarring."

"I've been spraining it since I was twelve," Cilla replied. "On horseback, on tennis courts, on boats, and on golf courses."

"You're going to have to stay off of it for a few days," he said, "and I mean off. Some of my patients believe that means on tippy-toe. It doesn't. If I apply a trusty elastic bandage, will you promise me to stay off it for four days?"

"*Four* days?"

"If you won't promise, I'll put a cast on it."

She sighed. "Oh, all right, I promise."

He taped the ankle, then gave her some folding crutches and two pill bottles. "One is a nonsteroid anti-inflammatory, the other is a painkiller, one that you can't combine with alcohol, unless you want to fall asleep and not wake up."

"You keep the painkillers," she said, "and I'll continue with my medication of choice."

The doctor packed up and Stone walked him to the door. "Send me the bill," he said.

"What's your connection with this ankle?" Dr. Kevin asked.

"It fell into my lap." Stone closed the door and made Cilla another drink. "How are you feeling?" he asked.

"Like a person who's had a couple of drinks," she replied. "I don't know how the ankle feels. It's not speaking to me."

"Just as well. I'd invite you out for dinner, but you aren't going anywhere tonight."

"Then I'll invite you to stay here for dinner," she said. "This hotel still follows the quaint practice of serving food in its suites."

"I accept," he said.

"Back to your interrogation," she said. "What do you do?"

"I'm a lawyer with a firm called Woodman & Weld."

"What is your specialty?"

"Practicing as little law as possible."

"Admirable. Where do you live?"

"I have a house in Turtle Bay."

"I know it well. I had an aunt who lived there until her death a few years ago. As a little girl I used to play in the gardens."

"It's hard to believe you were ever a little girl," he said.

"I still am."

"My turn: Where do you live?"

"In Greenwich, Connecticut, in a house I shared until recently with a husband."

"What brings you to New York?"

"I came to look for an apartment and to consult with my late father's investment advisors. He died last month, and I'm trying to get a grip on his estate."

"Do you have a Realtor?"

"No, I was going to ask you to recommend one."

Stone looked through his wallet until he found a card. "Margot Goodale," he said. "She's excellent."

"Thank you," she said, tucking the card into her bra. "Can you recommend a good divorce attorney?"

"I can," he said, taking a business card from the wallet and writing a name on it. "Herbert Fisher. Is your divorce likely to be contentious?"

"Aren't they all?"

"Is this your first?"

"Yes. I want to present the man with enough legal firepower to let him know I won't be a pushover."

"Herb is your man. He's our firm's lead attorney in that field. Your husband's attorney will know who he is and treat you respectfully."

She bra-ed the card with the other one. "Shall we look at a menu?"

Stone went to the desk and found one. "The dover sole looks good," he said.

"Same here, and the lobster bisque to start and some wine."

Stone made the call and ordered for them, then walked back and sat down. "Do you work?"

"Look at my manicure," she said, displaying her nails. "Does it look like I work?"

Stone laughed. "I wasn't thinking of something in the mines."

"I run two houses and this apartment," she said, "and supervise everything else except my husband's shopping."

"What is his name?"

"Donald Trask. I kept my maiden name, thank God. He operates a hedge fund that was built on referrals from my father and me."

"When did he start the firm?"

"Right after we were married."

"Good, then he won't be able to exclude the business from marital property."

"If I so much as whisper to a friend or two that I'm pulling my father's investment, he won't have a business by this time tomorrow."

"That sounds vindictive."

"It's not. Pulling the investment is why I'm meeting with the advisors. It's done less well than the market."

"Don't whisper to your friends," Stone said. "You might give him grounds for a defamation suit. Who owns the real estate?"

"We both own the Greenwich house and this apartment," she said, waving a hand. "The Maine house was my father's."

"So you'll sell both and divide the proceeds?"

"I believe that's how it goes. I'd keep this place, but you wouldn't believe the monthly maintenance charges."

"Are you angry with your husband?"

"No, just disgusted. He's the angry one because I caught him screwing around, and he's afraid I'll tell our friends."

"Once again, don't talk to your friends, until it's all over and the divorce is final."

"Good advice. I don't want to talk about it anyway."

Dinner came, and they washed it down with a good bottle of chardonnay.

"I'M SO GLAD I fell into your lap this afternoon," she said. "If I hadn't, I'd be languishing in some ER right now, waiting to be seen." She yawned.

"I expect you could use some rest," Stone said. "If you'd like to blindfold me I'll undress you and put you to bed."

"Thank you, but I remember how to undress. If you'll help me into the bedroom, I'll do the rest."

He did so, kissed her good night, and left her to it.

15

STONE WAS WORKING as lunchtime approached, when Joan rang. "Herbie Fisher on one."

"Good morning, Herb."

"And to you, and thanks so much for the referral."

"What referral?"

"Cilla Scott."

"Oh, she's called you already?"

"She's seen me. She just left."

"You're taking her on, then?"

"I certainly am. She's the ideal client—organized, prepared, and, most important, dispassionate. She wheeled in years of tax returns, financial statements, and annual reports for his hedge fund, along with her prenup. She's given me enough to put her husband into a homeless shelter, but she's instructed me to bend over backward to be fair to him. If I were being divorced, I'd love to have an ex-wife like that. How'd you come across her?"

"She fell into my lap. Who's representing her husband?"

"Terry Barnes, at Barnes & Wood. I'm expecting his call. He and Donald Trask are old fraternity brothers from Cornell. I'm guessing Trask will listen to him."

"That could be good or bad."

"No, Barnes will just want to be shed of all this, and he'll know how to give it to Trask straight and make him take it."

"Sounds like the ideal opponent."

"Just an honest one, which is what Trask needs to get him through this with some of his ego intact. The guy's been sucking at her family teat for the past eight years, and he should understand that it's over."

"Well, if anybody can explain it to him, Herb, it's you."

"Yeah, I'm putting on my Dutch uncle mask as we speak. Hang on."

Stone was put on hold for about a minute, then Herb came back.

"Terry Barnes is on the way over here. Things are moving fast and smooth."

"Do I have to remind you that where divorce is concerned, 'fast and smooth' are an illusion?"

"Hope springs eternal. I gotta go make some notes for this meeting."

"Keep me posted."

"Cilla has given me permission to do that; she seems to trust you implicitly."

"I'm flattered." He hung up as Joan buzzed again.

"A Ms. Scott on two."

Stone picked up. "Good morning. I hope you're staying off that foot."

"You and Dr. Kevin would be proud of me," she said. "I've

got myself a little cart to rest my knee on, and I scoot around like that. The concierge has furnished me with a minion to carry my purse and drag my wheelie around with all my documents. I left them all with your Herb Fisher."

"I heard. What do you think of him?"

"I think he's ideal."

"He said pretty much the same about you."

"I'm seeing my father's financial advisors, then having a quick lunch with your friend Margot, to hear about the real estate market, and then we're going apartment hunting."

"You move at the speed of light."

"Every step I take is one away from the marriage, and that's what I want most right now. Here's Margot, gotta run." She hung up.

Joan buzzed again. "A Mr. Trask to see you. He doesn't have an appointment."

"Who Trask?"

"Donald."

"Well, shit, send him in, I guess." Stone stood up to greet a very large man in a well-cut suit. Six-four and two-twenty, Stone guessed. Works out daily.

"Mr. Trask?" He extended a hand.

Trask shook it perfunctorily and accepted an offered chair.

"What can I do for you?" Stone asked, not very invitingly.

"You can stay away from my wife for a start," Trask said truculently. "I know you're behind all of this."

"All of what?"

"This divorce thing. You two have been planning it, haven't you?"

"Mr. Trask, please listen carefully, and remember what

I'm saying because I don't want to repeat myself. I met your wife less than twenty-four hours ago, entirely by accident, when she sprained an ankle in a shop I was visiting. I got her back to her hotel and arranged for a doctor to come and see her. When I told her I practiced law, she asked me to recommend a divorce attorney. I did so and, I might add, without regret. That is the sum total of her relationship with me. Do you understand?"

Trask glared at him, tapping a foot. Stone thought it probable that the man was accustomed to ending talks like this with his fists.

"Is that the truth?"

Stone nodded slowly. "Now, if there's nothing else, please excuse me. I have work to do." That last part was a lie, but Stone thought it sounded good.

"I expect you'll hear from me," Trask said, getting to his feet.

"We won't be speaking again," Stone said. "Your wife is represented by Herbert Fisher of Woodman & Weld. Your attorney can put you in touch with him, should you have any further questions." He stood and watched the man leave, then sat back down just as Joan came in.

"You all right?"

"I haven't been beaten to a pulp, if that's what you mean."

"I had a bad feeling," she said. That's when he realized she was holding her .45 behind her back.

"I don't think he'll be back," Stone said. "In any case, there shouldn't be any occasion for drawing weapons."

"What do you mean? Everybody in this house is carrying, including you."

"Well, yes, but that's another matter entirely. Mr. Trask is not a suspect in the case."

"Who is he?"

"An ex-husband-to-be."

"Oh, shit," she said. "The worst kind."

"He was operating on incomplete information," Stone said. "I augmented his education on the subject, so please decline any further calls or requests for meetings from him, and don't hesitate to call the police if he becomes persistent."

"I can't just shoot him?" Joan asked, half joking.

"Maybe later," Stone said, and she went back to her desk.

Stone took some deep breaths and went back to what he hadn't been doing.

16

STONE, on a hunch, called Dino.

"Bacchetti."

"Hi, will you run a name for me?"

"I'm sorry, you seem to have misdialed the number and been connected to our 'Services Not Available to Civilians Department.'"

"His name is Donald Trask of Greenwich, Connecticut. He also keeps a residence at the Carlyle. He runs a hedge fund."

Stone could hear the tapping of keys.

"I don't have time to read or explain this to you, so I'll e-mail it," Dino said, then hung up.

Stone waited a couple of minutes, found the e-mail, and printed it.

Donald Tyrone Trask had a record of scrapes, some of them violent, going back to college. He had done ten days in the local jail for beating up another student at a fraternity party, and he had had altercations with denizens of Greenwich, all of whom seemed to be service providers or blue-collar workers. Apparently, Donald Trask dirtied his hands only with those he thought to be his social inferiors, who might be less likely to sue or spread gossip among his peers. There was also a juvenile record, which was sealed, and Stone presumed it contained more of the same.

Stone called Cilla Scott's cell phone.

"Hey, there."

"Got a second?"

"Sure."

"Forgive me for prying, but I have a good reason."

"Pry away."

"During your marriage did Donald ever strike or otherwise physically abuse you?"

"You've met Donald, haven't you?" she asked after a pause.

"He called on me this morning. I made assumptions."

She was silent again. "On a couple of occasions he slapped me around. Once he sent me to the ER."

"What, if anything, did you do about it."

"I took a full swing at his jaw with a fireplace poker," she said. "It never happened again. He didn't like having his jaw wired shut."

That's my girl, Stone thought. "Did you mention this to Herb Fisher?"

"No, because I don't want him to use it, if this should go to trial."

"It's important that you tell him about it. You can discuss later how or if the information should be used."

"All right, I'll do that. Or, better yet, it would save me some pain if you told him."

"All right, and I'm sorry to cause you pain. Tell me, is your knee scooter restaurant-certified?"

"It is a fully certified knee scooter."

"Then have dinner with me this evening."

"I have a drinks date, but I'll meet you after that. Where and when?"

"Patroon, one-sixty East Forty-sixth Street, seven-thirty?"

"Poltroon?"

"No, *Patroon*. It's a Dutch title for a landowner. A *poltroon* is a spineless coward."

"I'll try to remember the difference. See you then."

Stone called Herb.

"Yeah?"

"Cilla Scott asked me to convey to you that Donald Trask has a history of beating her up, sending her to the ER on one occasion. It ended when she broke his jaw with a poker."

"Good to know," Herb replied.

"She will want that information used only in extremis, and with her expressed permission."

"Gotcha."

"I also caught a glimpse of Donald Trask's criminal record."

"Tell me."

"History of fighting, going back to college, maybe further; his juvie record was sealed."

"Did he win his fights?"

"I expect so. He chose people he thought were his inferiors, who were not likely to fight back."

"Good to know."

"See ya." Stone hung up.

———

HERB FISHER HUNG UP; his secretary buzzed him. "Terry Barnes to see you."

"Send him in," Herb said, arranging Cilla's documents in neat piles before him.

Barnes bustled in and tried to inject some bonhomie into the occasion. "Morning, Fisher," he said. "Good to see you again. How's the wife?"

Herb rose and shook his hand. "We've never met, Mr. Barnes, and I'm unmarried."

"Oh, ah, my fault. Mistaken identity." He took a seat. "I'm here in the matter of Trask v. Trask," he said.

"Actually, it's Scott v. Trask since Ms. Scott retained her maiden name at marriage."

"As you say. Only met the lady a few times."

"Tell me," Herb said, "are we going to settle this like gentlemen or go to trial?"

"Oh?" Barnes chuckled. "Have you met my client?"

"No."

"Well, if you had met him you'd know that he's a rather combative sort, more inclined to fight than to argue."

"And I understand he has a criminal record to support that position."

"Oh, that thing back at Cornell, you mean?"

"Before, during, and since," Herb said. "Your client and old friend is a nasty piece of work. I'd love nothing more than to depose him for a couple of hours, then examine him in court. He could go directly from the courthouse to the Y, where he would be living, subsequent to the ruling in my client's favor."

"You sound very confident, Herbert."

"That's only because I am confident. Your client, since his marriage to Ms. Scott, has not earned a dime that is not directly attributable to her father, her friends, or his wife's personal funds. His hedge fund is still in business only because of the record upturn in the market the past few months. He would fare poorly in the matter of New York State law requiring equitable division on property."

"What are you proposing?" Barnes asked.

Herb slid a single typed sheet of paper across the desk. "I think that, on reflection, you will find this offer to be much more generous than necessary," he said, "and it will not improve. Your problem is going to be to lead your client to face the reality of his situation. If he does, he can leave the marriage with some money, enough to maintain him in some sort of style. That's if he closes his hedge fund, of course."

"Why should he close it? It's profitable."

"When the investors learn of the divorce they will depart in droves," Herb said. "He would save face by just shutting it down."

Barnes reread the list to gain time. "I'll speak to him," he said.

"Remember, there will be no improvement in the offer, nor will there be in his reputation should we go to trial."

"I'll speak to him." Barnes got up and left without shaking hands.

17

S TONE WAS ABOUT TO WRAP up his day, a little late, when his phone rang. Joan had already left her desk. "Hello?"

"Is this Barrington?"

"It is."

"This is Donald Trask."

"I've no wish to speak to you," Stone said.

"You can speak to me, or I'll come over there," Trask said. "You wrote this document, didn't you?"

"Document?"

"My wife's demands."

"I do not represent your wife; I have not written or seen any document prepared for her; call Herbert Fisher at Woodman & Weld."

"Tell you what," Trask said, "you know the New York Athletic Club on Central Park South?"

"I do."

"Are you a member there?"

"I am not."

"Well, I am, and that's good enough for both of us."

"Mr. Trask, what are you talking about?"

"I'm suggesting that you and I meet there in an hour."

"I've no wish to drink or dine with you."

"They have a very nice boxing ring upstairs. I suggest we meet and settle the matter of the divorce terms mano a mano in the ring."

"Mr. Trask, I can suggest one of two options," Stone said. "First, seek professional help, which you are clearly in need of. Second, go to the New York Athletic Club gym, find a heavy bag, and punch it until you can't stand up anymore. Either of those options will keep you out of jail. Now, don't bother me again." Stone hung up. He thought a moment, then called Herb Fisher.

"Herb Fisher."

"It's Stone."

"Why do you sound exasperated?"

"Because I am exasperated."

"All right, tell me. Cry your heart out."

"I've just heard from Donald Trask, who persists in believing that I, not you, represent his wife in her divorce action."

"Hey, that's okay with me," Herb said. "I don't want him on my back."

"Well, that's where he's going to be, if I have to hit him over the head and deliver him to you personally."

"How kind you are!"

"I'm just letting you know that I think the man is unhinged and, as we know, prone to violence. He's been set off by a document containing his wife's demands that you apparently handed to his attorney, and eventually, after he's been told a few more times, he's going to finally get the idea that he should be dealing with you and not me."

"I suppose he will, after Terry Barnes explains it all to him."

"Have you met Donald Trask?"

"I have not."

"Well, physically, he makes one and a half of you, and you don't want to let him back you into a corner."

"Thank you. I will avoid corners until further notice."

"Have you heard back from Terry Barnes?"

"I have not."

"Well, I don't think you're going to—not today, anyway. I suspect that Mr. Barnes is in a dark bar somewhere, nursing loosened teeth, broken ribs, and a triple scotch."

"What do you advise?" Herb asked.

"Armed guards," Stone said, then hung up. He rang Fred on the house intercom.

"Yes, sir?"

"Fred, we have an imminent threat somewhere, possibly circling the neighborhood."

"Of what nature, sir?"

"Name of Donald Trask: tall, heavyset, in excellent condition for a man of his age, enjoys inflicting pain on those who annoy him."

"Have you annoyed him, sir?"

"Without even trying."

"Then I'll take a turn around the block, sir, and see if I can spot him."

"Be careful, Fred. Don't let him get a punch in."

"He'll be expecting you, not me, sir."

"A good point. Be careful."

Stone hung up and called Dino.

"And what service may the NYPD render to you this fine day?" Dino asked.

"I believe you employ people who are schooled in the art of removing dangerous characters from the street and housing them elsewhere."

"We've been known to do that."

"Well, there's one around my house somewhere: to wit, one Donald Trask, six-four, two-twenty, good shape, mean."

"Has he threatened you?"

"He has formed the opinion that I am representing his wife in a divorce action against him."

"Are you?"

"I am not. Herbie Fisher is, but I have not learned enough of the man's language to convince him of that. He invited me into the ring at the New York Athletic Club to settle the matter of his divorce."

Dino laughed heartily. "I'd pay for a ringside seat to that! Are you taking him up on it?"

"Are you insane?"

"Well, I don't think an invitation to a boxing match at a gentlemen's club constitutes a threat of actual violence, so I can't yank him off the street. You're lawyer enough to know that. Call me from the ER after he's found you, and I'll see what we can do."

"With friends like you, who needs assassins?"

"All right, all right, I'll get a couple of guys to brace him and tell him he'd be happier in a bar somewhere, getting unconscious."

"I think he may have already spent considerable time in that effort, and you should tell your guys to be careful with him, he's dangerous. Tell them to keep their Tasers at the ready."

"Yeah, I'll do that." Dino hung up.

FRED LEFT THE HOUSE by the front door, pausing to select a golf umbrella with a thick, heavy briar handle from the stand in the hallway. As he descended the front stairs he unbuttoned his jacket and transferred the umbrella to his left hand, leaving his right free for other action. He walked down the street to the corner of Second Avenue, stopped, and looked around. On the corner opposite him, looking thoughtful, was a man answering the description Stone had provided. Fred crossed the street.

The man looked up, saw Fred coming, and clearly dismissed him as a threat.

"Mr. Trask?" Fred asked. "Mr. Donald Trask?"

Trask looked down at him and shifted his weight, as if to be ready. "Yeah, what?"

Fred took hold of the golf umbrella with both hands and swung it at the load-bearing knee.

Trask made a loud noise and collapsed in a heap.

"Have a nice day," Fred said, "but do it in another neighborhood." He walked away, back toward the house.

STONE'S DIRECT LINE RANG. "Stone Barrington."

"It's Dino. My guys located your guy on the corner of Second Avenue, lying in a heap, clutching a knee."

"What happened to him?"

"He said he was attacked by a midget with an umbrella."

Not far wrong, Stone thought, given the disparity between Fred's size and Trask's.

"They got him into a cab and sent him home," Dino said. "Happy?"

"Happy," Stone replied.

"Dinner?"

"Sorry, otherwise engaged." They both hung up.

18

S TONE GOT TO HIS FEET at Patroon, but Ken Aretsky, the owner, was already assisting Cilla Scott down a step or two and restoring her knee scooter to its proper place. He waved to give her a target.

She made it with a few deft pushes of her other foot.

"You look as though you were born on that thing," Stone said, helping her to be seated.

"It feels like that long," she replied. "I'm going to try tippy-toe tomorrow."

"Don't rush it," Stone advised, "you could screw up things and make them worse."

"Do they sell alcoholic beverages in this restaurant?" she asked.

"My apologies. What would you like?"

"A very dry Belvedere vodka martini, olives."

The beverage was rushed to her.

"Two-legged days," she said, raising her glass.

"I'll drink to that, but you're supposed to wait four days before you try."

"Oh, all right, I'll wait until day after tomorrow."

"I had occasion to be introduced to your husband today," he said.

She looked surprised. "Where?"

"In my office."

"He doesn't even know your name," she said. "At least, not from me."

"Then he has a spy in your camp."

"What ensued?"

"I explained to him that Herb Fisher, not I, represents you. He seemed unable to make that leap. Perhaps you could tell him that?"

"I already have. Herb had his first meeting with Donald's attorney today. I'm told it went well."

"Then nobody told Donald. He's very upset about the deal offered him."

"Herb says my offer is more than a court would give him. I hope Terry Barnes can make him understand that."

"His judgment was probably impaired by alcohol. He called later in the day and offered to arrange a boxing match at the Athletic Club, in which he and I would duke out a settlement."

She placed her face in her hands. "That is so embarrassing," she said. "Please accept my apology."

"You've nothing for which to apologize. He was hanging out near my house, so Fred went out and had a word with him."

"Your Fred? That darling little man?"

"That darling little man reduced Donald to a quivering heap with a single blow from an umbrella," Stone said. "Two passing police officers got him into a cab and sent him home, wherever that is."

"The Athletic Club," she said. "He's taken a room there. I hope he'll take the opportunity to sober up."

"Is he an alcoholic?"

"Borderline, maybe. I'm not sure. He drinks to excess when angry or unhappy."

"That must be most of the time these days," Stone observed. "Still, I suppose he must have his charms or you wouldn't have married him."

"He used to, really he did. Strangely enough, the success of his fund in a rising market seemed to depress him. I suppose he realized that it was Daddy's money, and mine, he was riding on."

"The realization of one's inadequacies can be a trigger for depression, I suppose."

"Are you speaking from experience?" she asked.

"Inadequacies? Me? I assure you, I am a perfectly adequate person, if imperfect. On rare occasions, I can even rise above adequacy."

"Good to know," she said, taking a gulp of her martini. "God, that's good."

"Tell me," Stone said, "what's your game plan?"

"For how far ahead?"

"The next few months, say."

"One: get divorced. Two: get housed. Three: decorate housing. I haven't gotten much further than that."

"Those seem reasonable short-term goals."

"I've never really had long-term goals; I pretty much just wait for long-term to happen, then deal with it."

"Okay, let's see if you can look further ahead. Describe what you would like your circumstances to be a year from now."

"My circumstances? Still rich—richer, in fact, when I combine Daddy's estate with Mother's, which has been my only money, so far, exceeding any real need, except supporting Donald. Daddy liked it that way, because he could hang on to every dime of his own until the end. In fact, it wouldn't surprise me to learn that he'd found a way to wire-transfer it all ahead."

Stone laughed. "So he didn't coddle you?"

"Oh, he did, from time to time, but I've always been very good at coddling myself without the help of others. Are you rich?"

Stone managed not to choke on his bourbon. "Yes, fairly."

"The reason I ask is: If I'm going to end up supporting you, I'd rather know about it now than wait to find out. All I know about you is that you drive a Bentley—rented? borrowed?— that you are acquainted with a doctor, a divorce attorney, and a Realtor, and that you are known to the management of this restaurant. The rest is a blank slate."

"I own the Bentley, and please don't concern yourself: There are no conceivable circumstances under which you might ever have to support me."

"You understand my concern?"

"Yes, but what does your intuition tell you?"

"My intuition lies to me all the time. Who are you?"

"I believe it's the custom in this country to get to know people by talking to them, not by inquisition. If that's not sufficient, you can hire a private detective and have me investigated, which is probably what your father would have done in the circumstances. For the moment, however, all you need to know is what's on the menu."

She looked at the menu. "Caesar salad, strip steak medium rare." She put it down. "Where do you live?"

"A ten-minute walk from here, Turtle Bay."

"Ah, yes, you did mention that."

"I did."

"In which house?"

"I own two houses there, one for staff."

"Are those the only houses you own?"

"No, I also own houses in Los Angeles, Paris, London, Key West, and the South of England, with appropriate furnishings in each. I also own a jet airplane, a small yacht, and a partnership in a larger one. I don't think you'll ever be called upon to give me anything more boisterous than a necktie at Christmas, which I will return and exchange for one I like."

She threw up her hands in surrender. "Forgive me, that was a shitty thing to say to you. I suppose my wounds haven't healed yet from my last and only experience with a long-term relationship."

"How long have you been married?"

"Nearly eight years."

"It sounds like long enough."

"More than long enough," she replied. "I should have dumped him halfway through. Are you now or have you ever been married?"

"I was married."

"Ended in divorce?"

"Ended in death, hers."

"Again, it's my turn to apologize."

"It was a perfectly straightforward question."

"Why do you have so many houses?"

"Because I can. Anyway, I've always loved houses, and there came a time when I figured out that if I saw one I liked, I could buy it, just write a check. I'm trying to stop, but I can't make any promises."

"Promise me nothing," she said, "and I'll never be disappointed."

19

THEY WERE HALFWAY through their steaks.

"Do you have any children?" she asked.

"One, a son, Peter. He's a film director in L.A."

"Peter Barrington?"

"That's right."

"I have actually seen his work, and it's good."

"I'll tell him you said so."

"I'd like to tell him myself," she said.

"Well, if you someday decide that I meet your standards for male company, that might happen."

"I haven't told you what my standards are."

"I was guessing. All right, what are they?"

"Self-supporting, usually sober, intelligent, kind, and good company."

"Those sound like all the qualities not possessed by your current husband."

"A coincidence, but it's a start. What are your standards?"

"Pretty much the same as yours," he replied. "Oh, and two working legs. I insist on that."

She laughed. "All right, I know enough about you not to be paranoid anymore."

"Is paranoia your usual condition?"

"Only in dealing with men, and as I said, I'm over that now."

"What a relief. There's a Key lime pie in the fridge at home. Would you like to have a nightcap at my house?"

"I'd love that," she said.

Stone paid the bill, and they got into the Bentley. "Home, Fred," he said, "and pull into the garage, so we can take the elevator."

Fred did so, and Stone and Cilla got out at the living room level and made their way across it to Stone's study. He poured them each a cognac, found the pie in the fridge, and sliced it.

"Heavenly," Cilla said, taking a big bite. "This is a lovely house."

"Thank you. I inherited it from a great-aunt, my grandmother's sister, who thought I'd never amount to anything, so I should at least have a roof over my head. All the woodwork and much of the furniture was built by my father, who was a designer and cabinetmaker."

"A house with a heritage," she said. "I like that."

"I like it, too, and the staff lives next door."

"Why do you have a staff house?"

"The house next door came up for sale, and it's hard for working people to find affordable housing in this city, so I just moved them all in. Also, the purchase doubled the size of the garage."

"I saw another car under a tarp down there."

"That's a French sports car, a Blaise, designed by a friend of mine. I don't drive it very often; it's more convenient to have Fred drive the Bentley."

"Don't be surprised if you get a rock through a front window. That will be Donald's next move."

"The glass is armored, so it won't be a problem. Tell me, does Donald own a gun?"

"Several."

"I was afraid you'd say that. When he sobers up, is he going to come to his senses?"

"I wouldn't count on it," she said. "Are you unaccustomed to women with baggage?"

"Most people have baggage of one sort or another, and with women, it usually seems to be a disagreeable and unmanageable male former companion."

"*Unmanageable* is a good word to describe Donald," she said. "God knows, I tried hard enough, and the most it got me was a sock in the kisser."

"If you have any concerns at all about your safety, I can arrange for someone to watch over you."

"Like the Gershwin song?"

"Not quite. He'll be about Donald's size with a bulge under his arm."

"I think I'm all right for the moment; I'm sure his attorney has instructed him on behaving during trial."

"Do you think he'll go to trial?"

"Maybe, he's very competitive."

"If I may ask, what sort of deal did you and Herb offer him on the real estate?"

"Sell it and divide the proceeds."

"It might help you to avoid trial if you use some of your newfound wealth to just buy his half of the house and the Carlyle apartment. That would put some cash in his pocket almost immediately, which I'm sure he'd like. And there'd be less to argue about in court."

"I'm sure he'd like that, too," she said. "It's a damned good idea. How do we reach agreement on the value of the two properties?"

"Each of you hires your own appraiser, and the two of them pick a third. You take the average of the three appraisals."

"Brilliant!"

"Herb would have thought of it in the second round of negotiations. Wait and see if he doesn't bring it up."

"All right."

"How did you and Margot get on?"

"Blazingly! I forgot to tell you, she showed me three apartments, and I loved two of them. I'm leaning toward the one on Fifth Avenue in the Sixties."

"You can't go wrong there. Put down a deposit, but don't close until after the divorce is final. Another property in the mix might muddy the waters and slow things down."

"Where were you when I was making all the big decisions in my life, like whether to marry Donald?"

"Probably about that time I was a police officer."

"You? A cop?"

"A detective, thank you very much. I was invalided out—a bullet in the knee."

"Then how did you get to be a lawyer?"

"I had already graduated from NYU Law School when I

joined the force, so I just needed to pass the bar exam. I took a two-week cram course and passed, and an old classmate brought me into Woodman & Weld."

"My goodness."

"See how much you learn when you just talk to people?"

"You're absolutely right," she admitted. "And anyway, you're fun to talk to."

"Thank you."

"I'm sorry about my baggage," she said.

"Don't worry about it."

"I hope he doesn't make a further nuisance of himself."

"I hope so, too," Stone said.

HE PUT HER in the Bentley and Fred drove her back to the Carlyle.

20

STONE WAS SEEING CILLA off when he saw Faith walking past and up the front steps next door. He walked through the door to the next house.

"Oh!" she said, stepping back. "You frightened me."

"Apparently nothing else does," Stone said. "Forgive me for sounding like a father, but where have you been?"

"I left a few things at the hotel, and since it was such a nice evening, I walked over there to retrieve them." She held up a shopping bag as if it explained everything.

"Come with me," he said, holding the door for her. "Let's have a drink."

He settled her in the study with a cognac and took a seat. "Have you forgotten that we're in the middle of a wave of murders with victims who look just like you and who live in, roughly, the same neighborhood as that hotel?"

"Well, it seems to me that we're not in the middle of this wave, but at the end. Nobody's been killed for a week."

"And you took that as a reason to take a stroll in a danger-ous place?"

"Pretty much, I guess."

"Faith, you can't just do that."

"I'm a grown woman, I can do whatever I like."

"Not if you want to continue working for me."

"Are you threatening to fire me if I don't do as you say?"

"I'm threatening to fire you if you continue to risk your life by doing foolish things. I've no wish to have to ship your body back to your people in Georgia in a box, and I won't be a party to your murder. Do you understand me?"

She pouted, but said nothing.

"All right, tomorrow morning start looking for another place to live. I'll give you two weeks to move out, and your salary will continue until then."

Faith produced the ultimate feminine weapon, for which males have no defense: she began to cry.

"Oh, come on! You said you're an adult, start behaving like one. This isn't junior high."

"I don't want to lose my job," she said.

"You'll lose it instantly if you're dead. Has anyone told you what these killers do to the women?"

"I read the newspapers," she said.

"Well, sometimes there are things the police don't tell the press. Would you like for me to describe, in detail, what they're leaving out?"

"No!" she said. "Spare me."

Stone knocked off the rest of his cognac and set down his glass. "Come see me tomorrow morning and tell me what you want to do," he said. "Now, if you'll excuse me, I'm going to bed. Finish your drink here, if you like." He went upstairs, undressed, brushed his teeth, and got into bed. He was still angry with her, and it took him a while to get to sleep.

THE FOLLOWING MORNING, Stone made a call to Mike Freeman at Strategic Services and placed an order. The order arrived about an hour later and took a seat outside Joan's office.

Faith knocked and entered his office. "I've thought it over," she said, "and you're right. It was foolish of me to do that last night, and I don't want to lose my job, so I'll follow your orders on this until they catch these people."

"That's good," Stone said. "Now, I have a gift for you." He buzzed Joan. "Send in the gift."

A large man in a dark suit with a bulge under his arm walked into the office.

"Faith, this is Jimbo. He is going to be your constant companion whenever you leave the house, unless we're out of town, and until the killers are caught."

Faith was speechless. "You got me a minder?"

"That's a good way to describe Jimbo," Stone said. "He's your minder during the day. A woman named Sylvia will be on the night shift."

"That's outrageous."

"You're not required to continue to work here, but if you decide you want to, then Jimbo is part of the deal. I've known him a few years, and he's a nice guy. You'll get used to him. You might even begin to appreciate him. Jimbo, will you please see Faith to her office?"

"Certainly, Mr. Barrington," Jimbo replied. "Faith, right this way, please."

She stalked out of the room, followed by the faithful Jimbo.

Joan buzzed him. "Dino, on one."

Stone pressed the button. "Good morning."

"If you say so," Dino said grumpily.

"What's up today?"

"I thought you'd like to know. Yesterday, after my two guys put what's-his-name—?"

"Donald Trask?"

"Yeah, after they put him into a cab, they followed him to see if he went home. He didn't. He went down to the Lower East Side, where there's a gun shop used by a lot of cops, and tried to buy a gun."

"I know the place. He can't buy a gun in Manhattan without a New York City carry permit."

"He bought a gun."

"He has a carry permit?"

"He does, and before you ask, he hasn't done anything that would make it possible for me to have it canceled."

"He got drunk and tried to lure me into a fight."

"He got drunk, maybe, but I keep telling you, all he did was invite you to participate in a sporting event, which is not even a misdemeanor, let alone a felony."

"What did he buy?"

"A Beretta nine millimeter, the small one, and an over-the-belt holster—oh, and couple of spare magazines and a box of ammo."

"What kind of ammo?"

"Federal Personal Defense, the hollow points."

"So he's serious, you think?"

"I don't know," Dino said, "but if I were you, I'd behave as if he were serious."

"Where did he go from there?"

"To the New York Athletic Club."

"That's where he's staying."

"I wonder what their rules are about firearms on the premises?" Dino said.

"I don't know," Stone said, "but we could find out if one of your guys would call the club secretary and tell them there's an armed member in one of their rooms."

"I think you should perform that task yourself," Dino said.

"I would," Stone replied, "but I want to be able to deny having done it."

"Figures," Dino said.

21

S TONE THOUGHT ABOUT the dangers of having an armed Donald Trask loose in the city and what should be done about it. He put aside thoughts of his own safety and called Cilla Scott.

"Hello?"

"It's Stone, where are you?"

"In the rear seat of a black town car I've hired for the day, on the way to see Herb Fisher."

"Good. Do you have a will?"

"Yes."

"Who are the beneficiaries?"

"My father, a couple of charities, and Donald. Why do you ask?"

"When you arrive at Herb's office I want you to ask him to draw up a new will for you."

"Why?"

"Your father is dead, and I presume you don't want your

personal fortune to fall into Donald's hands in the event of your death."

"A good point."

"Don't leave Herb's office until the will is properly witnessed and signed."

"What's the rush?"

"Your position will be precarious until you have a new will."

She was silent for a moment. "You don't mean . . ."

"I mean that yesterday, after his encounter with Fred, Donald went to a gun shop downtown and bought a pistol, a holster, and ammunition."

"And you think . . ."

"At this moment Donald is the only person who stands to benefit from your demise."

"Oh, my God," she breathed.

"If you'll do as I ask, I'll give you dinner here this evening."

"How can I resist that. I promise I'll sign a new will."

"Keep your car and have it deliver you here. Call, and I'll open the garage door. Also, bring an overnight bag with a few things. I think it would be best if you stay here for a few nights."

"Well, that's subtle," she said.

"You may have your choice of six guest bedrooms, each with a lock on the door."

"And why do you think this is a good idea?"

"Does Donald have a key to the Carlyle apartment?"

"Oh. I'd be happy to accept your hospitality."

"One other thing. Ask Herb to let Donald's attorney know that you've signed a new will excluding him."

"I will. What time tonight?"

"Six?"

"See you then." She hung up.

HERB FISHER RECEIVED CILLA SCOTT and noted the absence of the knee scooter and the presence of a cane. He got her to a chair. "Are you sure you're ready for hobbling?"

"I spoke with my doctor and got his permission. The Carlyle supplied the cane."

Herb sat down. "I've heard from Donald's attorney. Donald is okay with the deal, but he wants ten million dollars."

"Ha!" Cilla replied.

"It's pretty much what I expected. I have a counteroffer in mind."

"And what is that?"

"You are cash-rich at the moment, are you not, what with your inheritance from your father?"

"I am."

"Offer to buy his share of both properties from him, in cash, immediately."

"That's clever," she said. "What should I pay him?"

"What do you think the properties are worth?"

"The Greenwich estate would probably go for ten million in today's market—there's a lot of land. The Carlyle apartment would probably go for four million. Those valuations are from my Realtor."

"So, we'll offer him seven million dollars for both properties?"

"That's good for me. I'll keep the Greenwich house and sell the apartment. I've already started looking for one."

"All right. Shall I call Terry now?"

"First, there's another matter," she said.

"Shoot."

"My will is among the documents I gave you at our first meeting."

"I saw it, but I haven't read it."

"The beneficiaries are a couple of charities, my father—who's now dead—and Donald. I don't want my death to be an advantage to Donald, and I want him to know I've changed the will."

Herb produced a legal pad. "Who would you like the beneficiaries to be?"

"For the moment, just the two charities, and I'd like to sign it before I leave here today."

Herb pressed a button on his phone. "Come in here, please."

Herb found the will and, momentarily, a young man appeared. "This is Devon, one of our associates; Devon, Ms. Scott." He handed him the will. "Ms. Scott needs a new will immediately, with the charities shown in the current will as beneficiaries. Eliminate the two other parties, print out a new will on our boilerplate, and bring it to me soonest."

"Ten minutes," Devon said, disappearing with the will.

"What sort of apartment are you looking at?" Herb asked.

"Three bedrooms en suite, living room, dining room, large kitchen, library, office, two maids' rooms, on Fifth Avenue, twelfth floor, terrace, park views, parking, twelve millionish."

"Sounds nice. Have you made an offer?"

"Probably today."

"Give them a six-million-dollar deposit, but insist that the closing must be after the divorce is final, so it won't get into the mix."

"All right."

"Are we ready to call Terry?"

"I am."

"If he doesn't bite immediately, can I sweeten the pot by another million dollars?"

"I'd do that to be rid of him immediately."

Herb made the call.

"Good morning, Herb."

"Good morning, Terry. I have a revised offer for you."

"Ready to copy."

"The offer is the same, but Ms. Scott will buy his share of both properties for seven million dollars cash, payable on final decree."

"That's interesting. Can you hold?"

"Sure." Herb turned to Cilla. "I think Donald is in his office now."

Terry came back. "Ten million dollars and we have a deal."

"Eight million, and that's our absolute, final offer—or we go to trial. Tell him for me, he's not going to enjoy it."

"Hold on." Terry was gone for a good three minutes before he came back. "You have a deal."

"I'll send the documents over to you within the hour," Herb said, "and I'll expect them to be returned, signed, today."

"And a down payment?"

"All of it at final decree. Lean on one of your judges, Terry, and we can wrap this up quickly. Oh, and let Mr. Trask know that Ms. Scott has signed a new will that excludes him."

"I'll tell him, and I'll see what I can do about a judge." Both men hung up.

"Okay," Herb said, "now we see if Donald signs."

"Do you think there's a chance he won't?"

"I doubt it, but I want to see ink on paper before I'm satisfied."

Devon knocked on the door and came in with the new will and three secretaries as witnesses. Cilla signed, and they were done.

Herb dictated the terms of the property settlement and sent Devon to print it.

"Are we done?" Cilla asked.

"Wait until we have a copy of the settlement for you to sign."

She waited, the copy came, and she signed it. "If you'll excuse me," she said, "I'm going to go take another look at that apartment."

"Margot will have the documents you'll need to sign. You should let your bank know you'll be writing a big check."

"Will do." Cilla hobbled out of Herb's office.

Herb handed the settlement agreement to Devon. "Hand deliver this to Terry Barnes's office, wait for it to be signed, and bring it back. Here's a copy with Ms. Scott's signature. When you're sure that Trask has properly executed his copy, hand him this one."

"I'm on it," Devon said, departing at a trot.

———

Cilla was packing a bag at the Carlyle when the phone rang. "Yes?"

"It's Herb Fisher. I wanted you to know that we've received the property settlement with Donald's signature on it, and we've given his attorney the copy with yours. All is now in order."

"Oh, Herb," she breathed. "Thank you so much."

"Terry is looking for a family court judge who will give us a quick final decree, so this could be over soon."

She hung up and headed for Stone's house with a light heart.

22

S TONE GOT THE CALL from Cilla and told her to take the elevator to the top floor, then he pressed the button on his iPhone that opened the garage door. It would close automatically when her car left.

He was standing next to the elevator when the door opened and took her bag.

"Where would you like to sleep?" he asked, kissing her.

"Wherever you're sleeping," she replied.

He walked her down the hall and put her bag in the second dressing room. "Unpack, freshen up, then come down to the study for drinks. Dinner is at seven."

STONE WENT DOWN to the study and called Fred on the house phone.

"Yes, sir?"

"Fred, I'd like you to have a look around the neighborhood again for our previous visitor."

"Yes, sir."

"If you find him, don't approach. He knows what you look like now, and he will be armed. Just come back here, and we'll let the police deal with him."

"Yes, sir."

Stone called Jimbo on his cell phone.

"Yes, sir?"

"Where are you, Jimbo?"

"In her sitting room, watching TV."

"Is she down for the night?"

"Hard to say. She's impulsive."

"Tell me about it."

"Sylvia comes on at ten. I'll be right here until then."

"If she doesn't want to go out, call Helene in the kitchen, and she'll bring dinner to you."

"Thank you, Mr. Barrington."

STONE LOOKED UP TO FIND Cilla standing in the doorway.

"Knock, knock," she said.

"Come in and have a seat. Martini?"

"Oh, please, yes."

He mixed the drink, handed it to her, and poured himself a Knob Creek.

"Did you have a good day?" he asked.

"I can't remember a better one in about two years. Herb reached a settlement with Donald's attorney, and we've both signed, and I've signed a new will and let him know it. I feel off the hook."

"That's because you are."

"Also, I've found an apartment. Margot is delivering an offer and a very large check as we speak."

"Closing date later?"

"After the final decree, but Herb is optimistic we can get that soon. I'm going to keep the Greenwich house for the time being, and Margot is going to sell the Carlyle apartment for me."

"Well, then, Margot's having a good day, too, isn't she?"

"She is. I can't thank you enough for all your help. A few days ago I couldn't walk; had an out-of-control, estranged husband; and was scared to death. And now . . ."

"I'm glad it's all better."

"Something occurred to me," she said.

"What's that?"

"I've signed a new will, so Donald has no reason to want me dead, but . . ."

"But what?"

"That doesn't mean that Donald feels any better about you. It troubles me that he went out and bought a gun, when he has half a dozen in the safe in Greenwich."

"Sounds rather like he had an immediate reason to do so, doesn't it?"

"It does, so please, please, watch your ass."

Stone laughed. "That's Fred's job," he said, "and he's good at it."

"How did you ever find that dear little man?"

"I didn't. He was sent to me by my French friend Marcel duBois, the same one who designed the Blaise. He gave me a year of Fred's time as a gift. I hired him after a month, then to seal the deal, he and Helene fell madly in love and moved in together."

"How convenient for you."

"Very much so."

A veal roast arrived. Fred served them and poured the wine Stone had chosen.

"So," Stone said, "what are your plans while you're here?"

"If my offer is accepted, I'm going to take a decorator over there and start measuring things, then start placing orders."

"Orders for what?"

"Orders for everything: furniture, beds, kitchenware, china, silverware, everything I need to get established. I have all that in Greenwich, of course, but since I'm keeping the house, I'll need to start afresh." Her cell phone rang. "It's Margot, please excuse me. Hello? Yes, Margot? That's wonderful! Can we gain immediate access? I want to take a decorator over there tomorrow. Let me know, and thank you!" She hung up. "They've accepted my offer, closing date and all."

"Congratulations." Stone's phone rang, and he looked at the caller ID. "It's Herb Fisher," he said, "excuse me. Herb?"

"Stone, can you get a message to Cilla for me?"

"I believe I can do that."

"Write this down."

Stone produced a pen and paper. "Okay."

"Cilla is to be in the chambers of Judge Mabel Watney tomorrow morning at eleven o'clock." He gave Stone the address.

"Okay, what for?"

"The judge is Terry Barnes's sister. She's agreed to issue a final decree, but both Cilla and Trask have to be there to swear that they both accept the property settlement."

"I promise, she'll be there." Stone hung up. "You are a very lucky woman," he said. "Donald's attorney has a sister who is a family court judge. She's going to sign your decree tomorrow morning at eleven, and you have to be there."

"Is that even possible?"

"It's unheard of, but a judge can do what she wants to do."

"I'm stunned. This means I can close immediately on the apartment."

"Let Herb know, and he'll do the legal work. It'll take a few days."

"Can you put up with me for that long?"

"I'll force myself," Stone replied.

23

THEY WERE ON COGNAC when the doorbell rang. Stone picked up the phone. "Yes?"

"It's Dino."

Stone buzzed him in. "You're about to meet my closest friend, Dino Bacchetti."

"Oh, good. Where have I heard that name?"

"He's the police commissioner of New York City. We were detectives together a long time ago."

Dino came into the room. "I didn't know you had a guest," he said.

Stone introduced him to Cilla.

"I don't suppose I can force a drink on you," Stone said.

Dino grabbed a chair. "Just try," he said, accepting a glass of Johnnie Walker Black Label. "Better days," he said.

"Cilla was just saying that they don't get much better than right now. She's getting divorced tomorrow, from Donald Trask."

"Ah, yes," Dino said. "The subject of my visit. And let me be the first to congratulate you, Cilla."

"You are that," Cilla replied, "and thank you. What has Donald done this time?"

"It's good news," Dino said. "When the New York Athletic Club heard about his weapon, they disarmed him and put the gun in their safe."

"He has no access to it?" Stone asked.

"Apparently not unless he moves out."

"Well, that is good news. Fred had a look around the neighborhood but didn't spot him."

"I don't want to throw cold water on good news," Cilla said, "but I should tell you that Donald is a very persistent person. Once he gets the bit between his teeth, he doesn't give up until he has what he wants."

"And is that Stone?" Dino asked.

"He may have been distracted by the news that he's going to get a very large check tomorrow, when he is divorced from me."

"That would divert a fellow's attention," Dino said. "Might it also cool his ardor?"

"Perhaps. His ardor is always cooled when he thinks he has won, and he probably thinks that about the settlement. What he doesn't know is, I was prepared to pay double what I'm paying him, just to be shed of him. So, if I ever want to get his goat, I'll just throw that into the argument."

"Please don't do that," Stone said.

"Don't worry, I'll resist the temptation."

"The City of New York would be grateful for that," Dino

said. "I was afraid we were going to have to arrest him tonight."

"What for?" Cilla asked.

"That's the problem. He has a carry license for the gun, so . . ."

"Hey, wait a minute," Stone said. "As I recall, a carry license lists the authorized weapons and their serial numbers, does it not?"

Dino brightened. "You're right, it does, so unless he had the presence of mind to add his new gun to the list, we've got grounds for canceling his license." Dino picked up his phone and made a call. "It's Bacchetti; I want you to run the carry license for one Donald Trask and tell me if he's added a new weapon, a Beretta, to his authorized list in the past few days. I'll hold." Dino covered the phone. "He's checking. What? No Beretta? Thank you." He hung up. "He hasn't registered it."

"Problem is," Stone said, "he's not carrying it. It's in the safe at the Athletic Club."

"Hoisted on my own petard," Dino said.

"Well, he won't carry it into the courthouse tomorrow morning, but after that, he could check out at any time."

"Jesus, but you're a lot of trouble," Dino said.

"Me? What'd I do?"

"Now I'm going to have to put a man on him, so, if he has a bulge under his coat when he leaves the club, we can bust him."

"How long does he have to register the new weapon?" Stone asked.

"I'm not sure. Three days, maybe."

"I think I can get him to check out of the Athletic Club," Cilla said.

"How are you going to do that?" Stone asked.

"I'll see him in court tomorrow morning, and as soon as we get the decree, I'll tell him I want him out of the Greenwich house by the weekend. He'll have to go up there and pack up his stuff, so he'll check out of the club and sleep in Greenwich, until he leaves the house."

"So," Stone said. "He'll probably check out of the club tomorrow after his court appearance, so Dino's guys can roust him when he's on the way to catch his train."

"That works for me," Dino said, tossing off his drink. "Okay, I'm going home. We'll pick up Mr. Trask's tail when he leaves the courthouse. Which court?"

"Family court, chambers of Judge Watney," Cilla replied.

"Then we'll follow him to the Athletic Club and let nature take its course."

"Cilla," Stone said, "where is he likely to stay after he leaves the Greenwich house?"

"Normally to the Carlyle, but after our hearing he won't have access to that anymore. Margot will be getting it ready to show it."

"So, back to the Athletic Club?"

"Maybe, but there he'll have the inconvenience of checking his gun. Maybe the Yale Club; he's a member there."

"Is there anyone at the Greenwich house you could have call you when he leaves?"

"Yes, the housekeeper, who will be glad to see the back of him."

"Good. Tell her to ask him for a forwarding address and number when he leaves, then call you."

"I can do that," she said. "I'll be speaking to her in due course."

Dino said good night and left.

Cilla finished her cognac, then stretched and yawned. "You can take that as a hint," she said to Stone.

Stone turned out the lights and escorted her upstairs.

He got undressed and into bed, and she went into her dressing room and was there for a half hour. When she came out she was wearing a long negligee.

"Why is it," he said, "that it takes so long for a woman to take her clothes *off*?"

She stood by the bed, slipped the straps off her shoulders, and allowed the negligee to fall to the floor. "I guess I'm just going to have to make that up to you," she said, climbing into bed.

And she did.

24

AT TEN O'CLOCK the following morning, Cilla got into Stone's Bentley, and Fred drove her downtown to the courthouse. They were a few minutes early, so Fred parked near the front steps with the engine idling.

"Fred?"

"Yes, ma'am?"

"Stone told me how you handled my, ah, former husband the other day, and I want to thank you."

"It was my pleasure, ma'am. Please let me know if it needs doing again."

AT TEN MINUTES before the hour, Fred pulled up to the broad front steps and opened the door for her. As she got out, he handed her a card. "I'll be nearby, Ms. Scott," he said. "Please call me when you're on the way downstairs, and I'll pull up right here."

"Thank you, Fred." She walked up the front steps and

found Herb Fisher waiting there, briefcase in hand. They shook hands.

"Donald and his attorney are on their way upstairs to the courtroom," he said. "We'll wait there, until the judge calls us into her chambers."

They went through security, and she drew some comfort from the metal detector. Surely, Donald would not have tried to carry a gun through that. They rode up in the elevator. In the courtroom, Donald and his attorney were sitting in the front row. Herb directed her to a seat a few rows behind them. They sat quietly until a clerk came into the courtroom.

"Scott v. Trask," he called out.

They all stood and were directed into the judge's chambers. She was a small woman, wearing her robe. They were not offered seats but stood before her.

"Your Honor," Terry Barnes said, "these are Ms. Scott and Mr. Trask, and Herbert Fisher for the co-plaintiff." He placed a sheaf of documents on the desk before her. "Both parties have had counsel review the property settlement, and they have both signed. I believe everything is in order. I've printed out a decree, which both counsels have reviewed."

The judge scanned the property settlement and nodded.

Cilla found herself breathing more rapidly. Donald was going to somehow torpedo this, she thought. Perhaps he would produce a weapon and kill them all.

"Are both parties satisfied with the agreement? Ms. Scott?"

"Yes, Your Honor."

"Mr. Trask?"

"Yes, Your Honor."

"Ms. Scott, do you have a financial instrument that will effect settlement?"

"Right here, Your Honor," Herb said. "A cashier's check in the amount of eight million dollars for Mr. Trask, and transfer documents to be signed by him. They already bear Ms. Scott's signature."

Trask signed the transfer documents, and the judge handed him the check, then she signed two copies of the decree and handed them to the lawyers. "If you have nothing else before the court, this matter is adjourned," she said, and everyone filed out of the room.

The attorneys shook hands.

"Donald?" Cilla said.

"Yes?" He seemed surprised to be addressed.

"I have guests coming to Greenwich for the weekend, and I'd be grateful if you would remove your personal effects by five PM on Friday."

"I've already arranged a mover for Friday," Donald replied.

"Then goodbye."

"Goodbye."

They left the courtroom together but took separate elevators down. Cilla called Fred to let him know she was coming.

"Herb, can I give you a lift uptown?" she asked.

"Thanks, but I have a car and driver."

"Oh, by the way, my offer for the apartment was accepted last night, so I'll need you to arrange a closing as soon as possible."

"Have the seller's attorney call me, and I'll get right on it."

"How long should it take?"

"Assuming a clean title, say next Monday, at ten AM?"

"Fine."

"I'll need a cashier's check for the balance on the apartment."

"Here you are," she said, handing it to him. "I'll see you next Monday at ten."

They air-kissed and Cilla got into the Bentley.

"I'm a free woman, Fred," she said.

"My congratulations, miss. Where would you like to go now?"

She gave him the address. "I have a one o'clock appointment there."

THEY MADE IT WITH TIME to spare, and Margot was waiting out front for her. "Here's my check for six million," Cilla said.

"Great. I'll give it to her Realtor. The seller is away for the weekend, so the place is ours." She handed Cilla a set of keys.

"The seller has tagged some pieces of furniture that are for sale; she's downsizing, so she won't need to take a lot of things."

When they were let into the apartment, Cilla's decorator was already there. Margot received the signed contract document and handed the deposit check to the Realtor. "We'll be ready to close next Monday morning at ten AM at my attorney's office." Cilla handed her a card. "Please have your closing attorney call him."

"The place is all yours," the Realtor said. "I'll stay for a few minutes to record which pieces of furniture you wish to purchase."

Cilla went straight to the grand piano at one end of the living room. It was a Steinway Model B, in walnut. She sat down and played for a minute, then checked the tag. "I'll take this," she said to the Realtor. She continued around the apartment with the Realtor and her decorator, taking some things, leaving others. "I'll want the two sofas reupholstered," she said. "And I like the style of the living room and dining room curtains, but I'll want new fabrics."

"I'll get some samples together."

In the kitchen, she was introduced to the middle-aged couple who cared for the place and, after a brief chat about their duties, hired them on the spot, then she continued her tour. When she was done the Realtor added up the prices of the pieces she had chosen, and Cilla wrote a check for them.

IT WAS AFTER FIVE before Fred returned her to Stone's house; she found him in his study and flopped down on the sofa. "What a day! We close next Monday morning, and I've bought enough furniture from the seller to allow me to move in immediately!"

Stone fixed them drinks and sat down beside her. "I haven't heard from Dino yet. His guys are camped out at the Athletic Club."

"I don't care about that anymore," she said. "I'm free of him—signed, sealed, and delivered!"

Stone hoped he would be free of the man, too, and soon.

25

THE TWO DETECTIVES, Sharkey and Paulson, made themselves at home in the commodious lobby of the New York Athletic Club and flashed a badge when a retainer asked their business.

"This is quite a place," Sharkey said.

"You wouldn't believe," Paulson replied. "I used to work out here with a friend who was a member—until he couldn't pay his dues anymore, and they kicked him out. There's twenty-six floors here, a couple of restaurants and bars, gyms, steam rooms, a pool, a running track, everything you could imagine in the way of indoor sports."

"And rooms for the members?"

"A couple of floors of them—for guys whose wives have kicked them out, or guys between apartments, or out-of-towners."

"So, I guess Donald Trask is a regular member."

"I guess so. The commish says he's a member of the Yale

Club, too, and might move over there because of the gun thing. But he's supposed to be going to Connecticut from here, so we can bust him at Grand Central Station."

"Twelve-thirty," Sharkey replied. "And there he is."

Donald Trask entered the lobby from Central Park South, stopped at the front desk for a brief conversation, then got onto an elevator. The detectives walked over and noted the floor number of his stop, then took their seats again.

"Maybe he's packing up to move," Paulson said.

"We'll see."

Shortly after one o'clock, Trask got off the elevator in the lobby, towing a large suitcase and carrying a smaller one. They followed him to the door he had entered. Outside, a black town car was waiting for him. Sharkey trotted around the corner to get their car. The driver stowed the luggage and drove away, making a U-turn toward Columbus Circle, with the detectives following half a block back.

"We'll brace him at Grand Central and take his gun and license," Paulson said.

"Then where the fuck is he going?" The town car had turned uptown on Broadway.

"Beats me."

The town car turned west on West 72nd Street and drove all the way to the West Side Highway, where it turned onto the ramp and headed north.

"Maybe he's staying with friends on the Upper West Side," Paulson said, but near the George Washington Bridge exit, the town car turned east.

"How long do we follow?" Paulson asked.

"I don't know—to the city limits, maybe?"

The town car turned north, and still the two cops followed.

"Suppose he's headed for Boston?" Paulson asked.

"I'm good as far as the Connecticut state line," Sharkey replied, but when they reached that point, he kept going.

"We're out of state now," Paulson pointed out.

"Yeah, but now I'm curious."

Twenty minutes later they were in Greenwich, following the shoreline, and the town car turned through large stone and wrought-iron gates and went up the drive to a large, Georgian-style house, where, from the street, Donald Trask could be seen taking his luggage through the front door.

"All right," Sharkey said, getting out his cell phone and pressing a button. "Detective Sharkey for the commissioner."

"Bacchetti," Dino said.

"Commissioner, Donald Trask didn't go to the Yale Club, and we never had a chance to brace him. We followed him to a big house in Greenwich."

"Connecticut?"

"Yes, sir."

"You know we don't operate up there, unless we're serving a warrant."

"Yes, sir. It looks like he lives up here."

"Not for long," Dino said. "He got divorced this morning, and he's got to clear that house by Friday afternoon at five. Pick him up then, follow him to the city, and do what you've got to do."

"Yes, sir."

"Now get your asses back to New York, where you belong."

Sharkey hung up and reported the conversation to his partner. "I think we should take his suggestion."

"Doesn't sound like a suggestion," Paulson said.

The two drove back to the city.

A WEEK LATER, on Monday morning, a meeting attended by Cilla Scott, the two Realtors, and the seller's attorney, took place in Herb Fisher's office. Cilla signed many documents— the seller had already signed—and handed over a check.

"Congratulations," the seller's attorney said. "The apartment is yours." He handed over four sets of keys and a bill of sale for the furniture she had bought, then departed.

Cilla thanked Herb for everything, then she and Margot left.

"I have an offer on the Carlyle apartment," Margot said.

"Already?"

"I think we priced it right."

"What's the offer?"

"He offered $3,500,000; I countered with four and a half, and he came up to $4,250,000."

"Accept it," Cilla said. "He can close anytime. I'm moving this afternoon."

"May I help?" Margot asked.

Back at the Carlyle, Cilla packed, while Margot phoned and accepted the offer, then they put Cilla's things into a hired town car and ferried it over to Fifth Avenue.

The apartment was neat and spotless, and there were fresh linens on the beds. Cilla hung her things in the dressing room. "Now I have to go buy a car," she said. She found Paul, the male half of her newly hired couple. "Paul, do you drive?"

"I drove your predecessor everywhere."

"Then come with me."

Downstairs, Margot excused herself to deliver the signed offer of the apartment to the buyer's Realtor.

Cilla thanked her profusely. "Margot, do you know where the Bentley dealership is?"

"It's called Manhattan Motorcars, and it's on Ninth Avenue, below Forty-second Street."

Cilla and Paul got into a cab, she googled the dealership for the correct address, and they were there in twenty minutes.

Cilla walked into the showroom, followed by Paul, and a salesman approached.

"May I show you something?" he asked.

"You can show me that," Cilla said, pointing at a silver Flying Spur.

He did so, and she examined the window sticker carefully. "How much of a discount can you offer me?" she asked.

"None, I'm afraid. Everything here is sold at list price. I can offer you your first detailing free, though."

"Write it up," she said, digging in her bag for her checkbook.

A half hour later as they were driving uptown, she caressed the beautiful leather of the seats. "This is going to be your second home, Paul," she said.

"Yes, ma'am," Paul replied. "And a fine home it is."

26

CILLA CALLED STONE.

"Hello?"

"I feel in a celebratory mood," she said. "Can I take you to dinner?"

"Sure. What time should I pick you up?"

"I'll pick you up," she said. "Be downstairs at seven o'clock."

"As you wish."

THE SILVER FLYING SPUR glided to a halt in front of Stone's house, and the driver held the door for him.

"This is beautiful," he said, climbing in.

"It's not as big as your Mulsanne," she said, "but it had the virtue of being on the showroom floor, ready to drive away. I was in no mood to wait three or four months for delivery."

"Where are we headed?"

"Brooklyn," she said.

"I'm in your hands." They crossed the Brooklyn Bridge,

took a right or two, and drove up to the River Café. "Ah, one of my favorites," Stone said.

"They know me here, so I was able to get a table on short notice."

They were seated, ordered drinks, and perused the menu. When they had ordered, Cilla spoke up. "Do you know why I'm so happy?"

"Because you're divorced?"

"That was last week. Now I'm happy because I moved into my new apartment today."

"What are you doing for furniture?"

"The previous owner was a recent widow who was downsizing, so I bought enough of her furniture to live with. Oh, I'll re-cover some things, and buy many others, but I'm comfortable."

"Anything else?"

"Donald is out of the Greenwich house. I expected him to take his clothes and personal things, but according to my housekeeper he took everything—furniture, books, art, TVs, rugs—and he took an early Picasso that was my mother's. I'll probably have to sue him to get it back. Herb is on it."

"What is it worth?"

"Millions, I expect."

"Where did Donald move to?"

"He's rented an apartment on the Upper East Side, in a nice building, far enough from me."

"Good," Stone said. "Just think of the stuff he took as a challenge to your decorating skills."

"I'll do that."

"He took the safe in the study, too. That's where he kept his guns."

"So, he's armed again? Dino's guys never caught him with a gun; they didn't know about his new apartment."

"Herb is going over there as we speak, to get the Picasso back."

"Does he know that Donald is armed?"

"He's taking backup, don't worry."

HERB FISHER, accompanied by two uniformed NYPD officers hired for the occasion, rang the doorbell of Donald Trask's new apartment. Trask opened it, wearing a new-looking silk dressing gown. "Hi, remember me?" Herb asked.

"All too well," Trask replied. "What the fuck do you want?"

"The Picasso," Herb said.

"What Picasso?"

"The one you stole from Ms. Scott's Greenwich home."

"I didn't steal it. It was hanging in my study."

"You also stole the furnishings of the study. There was no such right given to you in the separation agreement. May we come in, or do these two gentlemen have to arrest you first for grand larceny?"

"I want to call my lawyer," Trask said.

"Call whoever you like," Herb replied, brushing past Trask with the cops close behind. He walked quickly around the apartment, which was filled with unpacked boxes, until he found the Picasso on the mantelpiece in a small study.

"That one," Herb said to the cops, taking it down. He

found a sheet of Bubble Wrap in a pile of trash and wrapped the picture in it. "That's it," he said to the cops. "Let's go."

"I'm going to get that picture back," Trask said.

"No, you're not. It wasn't marital property—Ms. Scott inherited it from her mother. If you try, you'll end up in jail. Good evening."

The three men left, slamming the door behind them.

CILLA'S PHONE RANG, and she answered it and listened. "Thank you so much," she said, then hung up. "That was Herb. Picasso recovered and on its way to its new home on Fifth Avenue."

"I expect Herb short-circuited the process," Stone said.

"As long as the picture is mine again," she replied.

UPTOWN, IN TURTLE BAY, Faith went downstairs and looked around for Jimbo. It was past ten, so his relief was due. Impatiently, she left the house and began the walk to Lexington Avenue. "I'm not a baby," she said aloud to herself.

Jimbo came out of the downstairs powder room as his relief rang the doorbell, and he let her in.

"Evening, Jimbo," she said.

"Evening, Sylvia."

"Is she ready for the hand over?"

"Let's go upstairs." They took the elevator to the top floor and let themselves into Faith's apartment. "Faith?" Jimbo called out. No reply.

Jimbo and Sylvia quickly searched the apartment. "She's gone out, and without me," he said.

"Why would she do that? She had the riot act read to her by Barrington."

"She's impulsive," Jimbo said, "and impatient." He dialed her cell number, which went immediately to voice mail.

"Faith," he said, "this is Jimbo, please call me immediately."

Faith had the bell turned off and didn't hear the cell phone. She continued her trip uptown, where she wanted to visit the Caswell-Massey pharmacy on Lex. All she needed was some soap; she'd go straight back to the house after she'd bought it.

She spent a half hour in the drugstore, sniffing things, then bought her soaps and left. She vanished into the night.

27

JIMBO AND SYLVIA walked around the block, each in opposite directions, looking for Faith. She was nowhere in sight. Jimbo called Stone Barrington.

Stone and Cilla were finishing up dessert at the River Café when his phone rang. He glanced at the caller ID. "Please excuse me." He pressed the recall button.

"Stone?"

"Yes, Jimbo, what is it?"

"Faith has disappeared. At change of shift, I was in the downstairs powder room, thinking she was upstairs. Then, when Sylvia arrived, we went up to her apartment and found her gone. We made a quick search around the block, but no joy."

"Go up to that hotel on Lex where she used to stay and start a new search there," Stone said.

"Right."

Stone hung up and called Dino.

"Bacchetti."

"Are you at home?"

"With my feet up," Dino replied.

"I just got a call: Faith has disappeared."

"How'd that happen with her security on the job?"

"She left the house at the change of shift, while one of them was in the john. They've had a look around the block, but no luck. I've sent them up to that hotel where Faith used to stay."

"I'll call it in," Dino said. "We'll saturate the neighborhood." He hung up.

Cilla was signing the check. "I heard, we'll use my car," she said.

JIMBO CALLED STRATEGIC Services for a patrol car, and they went immediately to the hotel. Once there, he and Sylvia walked into the lobby and encountered only a janitor mopping the floor. They went to the front desk.

Jimbo showed his private badge to the desk clerk. "Do you remember Faith Barnacle?" he asked. "She used to stay here."

"The little blonde? Sure, I remember her. I heard she got a job flying private."

"Has she been in here in the past hour?"

"Nope. Hey, Sid!"

The mopper paused in his work. "Yeah?"

"You seen the little blonde, Faith, in here tonight?"

"Nah, not for two or three weeks."

"You're sure she didn't come in during the past hour?"

"I've been mopping for longer than that; she didn't come in."

The clerk turned back to Jimbo. "Sorry, sir, we haven't seen Faith tonight, and not for some time."

"Thanks," Jimbo said, then rejoined Sylvia. "Okay," he said, "you take this side of Lex, I'll take the other; we'll walk uptown and check every side street."

"Right," Sylvia said, then watched Jimbo cross to the other side. They started walking uptown.

Jimbo heard a police car in the distance, then another. He could see the flashing lights way up Lex, coming his way. He flagged down one of them. "You guys looking for Faith Barnacle?"

"Yeah," the cop replied.

"So are we. Any sign of her?"

"Nothing, and there aren't that many people on the street, except around Bloomie's.

Jimbo showed his ID. "I'm from Strategic Services—mind if my partner and I ride with you?"

"Hop in."

Jimbo whistled up Sylvia, and she joined them. They drove up Third Avenue, vainly seeking Faith.

"We haven't had a call on this thing for a week or more," said the cop who was driving. "I had hoped it was over."

"I don't think it's over," Jimbo replied.

STONE AND CILLA got onto Lexington at 86th Street and cruised slowly downtown. Stone's phone rang. "Yes, Jimbo?"

"We're in a patrol car, going up Third, then down Lex."

"Good. We're doing much the same thing. Keep in touch if something happens."

———

FAITH CAME TO SLOWLY, but she couldn't see anything. A soft cloth bag was over her head, there were some holes around her mouth that enabled her to breathe. She could hear the muffled sound of classical music. Her hands were bound to a wooden chair that should have had a wicker seat, but didn't. "Hello?" she said. Then she heard the sound of a heavy door closing and being locked. "Hello!" No response. She squirmed, trying to loosen her bonds, but they were too tight.

Then she realized that she was naked.

28

IT WAS NEARLY TWO AM when Cilla dropped Stone off at his house. "Let me know if you hear anything," she said.

"I will."

He was getting into bed when Dino called.

"Did I wake you?"

"You would have in another ten minutes," Stone said.

"We've got nothing, not a trace. She went into the Caswell-Massey store on Lex and bought some soap, but after that, nobody saw her on the street."

"This is bad," Stone said wearily.

"The search is still on," Dino said. "Not to be pessimistic, but nobody will be able to dump a body in that neighborhood without being seen."

"I don't think it will happen tonight," Stone said. "The kinds of injuries the ME described won't happen fast. He'll want to enjoy himself."

"Until he gets tired of her," Dino added. "Talk to you in the morning."

Dino hung up, and Stone fell into bed, exhausted by his worry and his inability to do anything to help Faith.

FAITH KNEW THE MAN would be coming back for her. She managed to get the cloth between her chin and her shoulder and move it until, with her head pitched back, she could see out through one of the small breathing holes if she tilted the chair back a bit. She nearly went too far and fell on her back, but caught herself in time.

She could see a stool on the floor in front of her, next to the wall, and there was a window above it. The window appeared to be fixed, with four large panes. There was no sign of a lock. Then she heard a noise: the sound of an elevator running. She had an idea, but she would have only one shot at it before the elevator reached wherever she was.

She stood on her feet, bent over because her hands were tied to the chair. For an instant she wondered what floor she was on, but she pushed that thought out of her mind. If she was going to die, then better to do it now.

She backed up against the wall behind her and judged the distance to the stool, then, leaning into it, she began to run as fast as she could under the circumstances. She knew she needed momentum, and her thoughts went back to the high school track team, when she would lean forward into the tape at the finish line for that last bit of speed.

She leapt and got a foot on top of the stool and pushed off, as high and as fast as she possibly could, and dove headfirst into the window. There was the crash of breaking glass, then she was falling in cold air, falling and falling.

IT WAS NEARLY FIVE AM as two uniformed cops sat in their patrol car at the corner of Lexington Avenue, facing downtown. One of them reached for the radio's microphone and called in their position. "We've made two dozen sweeps uptown and downtown and found nothing. Are we getting a shift change soon?"

"Come on in to the precinct," the operator said.

"Let's go, Max," the cop said to the driver, who put the car in gear. Then there was a very loud noise heard from the direction of the driver's window. He stopped the car and reversed a few feet. "What the fuck was that?" he asked.

"I don't know, but I heard it, too."

They both stared east, at the empty street. Nothing was moving or making more noise.

"It sounded almost like a car crash," the driver said.

"I don't see anything," his partner said.

"Let's take a stroll," Max said.

They got out of the car and began to walk east.

"You take the other side of the street," Max said. Halfway down the block he encountered some broken glass on the sidewalk, but he could find no broken windows.

The two cops continued to Third Avenue, then turned and walked back toward Lexington. Halfway up the block, in line with the broken glass, he passed a dumpster and thought he heard a small sound from its direction. He looked up and could see that both of the steel lids were propped open. They should get a ticket for that, he thought.

"Max, where are you?" his partner called from across the street.

Max walked to the east end of the dumpster, stepped up on the bumper of a car parked next to it, and got out his flashlight. He played it over the contents: broken drywall, short pieces of lumber, broken glass—the detritus of demolition. He saw a wooden chair, broken, and fixed on that for a moment. He was about to get down from the bumper when he saw something else that transfixed him.

There was a hand—a woman's hand from the size of it—tied with rope to the chair.

He reached for his radio and called in his location. "I've found something: requesting an ambulance *right now*!"

"Harvey!" he yelled at his partner. "I got something here. Get to the car and turn on the flashers, so an ambulance will see it."

"What have you got, Max?"

"At least part of a woman!" Max yelled back, wading into the dumpster.

STONE'S PHONE RANG, causing him to sit straight up in bed; he was unaccustomed to calls at this hour. "Hello?"

"It's Dino. I thought I'd call you because I'm awake, and I'm not going back to sleep."

"That was thoughtful of you."

"My people found Faith. At least, we think it could be Faith. She's about the right size."

Stone's heart sank. "Is it so bad that she can't be iden-tified?"

"Not yet, not for sure. They're taking her to Bellevue."

Stone woke up a little more. "Why not the morgue?"

"Because she's still alive," Dino said. "At least, she's not dead yet."

"Thank God."

"Don't thank Him too soon," Dino said. "This is really bad."

"Where are you?"

"About to leave home. Shall I pick you up on the way?"

"Please. See you shortly."

Ten minutes later, Stone stood at the curb, watching the black SUV turn the corner. He got into the backseat with Dino. "Anything new?"

"Nope, and no news is good news," Dino replied.

29

THE CAR ROLLED to a stop at the ER entrance to the huge hospital. Stone and Dino jumped out and ran down the hall to a nurse's station.

Dino flashed his badge at a nurse. "Where is Faith Barnacle?"

The nurse consulted a list. "We've got no Faith Barnacle, but there's a Jane Doe in exam room two, Commissioner," she said, jerking a thumb down the hallway.

They ran another fifty feet and nearly collided with a nurse coming from behind the curtain, bearing a pan filled with blood-stained gauze and other horrible things.

"Get back," she ordered the two men. "There're two very busy doctors working in there, and you don't want to screw with them. Siddown!" She jerked her chin in the direction of a row of chairs, and they meekly followed her orders.

"Hey, how is she?" Dino shouted at the nurse's back as she walked away.

"Stick around!" she shouted without turning.

———

THE BETTER PART of an hour passed before a young physician in bloody scrubs came out of the curtained room and was replaced by another.

"Doctor!" Dino shouted.

The man walked wearily over to where they were getting to their feet. "What?"

"How is she?"

"Awful," he said. "I've rarely seen such a mess. I had to bring a fresh doctor down here just to suture her wounds."

"Is she going to make it?"

"She's taken about as much abuse as a human being can stand and still live, but she's stable. She's got some broken ribs and a thousand cuts, but she's been conscious off and on, and that's a good sign."

"How were all these cuts inflicted?" Stone asked.

"Not with a knife or razor," the doctor said. "As I hear it, she fell from three or four stories into a dumpster filled with chunks of old drywall and glass. There must have been enough air in there to offer some kind of cushion. Oh, and her hands were tied to what remained of a chair. That's all I can tell you."

Dino thanked him and got on his phone. "Listen, you've got to figure out which window she fell from," he said. "We've gotta get an arrest out of this." He listened for a couple of minutes. "Keep me posted," he said and hung up.

"They found the room, twelve stories up. It looks like, while tied to the chair, she made a head-on run at the window and crashed through it. Two cops were sitting in their patrol car on the corner and heard the noise when she hit the dumpster. One of them found her and called it in. He thought she was dead."

Stone collapsed into his chair. "Christ, she's got guts, you have to give her that."

"She must have had some idea of what was coming," Dino said. "I hope I'd have done the same thing in the circumstances."

Another doctor came out of the exam room, and Dino braced him. "Can we see her?"

"She's out like a light on morphine," he said. "She may be talking tomorrow, but I'm not promising you anything."

"But she'll live?" Stone asked.

"She's a tough one," the doctor said. "The ribs will be painful, but she doesn't have any internal organ damage, and that's remarkable. She'll be recovering for quite a while."

Stone and Dino made a move toward the exam room.

"Forget it," the doctor said. "There's a doctor and a nurse at work in there suturing, and believe me, you don't want to see her in her current state. She was naked when she went into the dumpster, except she had a hood over her head, so the cuts to her face are less bad. Go home and call here tomorrow before you come over. She needs rest, not questions."

They thanked the man and reluctantly left the hospital. By the time Stone got home, Joan was at her desk. He told her what had happened.

"That poor girl," Joan said, brushing away a tear.

"Where are Jimbo and Sylvia?"

"At home. They're both crushed, but there was nothing more they could do. I'll call them."

"Tell them to put a guard on her room at Bellevue," Stone said. "When word gets out that she's alive, somebody could come after her."

"Will do," Joan said, picking up her phone.

"Send a whole lot of flowers and a cell phone to her room, with a note from me saying that when she feels like talking to call me, but not to rush it."

"All right."

Stone went back upstairs to try to get a couple more hours of sleep. Dino called as he was getting into bed.

"I got a look at the room," he said. "It's in one of two buildings built into the hotel. Apparently, when it was built, the property owners wouldn't sell, so the hotel was built around them. Down a hallway was a door leading to an attic, and through there you could get to the hotel."

"There are those three night guys there," Stone said, "night clerk, elevator operator, and janitor."

"They're at the precinct being separately sweated as we speak," Dino said. "So far, nobody knows nothing."

"Okay, I'm going to sleep. I told Strategic Services to put a guard on her room."

"Already done," Dino replied.

"And I sent her some flowers and a cell phone so she can call when she feels like it."

"Good idea. Let me know if you hear from her."

"Okay, now I'm going back to bed."

"Lucky sonofabitch, I wish I could do that."

"Don't call me before noon, unless something breaks."

"Sure." Dino hung up.

Stone pulled the blinds and lay on the bed in the dark,

wondering what he could have done different that would have avoided this. Finally, he decided that there was nothing he could have done, unless Faith cooperated, and she was clearly not the cooperative sort.

He fell asleep finally and dreamed of falling twelve stories into a dumpster.

He was awakened by the phone at the stroke of noon. "Yes?"

"We're not getting a whole lot out of the three," Dino said, "but everybody's money is on the janitor."

"It's got to be all three of them," Stone said. "He couldn't have done it unless the other three were in on it—or, at the very least, covering for him."

"I won't argue with that," Dino said. "Now, I'm going to lock myself in my office and take a nap on the sofa." He hung up.

30

STONE WAS GETTING HUNGRY for lunch when Joan buzzed. "You had a message," she said.

"Why didn't you put the call through?"

"It wasn't a call, it was a message from Mikeford Whitehorn."

Mikeford Whitehorn had served in three cabinet positions and, in between, had expanded his family's legendary fortune in investment banking. Stone had met him once, three or four years before, at a dinner party. "What's the message?"

"He would be grateful if you would call on him at his home at three o'clock this afternoon. He's at 740 Park Avenue."

"Any idea what he wants?"

"That was the entire message. He didn't ask that you call and confirm, either."

"That was pretty confident," Stone said.

"I guess he's not accustomed to people saying no."

"I guess not." As Stone hung up, his cell phone started vibrating. "Hello?"

The voice was a hoarse whisper. "It's Faith. I'm so sorry."

"Listen, you need rest. You don't have to talk now, not even to the police."

"I'm going to be all right. I'll call tomorrow. I just wanted you to know I'm sorry I didn't listen to you." She hung up.

740 PARK AVENUE was the grandest and, legend had it, the most expensive apartment building in New York. It was built at the dawn of the Great Depression by Jacqueline Kennedy's grandfather and was made up almost entirely of large duplexes and triplexes, one of which was occupied by John D. Rockefeller, Jr., from the mid-1930s. Some of the apartments had been described as "country houses in the city." Stone knew a couple of people who lived there, but he had never visited Mikeford Whitehorn's apartment.

He was admitted by a uniformed butler, seated in a large, paneled library stocked with leather-bound volumes on two levels that were joined by a spiral staircase, and asked if he would like a drink.

"No, thank you," Stone said and was left alone.

A moment later Mikeford Whitehorn entered the room as a bull might enter the ring in Madrid. He was six feet, six inches tall and weighed, probably, two-fifty pounds—his slim weight. He had been an all-American football player at Harvard, back when that school had still produced all-Americans, and was known to intimates—but no one else—as "Swifty."

Whitehorn enveloped Stone's hand in a brief handshake, then he took a chair and ordered a large Laphroaig, a single-malt scotch whisky, neat. Stone reconsidered and ordered a Knob Creek.

"I remember our conversation at that dinner party a while back," Whitehorn said.

That surprised Stone because it had hardly been a conversation: he had just listened while Whitehorn rattled on about whatever crossed his mind. "I remember it, too, Mr. Secretary," Stone replied, "but I don't remember talking much."

Whitehorn laughed. "Maybe not, but you asked the right questions."

"I was surprised to hear from you, Mr. Secretary. Is there something I can do for you?"

"I need some advice from a person of your background," Whitehorn said. "The police thing, you know."

"I used to be a police detective," Stone said.

"Exactly. I don't want to ask my grandson's lawyer about this."

Stone had not known that Whitehorn had a grandson. "I see," he said.

"My grandson is named Michael Adams," he said. "My daughter's boy. He has never amounted to much of anything. He has what I consider to be a menial job, and he is supported by a trust fund I set up for him at his birth."

"Is he in some sort of trouble?"

"He has been arrested, and it looks as though he may be charged as an accomplice in an attempted murder."

"What are the circumstances?"

"He is a night clerk at a fairly seedy hotel on Lexington Avenue in the Forties, and it appears that at least one of his colleagues, the janitor there, is a suspect in half a dozen murders."

"Let me stop you there for a moment, Mr. Secretary, while I declare a conflict."

"A confict?"

"A young woman I employ as an aircraft pilot is a victim in this case, although she did not die."

"How is that a conflict?"

"I can't represent your grandson and advise the young lady simultaneously."

"I'm not asking you to represent my grandson. He already has a competent attorney. I'm asking you to advise me, not him."

"Well, as long as it's only informal advice, not actual representation, I suppose we can talk about it."

"Good. Now, my grandson's attorney is urging him to accept a plea deal, guilty, in exchange for a five-year sentence, but Mike maintains his innocence and doesn't want to do it."

"I know that there are three suspects," Stone said, "and that the police feel the chief among them is the janitor. However, they don't believe he could have pulled off these murders without help, and that leaves the elevator operator and your grandson in a bind, I'm afraid."

"What do you think the boy should do?"

"I think that if he continues to maintain his innocence, he should instruct his attorney to ask for immunity from prosecution, in exchange for Mike testifying to everything—absolutely everything—he knows about the attack on my employee and a number of previous murders, which seem to have been perpetrated by the same person or persons. I should warn you that this is not going to work unless he actually has information that would help convict the janitor and maybe the elevator operator, too, and that once he agrees to help, he must withhold nothing from the police, nothing at all."

"Is that his only option?"

"No, he can refuse to answer any questions, which I'm sure his attorney has already instructed him to do, and go to trial. Whether he does that would, of course, depend on the strength of the prosecution's case, as determined by his attorneys. If he should go to trial, he will need the best criminal defense attorney available, who may not necessarily be his current attorney."

"Can you recommend someone?"

"One of my law partners, at Woodman & Weld, Herbert Fisher, is an excellent trial attorney, and I recommend him unreservedly. However, I must ask you not to use my name as a referer, if you call him, or mention me to anyone else, for the reason of the possible conflict, which I have already expressed."

"I understand," Whitehorn said. "You may rely on my discretion."

Stone nodded. "Thank you, sir."

Whitehorn tossed back his scotch and stood up.

Stone stood as well, leaving half of his bourbon in the glass.

"Can you come to dinner here on Saturday evening?" Whitehorn asked unexpectedly. "I usually entertain on Saturdays, which often causes my invitees to have to choose between my table and others, which sort of tells me who my friends are."

"Thank you, I'd be delighted."

"It's black tie, six-thirty for seven-thirty, and—are you married or have a regular woman in your life?"

"No on both counts."

"Then come alone. I need an extra man."

They shook hands.

"Thank you for your advice. May I call you Stone?"

"Of course, Mr. Secretary."

"Good. Call me Swifty, all my friends do."

"As you wish."

The butler appeared as if by magic and escorted Stone to the door.

Stone checked his watch: he had been there no more than fifteen minutes. Swifty was nothing if not efficient with his time.

31

STONE WAS HALFWAY home when his cell went off. "Hello?"

"It's Faith." She sounded stronger and spoke more confidently.

"It sounds as though you're getting better fast," Stone said. "How are you feeling?"

"Better, fast. This morning I hurt all over, but they've given me morphine for that, so I can relax. I'm going to take a nap shortly, and I thought maybe you could tell Dino something for me, so his cops won't have to come and question me. I'm not up for that."

"Of course. What would you like me to tell him?"

"Tell him I remember going into Caswell-Massey and buying some soap and walking out the door to Lexington, but absolutely nothing else until I woke up in that room. I had a bag over my head, but I could see out a little through a hole, and I saw the stool and window across the room. I heard the elevator coming, and I decided I'd rather die quickly than slowly, so I used the stool as a running step and went head-first through the window. I remember cold air, then nothing, until I woke up in the hospital. That's it, that's everything."

"Do you remember ever being in the room with someone else?"

"No, but since I was naked and tied to a chair, I knew someone had been there. I feared he was coming back."

"All right, I'll pass that on and see if we can keep the investigators off your back for another day."

"I'd really appreciate that."

"Can I come and see you?"

"Maybe tomorrow. The morphine is putting me to sleep right now. Oh, the flowers are beautiful, and thanks for the phone." She hung up.

Stone called Dino.

"Bacchetti."

"Our victim woke up and called me."

"I'll get somebody over there right now."

"No, she doesn't want that until tomorrow."

"This isn't about what she wants."

"She told me what happened, and I'll tell you."

Dino sighed. "All right, what?"

Stone related Faith's account of her evening.

"That's it?"

"That's it, every word of it, and I believe her. I told her your guys would be there tomorrow. Right now, she's asleep on morphine."

"Well, if she's all doped up I guess that's the best we can do."

"I guess so. Oh, there's something else I have to tell you. How about dinner tonight?"

"P. J. Clarke's at seven?"

"See you then." He made it back to his desk before the phone rang again. "Hello?"

"Hi, it's Cilla. How about I cook you some dinner tonight?"

"I'd love that, but I'm dining with Dino, and we have some business to discuss."

"Saturday?"

"I'm sorry, I have a previous invitation to a dinner party, and I was asked to come alone. I expect I'll be seated next to some highly perfumed, heavily bejeweled deaf dowager."

"If you can't be with me, then I wish that for you. I'm afraid I'm tied up on Sunday, but I cook to order on Mondays."

"Perfect."

"Come at six-thirty, and I'll have a bottle of Knob Creek and a straw waiting." She gave him the address and apartment number.

Stone entered his plans into his iPhone calendar.

DINO WAS HALF A DRINK ahead of him when he arrived at Clarke's, and Stone started catching up. Shortly, they were seated at a table in the back room, ordering dinner.

"Tell me," Stone said, "how is the interrogation of your three suspects going?"

"They've lawyered up, and they're holding their water."

"I can make a suggestion that might help."

"Any help at all would be appreciated."

"One of the suspects, Mike Adams, has been offered a

deal: he testifies and gets five years. However, he stoutly maintains his innocence."

"And how would you know that?"

"You can't ask me, and I can't tell you, but here's what I think might work: ask the DA to give Mr. Adams immunity, and he'll tell everything he knows about the other two."

"Yeah, but what does he know?"

"Listen, he works with the other two guys every day of his life, and the three of them are very frequently alone in that hotel lobby. Even if he didn't watch them kill those girls, he'll know something about their whereabouts on the relevant evenings."

"And what if he was a cheerful participant in the rapes and murders?"

"It's the old choice," Stone said. "One, perhaps two birds in the hand and one out the window."

"You think the desk clerk will crack, huh? I'd sure like to know how you know that."

"I don't know it, but I have every reason to believe that he'll take the deal."

Dino heaved a deep, sorrowful Italian sigh. "All right, I'll suggest it to the DA."

"There's one other piece of information you might drop while you're suggesting it."

"What's that?"

"Young Mike Adams is the grandson of Mikeford Whitehorn."

"You're shittin' me! That little creep is of Swifty Whitehorn's blood?"

"I shit you not. Mike is his daughter's son."

"Then what's he doing working in that fleabag hotel?"

"Mike appears to be the black sheep in the family. I think they're grateful that he has a job, even that one, although he has a trust fund."

"You're just a fountain of fucking information, aren't you. I didn't even know you knew Swifty Whitehorn."

"You still don't," Stone pointed out, "although I'll tell you we were at the same dinner table a few years ago, and I spent the evening listening to him talk about himself."

"And that's where you got all this information?"

"I didn't say that. In fact, that dinner is not the source of my information."

"But . . ."

Stone held up a hand. "Don't ask," he said, smiling a little.

"I'll call the DA."

32

ERB FISHER was at his desk the following morning, dictating a memo, when his phone rang. He answered. "Herb Fisher."

"Herb, this is Ted Faber, over at Littlejohn & Brown. How are you?"

"Real good, thanks. Have we met?"

"At a Bar Association cocktail party a long time ago, but that's not why I'm calling. I may have a client for you."

"Who referred you to me?"

"I can't say, but why don't I buy you a good lunch, and we can talk about it."

"As long as it's a *really* good lunch."

"How about The Grill, formerly the Four Seasons Grill?"

"That'll do."

"Twelve-thirty?"

"Good."

———

HERB WALKED UP THE STAIRS and past the busy bar, and a young man stepped forward and offered his hand. "Herb, I'm Ted Faber."

They shook hands and were seated.

Herb looked around. "Thank God for the Historical Commission," he said.

"Beg pardon?"

"They kept the new building owner from ripping out the interior and starting over. It's exactly as Philip Johnson designed it."

"Right."

They ordered drinks and lunch.

"So," Herb said, "what kind of case have you got?"

"A high-profile criminal one. You know the murders of the small blondes on the East Side?"

"Who doesn't?"

"Well, our client is a suspect."

"It doesn't get any more high profile than that," Herb responded. "Who represents the other two?"

"Two other attorneys from two other firms. They've clammed up their clients."

"Good. How's your client going to plead?"

"Not guilty. He's adamant that he had nothing to do with it, says he'll go to trial."

"What if the other two implicate him?"

"We'd like to head off that possibility at the pass."

"How are you planning to proceed, then, and why do you want me?"

"We've had some very specific instructions about that from a relative of our client, the one who's paying the bills."

"What instructions?"

"First, he's instructed us to hire you. He won't say why."

"And, I take it, he won't let you say who he is?"

"Later," Ted said. "Second, he's instructed us, or you, rather, to make a proffer to the DA: immunity on all charges in return for his testimony against the two other suspects."

"And who are these three?"

"Our client is Mike Adams, the night clerk at a hotel on Lexington Avenue; the other two are the janitor and the elevator operator. We have it on good authority that the cops and the DA favor the janitor as the perp, but they figure he needed help, so they're charging all three."

"That's odd. Hasn't the DA made an offer?"

"Five years."

"And Adams won't take it?"

"He will not, and he is adamant."

"But he's agreed to testify?"

"We believe he will, with full immunity."

"I don't get it. Why do you need me?"

"Two reasons. First, as I said earlier, the relative of our client has specified you. Second, the ADA on the case is Cheray Gardner."

"Ah," Herb said. He and Cheray had had a torrid, albeit brief, affair the year before.

"Did you part on good terms?"

"She still winks at me in the courthouse elevator."

"I'll take that as on good terms."

"So will I," Herb said. "Okay, who's the relative?"

Ted sucked his teeth.

"I need to know that. I don't want to be blindsided later."

"First, let's discuss your fees—with or without trial."

Ted's reluctance to reveal the name more than doubled what Herb had intended to ask. "Twenty-five grand, if I get him immunity. If it goes to trial, a hundred grand against a million-dollar fee, calculated at a thousand dollars an hour."

"I can do that," Ted said.

This indicated to Herb that Ted had already gotten an approval for the fees. "Then all I need is the name."

"Mikeford Whitehorn."

"He's a relative?"

"A grandfather. Adams is his daughter's son."

"What's the kid doing working at a fleabag hotel?"

"Let's just say that Mike is something of a disappointment to his family. He's not starving, though; he has a trust fund from grandpappy."

"Okay, I'll go for the deal, but I want permission to use Whitehorn's name in my dealings with the ADA, and I want to talk to Whitehorn. Phone is okay."

"I don't know about that," Ted replied.

"Tell old Swifty this: if it goes to trial, he's going to be all over the papers and TV, guaranteed. The media will find out; they always do. However, if I can whisper his name into Cheray's shell-like ear, it might carry some weight. It certainly will if she needs an approval from the DA himself to make the deal."

"All right, but I don't think you need to talk to grandpappy."

"All right, but find a way to intimate to him that if he

doesn't know the DA, which he certainly does, but it would be gauche for him to make a call himself, then he might find a mutual acquaintance who can whisper to the DA that he should smile on immunity."

"I can do that," Ted said, "and I'm sure Swifty can, too."

"Before I call Cheray."

"Right after lunch."

"When do I meet my client?"

"How about in an hour at Riker's Island?"

"I can make that. Has anybody grilled young Mike about what he can give the DA?"

"I have. He says he's worked with the janitor and the elevator operator for a year and a half, and he knows they did it, and he can shred any alibi they might have. And he keeps a diary."

Herb looked at his watch.

"Give me a couple of minutes, and I'll give you an answer," Ted said.

Herb went to the men's room, and when he came out, Ted was waiting in the entry hall.

"You can whisper, but not shout, grandpappy's name," he said.

"I'll call you later this afternoon," Herb said. "Thanks for the lunch."

"My car and driver are outside. Take it to Riker's and he'll take you back to your office."

They shook hands, and Herb went outside to the car.

33

HERB WAS LET into a room containing two steel chairs and a table, all bolted to the floor. He sat down and tried to check his phone for messages, but there was no signal.

Five minutes later a guard opened the door, and a tall, slim young man with thinning dark hair and glasses entered the room. His handcuffs were removed and he shook Herb's hand firmly. "I'm Michael Adams," he said, then sat down.

"I'm Herb Fisher. Your grandfather has retained me to represent you."

"He spoke to you directly?" Adams asked, sounding surprised.

"No, through your previous attorney, Ted Faber."

"I'm glad he found you. Faber didn't impress me."

Herb was surprised at how calm and confident Adams seemed. In these circumstances, his clients were usually shaken and worried. "I've been told by Ted Faber that you're willing to answer all the DA's questions, in exchange for immunity from all charges."

"Who wouldn't?" Adams asked.

Herb smiled. "Of course, but I'm going to need to hear your story before I attempt to make that deal."

"Okay, ask me whatever the DA will. This can be a rehearsal."

"Let's avoid that term and just call it a client interview."

"Sure."

"All right, Mike, give me your sixty-second biography, right up to this minute."

"Born New York City twenty-nine years ago, educated at Buckley, had a shot at Yale, but didn't make it there. Got my degree at Fordham."

"Is your grandfather Catholic?"

"You guessed it."

"And after Fordham?"

"I got into law school but left after a year."

"What did you do for work?"

"My father got me a job at his commercial real estate firm, but it didn't suit me. Neither did a couple of other things, but old Dad got me the night clerk gig at the hotel, which his firm owns. It suits me well. I can read and watch a lot of TV and, sometimes, work on my novel."

"When did you begin?"

"A year and a half ago."

"Any problems at work? You get along with your boss?"

"No problems. Everybody there works for my father's firm, and my boss works days, so we don't see each other that often."

"When did you meet your two coworkers?"

"Sid Francis, the janitor, and Larry Cleary, the elevator operator?"

"Right." Herb made a note of the names.

"They were already working there when I arrived. Nominally, I'm their boss; they're night workers, too."

"And who do you report to?"

"The assistant manager, Harmon Wheeler, Jr., who reports to the manager, Harmon Wheeler, Sr., who reports to my father's firm."

"And what were your first impressions of Sid, the janitor, and Larry, the elevator operator?"

"Slackers. They worked slowly, and they paid a lot of attention to the airline girls who stayed with us."

"Flight attendants?"

"And pilots. They worked for a couple of charter airlines that had a deal with the hotel. Until recently."

"What happened recently?"

"My dad's firm decided to gut the hotel and remake it as something that would appeal more to business travelers, so the airline people looked for beds elsewhere."

"How recently?"

"A few weeks ago. There's very little business now because as their contracts expire, they aren't renewed."

"So Sid and Larry liked the girls."

"They did and do. Their problem was the girls didn't like them much. Their approaches tended to get rebuffed, so I guess they looked elsewhere."

"With what result?"

"I noticed that Sid and Larry tended to disappear for an

hour or two late at night—rarely together—one at a time. Sid would cover the elevator when Larry was gone."

"Did you know where they went?"

"I assumed they were taking naps or watching porn in one of the vacant bedrooms. I found some videos in a room on the second floor once, when I was making my rounds."

"How often did you make rounds?"

"When I felt like it, which was not often, but I got curious about where Sid and Larry were going, and I couldn't catch them actually in a room. Then, last week, I noticed the door."

"What door?"

"On the top floor. It's a pull-down door to what I assumed was the attic."

"Did you have a look up there?"

"Once. I found that you could get into the attic in the building next door from there."

"Did you explore that further?"

"I intended to, but then, suddenly, the lobby was full of cops, and there were a lot of sirens outside. This was the night they found the girl in the dumpster."

"How did you hear about that?"

"They arrested me, and the subject came up."

"Did you withhold any information?"

"No. I told them about the attic door, and according to my attorney, that led them to the room the girl jumped from."

"Did you refuse to answer any questions?"

"Not until I got the feeling they thought I was implicated, then I shut up and demanded an attorney. A firm, Littlejohn & Brown, that represents some of my grandfather's interests, sent me Ted Faber. The only advice he gave me was to shut up, which I was already doing. Then he brought me an offer, five years, if I'd testify against Sid and Larry. I told him I wanted to walk on all charges, and then I'd talk to the DA."

"Well, you sound like an ideal client, Mike. I understand you're saying you're innocent of all charges, is that right?"

"That's right. I had absolutely nothing to do with harming those girls. I'm not put together that way."

"All right, tell me what you're going to tell the DA that will want her to make the deal."

"I keep a journal, every day. I have lots of time every night."

"And where is this journal?"

"In a safe place."

"How long would it take for you to produce it?"

"As long as it takes for you to go get it from the safe place."

"And how does the journal relate to the murders?"

"I noted the times when Sid and Larry disappeared. I expect that if you compare them to the dates the girls were murdered, you'll get some matches."

"That's good, but I think we need a little more than that. Are you aware that a murder almost identical to the ones in New York occurred in Los Angeles almost simultaneously?"

"I was not aware of that, but Sid was in Los Angeles for a few days during that time. He took some vacation time to visit his mother, he said."

"The name of the girl who jumped from the building is Faith Barnacle. Did you know her?"

"Sure, she was a pilot with a charter airline; she stayed there at least a dozen times, maybe more."

"Did Sid or Larry pay any attention to her?"

"Yeah, it's the old story: Sid tried to chat her up, but what girl wants to be chatted up by a guy who's mopping the floor?"

"And you saw this happen?"

"I did, and Sid was plenty pissed off about it. I heard him call her a 'fucking bitch,' after she walked out of earshot."

"How about Larry?"

"He was always pretty quiet. Sid did the talking to the girls."

"Anything else, Mike?"

"Have you spoken to my grandfather?"

"No, he preferred to deal through Ted Faber."

Adams snorted. "Yeah, he would. He'd want to keep his hands clean."

"Mike," Herb said, "let me give you some advice. Be grateful to your grandfather. He's the one who's ultimately going to get you this deal."

"Okay, I understand. When will I get out?"

"Not for a while, but I think we can improve your circumstances. If they go for the deal, they'll move you to a hotel, and you'll probably be there until you testify."

"Why?"

"Maybe Sid and Larry have other friends, who might take exception to you testifying."

"Oh, I hadn't thought of that."

"One more thing, Mike. Where's the diary?"

"It's in my office, behind the front desk, in a small safe under the floorboards."

"Haven't the police already searched it?"

"Maybe, but they can be pretty perfunctory."

"What's the combination to the safe?"

Adams gave it to him.

"How do I locate the floorboards?"

"They're under the document shredder."

Herb gave Adams his card. "Call me if you need anything."

"How soon will we know about the deal?"

"Soon," Herb said. He shook Adams's hand, then banged on the door and was let out.

34

ERB GOT BACK into Ted Faber's car and asked to be taken to the hotel on Lex. He walked into the lobby and found it deserted. "Hello?" he called, but got only an echo for a response.

He flipped up the part of the desktop that admitted him to the front desk, then found the door to the small office behind. He dragged the document shredder to one side, found the safe under the floorboards, and entered the combination. The journal was on top of some other items; Herb put the journal into his briefcase and looked through the safe. He found a .380-caliber semiautomatic pistol, some ammo, and a spare magazine. There was also a thick manuscript entitled "Night Job in Hell." Pretty florid for a front desk, he thought. He closed the safe and left the hotel, checking his watch. It was a little past five. He wanted to see Cheray Gardner, and he knew where he was likely to find her. He told the driver to take him back to the courthouse. On the way, he googled the murders and noted the dates of each, then he compared the dates to the notations in Mike Adams's diary. They all matched, even the one in L.A. He marked the entries with his business cards and put the diary back into his briefcase.

Once at the courthouse, he directed the driver to a bar a couple of blocks away. "Wait for me," he said, taking his briefcase inside with him.

The place was going full blast, filled with lawyers, detectives, and court employees. Herb checked his watch and took a seat at one end of the bar. He didn't have long to wait. Cheray Gardner entered the bar and immediately spotted him in her usual corner. She came over and permitted herself to be air-kissed.

"Well, Herb, you're out of your neighborhood, aren't you? Or are you actually trying a case?"

"Certainly not. When all your clients are innocent, why bother with trying cases?"

She laughed heartily. "Yes," she said, "you can buy me a drink."

"Bartender," he said, "a very dry Belvedere martini with four olives, straight up."

"You remembered," she said. "How sweet of you."

"What are you working on these days?" he asked.

"Oh, the usual," she replied. "Why do you ask?"

"Just making conversation."

"How about you?" she asked. "What're you working on?"

"Oh, a very nice divorce case and some real estate work attendant to that."

"Funny," Cheray said, looking at him questioningly. "I thought you might be working on one of my cases."

"What case is that?"

"Oh, just a team of serial rapists and killers who've been terrorizing the Upper East Side."

"I've read about that one, of course, and this afternoon I was asked to represent one of them."

"Which one?"

"The innocent one," Herb replied.

"Oh, ho, ho! Am I supposed to ask which one?"

"You already know which one," Herb answered. "So do the cops."

"Oh, really?"

"Yes, really, Cheray. You're just waiting for one of the three to break and rat out the other two, and you don't really care which one."

"That's not a bad guess," she said.

"Maybe I can help you out," Herb said. "Suppose I can get the innocent one to flip and give you enough to convict the others?"

"Then I'll buy you a very good dinner," she said.

"Tell you what, I'll settle for a steak here. Shall I find us a booth?"

"Sure. We can figure out who's buying over dessert."

"I'm just accepting your offer." Herb went to find the headwaiter and slipped him a fifty. He beckoned to Cheray, and she came over.

"Oh, and the nicest, quietest booth, too."

"Nothing but the best for us." They sat down, and Herb ordered them another drink. Cheray always drank her first martini quickly. They ordered steaks.

"Why don't we get business out of the way?" Cheray proposed. "I don't want it to get in the way of . . . my steak."

"Sure. All Mike Adams needs is immunity on every count of the case and protection from the other two until the trial."

"I've already offered him five years," she said. "Why should I improve on that?"

"Why would an innocent man plead guilty to something he didn't do and serve five years for it?"

"So, he gets himself a smart lawyer, and . . ."

"He didn't hire me, his grandfather did. Old Swifty must have heard about me somewhere."

"'Swifty'? His grandfather is Mikeford Whitehorn?"

"Oh, shit," Herb said, slapping his forehead. "I did not say that, you hear me? The name never passed my lips."

"Well, it passed my ears."

"Cheray, promise me you won't mention that name to anybody, and I mean anybody, in connection with this case."

"Why, is he getting publicity shy?"

"Promise me, or you'll be eating two steaks."

"Oh, all right, I promise. Not that I couldn't eat two steaks. Tell me, how did your relationship with this . . . anonymous person come about?"

Herb shrugged. "I've never met the man. Apparently, my reputation precedes me. So, you want to do this deal and make yourself famous overnight, without all the bother of a trial?"

"First, I want to know what your client has got on the other two that will get them to plead and take a life sentence."

"He worked in that hotel as the night clerk with them for a year and a half. He noticed that one or the other would disappear for an hour or two—never together."

"I'll need more than that," she replied.

"Suppose my client kept a journal of his evenings and noted the dates and times when one or the other was out of sight, and suppose one of them was in L.A. at the time of the copycat murder? Would that be enough to sway you to do the right thing?"

"I'd have to see the journal," she said.

Herb unsnapped his briefcase. "What a coincidence!" he said. "I just happen to have it right here." He handed it over. "Save time and go where the markers are."

Cheray went through the diary, between sips of her martini. "Well, shit," she said. "A chimpanzee could get a conviction with this."

"Not just a conviction, a couple of confessions," Herb said. "Save the DA the time and costs of a trial." He extended his hand across the table. "And all that anxiety, waiting for the jury to come back with a verdict."

Cheray thought about it for a moment, then took Herb's hand. "Counselor, you've got your client a deal," she said. "Subject to the old man's approval, of course."

"Oh, I don't think you'll have any problem getting that," Herb said. He tucked the journal back into his briefcase. "You'll get this in exchange for the written offer."

After dinner, they went back to her place, dismissed the driver, and sealed the deal with an enthusiastic roll in the hay. Herb got back to his own apartment in time to shower and change for the office.

35

As Stone was finishing up his day, Joan came in. "Mr. Mikeford Whitehorn's assistant called and asked if you'd turn up at his dinner party tonight a few minutes early. I accepted for you."

"Thanks for saving me the trouble," he said, glancing at his watch. He could make it. "And please tell Fred we're leaving early."

She returned to her office, and Stone went upstairs to shower and dress. He found a tuxedo that had recently been pressed, buttoned on the suspenders, and got into it. He chose a black tie and neatly knotted it in one smooth motion, something he had once seen Cary Grant do in a movie. He had practiced for days until he got it right, and he regretted that there was no witness to compliment him. He slipped into the waistcoat and got his gold Patek Philippe pocket watch and chain from the safe, wound the watch, attached the bar to its little buttonhole, and slipped the watch into its right pocket. The counterweight, a small gold folding knife, went into the left. He put on the jacket and selected a white silk pocket square and tucked it into the breast pocket. He put his iPhone and pen into their proper pockets and examined the result: presentable. His dowager dinner partner would be knocked out.

Fred was waiting downstairs and drove him uptown to 740 Park. The elevator opened onto a private foyer, where the butler was waiting to show him into the library. There was a Knob Creek on the rocks waiting for him on a small table between two wing chairs facing the fireplace, where a cheerful blaze burned.

Mikeford "Swifty" Whitehorn appeared almost immediately, right after his own glass of scotch. "Good evening, Stone," he said.

Stone stood and took his hand. "Good evening, Swifty," he replied. They sat down, raised their glasses, and sipped.

"Thank you for coming early," Whitehorn said. "I thought, perhaps, I'd give you the news, if you haven't heard."

"I haven't seen or heard any news since the *Times* this morning," Stone replied.

"Well, in tomorrow morning's *Times* you will learn that the district attorney has given my grandson immunity in return for his testimony, and the DA has used that news to persuade the two perpetrators to accept life terms with the possibility of parole."

"Which they are unlikely ever to receive, because of the number and savagery of their crimes," Stone said.

"Your Herbert Fisher wrapped up the whole thing in an afternoon, apparently sealing the bargain in the assistant district attorney's bed, if my driver's judgment is any good. I loaned Mr. Faber my car for the day, and he passed it on to Mr. Fisher."

"I'm delighted to hear it went well," Stone said. "If you're pleased with the outcome, perhaps you might sometime direct some business Herb's way. He's very versatile and can handle just about anything."

"I have already done so," Whitehorn replied.

"On Herb's behalf and that of Woodman & Weld, I thank you."

"And now I'd like to do something for you," Whitehorn said.

"That's not necessary," Stone replied.

"Such things are always necessary," Whitehorn replied, "or Earth would not turn on its axis. Your dinner partner this evening will be an old friend of mine, Edith Beresford. Edie is a widow and a divorcée, the two events occurring almost simultaneously—fortunately before her ex-husband had time to change his will. So, instead of getting half his estate, she got everything, there being no children to squander it all."

"She's to be complimented on her timing," Stone said.

"Edie needs a bit of help in setting her affairs in order," Whitehorn said. "She tends to be impulsive about such things and is sometimes inclined toward people whose motives are, shall we say, questionable."

"I suppose that's always a danger for wealthy widows," Stone said.

"I ran a Dun & Bradstreet on you and poked around in other places, and I'm satisfied that you don't need her money."

Stone didn't think thanks were in order for Swifty's prying, so he said nothing.

"I hope that doesn't offend you," Whitehorn said after a pause, "and if it does, well, tough."

Stone laughed into his bourbon. "I'm not offended, Swifty. You're not the first to have a look under the stones of my life." He was already wondering who he could palm off Edith Beresford on—not Herbie Fisher—perhaps Bill Eggers, who liked old ladies with piles of money for clients.

"There's another matter I'd like to discuss with you, Stone," Whitehorn said, staring into his scotch.

"Certainly," Stone replied.

"It's my grandson, Mike Adams, who this afternoon received his freedom."

"How can I help?"

"I realize you haven't met the boy, but I've always felt he had more to offer than we've seen from him. His father, Howard Adams, is not very well, and I fear we'll lose him in a year or two. Then Mike will be awash in money, which may not be the best thing for him. Howard owns the commercial real estate company that owns the hotel where Mike was given the night clerk's job. They're going to close the hotel immediately; it was scheduled for a gutting and renovation anyway, but its new infamy would kill any existing business. They want to turn it into more of a businessman's destination."

"Do you think that Mike, if given major responsibility, might rise to it?"

"That is in line with my assessment of him. However, he has disappointed his father so often that I think he is unlikely to be given such responsibilities."

"Do you have any influence with the boy's father?"

"I daresay I do. I put him in business and invested heavily with him."

"Has your investment paid off?"

"It certainly has, and beyond my expectations."

"Then, perhaps, his father might be susceptible to a suggestion from you that he put Mike in charge of the revitalization of this hotel. The boy should know something about it, having worked there for a year or two."

Whitehorn looked thoughtful. "And, if Mike looks like he is screwing it up, the brakes could be applied."

"He could start by reconceptualizing the hotel, perhaps as something better than a businessman's destination. There are a lot of hotels in the city that cater to a younger crowd, who seem to have a lot of money to spend, but they're mostly downtown; none in that neighborhood."

"By God, that's a fine idea!" Swifty said. "I'll have lunch with Howard tomorrow and put it to him."

The butler entered the room. "Mr. Whitehorn, Mrs. Edith Beresford," he said, "and there are others arriving, too."

The butler was followed into the library by a tall, slim woman in her thirties, wearing a clinging sheath of a dress that featured a lot of gold thread and accented her full breasts.

"Edith," Swifty said, "may I present Mr. Stone Barrington? Stone, this is Edith Beresford."

36

STONE SHOOK EDITH'S HAND. "How do you do?"

"Very well, thank you."

Her voice reminded Stone of that of Ava Gardner, smooth and a little Southern.

"Tell me," he said, "were you, by any chance, born in a small Georgia town called Delano?"

"No," she replied, "I was born in a slightly larger Georgia town called Atlanta."

"Ah," he replied. "I seem to meet so many people from Delano."

"I'm afraid I don't have an answer for that," she said. "I believe you must be the attorney Swifty says can put all my affairs into order."

"He did mention something about that," Stone replied, "but frankly, you don't look like a woman who needs her affairs put into order. The impression you give is one of confidence."

She smiled. "Thank you. That sounds like a very good excuse for you to avoid the job."

"I have a better excuse than that," Stone said.

"And what would that be?"

"I would prefer a personal relationship to a business one, and the two are often incompatible. However, I can recommend an excellent person for the job."

"And who might that be?"

"Bill Eggers, who is the managing partner of my firm, Woodman & Weld."

"I've heard good things about the firm," she said, "but why Mr. Eggers? Surely someone a bit further down the ladder—but not too far—might be more interested in my situation."

"Well, Bill has something of a specialty in dowager widows and divorcées, you see." He held up a hand. "I know, but if I tell him you're a dowager, he will have a more immediate reason to see you. Then you can surprise him at your first meeting."

"As I surprised you, Mr. Barrington?"

"I confess you did," Stone replied. "Please call me Stone."

"And I'm Edie," she replied. "What sort of 'personal relationship' did you have in mind?"

"Why don't we start with dinner and see where that leads us?"

"But we're having dinner this evening," she said.

"Of course, but this evening I'll have to share you with whoever is seated on your other side, and while I'm not the jealous type, well, my personal motto is *Si non nunc quando*."

She laughed. "'If not now, when.'"

"Your Latin is very good."

"It comes from having been a classical scholar. How's yours?"

"I have just exhausted my entire Latin vocabulary," he said.

"All right, we can have half a dinner tonight and a whole one tomorrow evening?"

"What more could I ask?" Stone said.

"I'm sure you'll think of something."

They were called in to dinner. It was a table for twelve; Stone was on Edie's right, and another gentleman, whose place card read "Dr. Johnny Hon," was on her left.

Edie and Dr. Hon exhibited an immediate affinity for each other, and Stone was having difficulty getting a word in edgewise. Between courses, Dr. Hon excused himself for a moment.

"Whew!" Stone said. "I'm glad to see the back of him."

"Why?" Edie asked. "He's perfectly charming."

"I expect that's why I'm mostly seeing the back of you."

She laughed. "And you struck me as a competitive sort. Was I wrong?"

"Well, I could arm-wrestle him for the privilege of your attention, I suppose."

"Think of it as football," she said. "What you need is a turnover."

Dr. Hon returned, and Stone lost the ball again. After dinner, when Dr. Hon's attention was diverted, he took the opportunity to whisk Edie into the library, where they were alone.

"Turnover accomplished!" Edie said.

"Now I have to score?"

She laughed again; he liked it when she laughed. "You'll have to run up a lot of yardage rushing," she replied. "The forward pass doesn't work every time."

The butler appeared with a tray of after-dinner drinks, and they both chose cognac.

"Let me ask you a question," she said, "the answer to which I have always found to be revealing."

"Then I'll be sure to give you a straight answer."

"Where is your second home?"

Stone burst out laughing. "That's a more difficult question than I anticipated," he said.

"Why?"

"Because I have more than one second home. But for purposes of this discussion, and because it's the closest, my reply will be Dark Harbor, Maine."

She looked surprised. "Nothing in the Hamptons?"

"I'm afraid not. I don't think I'd fit in very well out there."

"Very good," she said. "I despise the Hamptons. Now, since you have more than one second home, where is your favorite one?"

Stone thought about it for a moment before replying. "South Hampshire, England," he said. "On the Beaulieu River."

"And why is it your favorite?"

"I like the climate."

That made her laugh again. "Oh, really?"

"There's nothing like curling up with a good book and listening to the rain beat against the window."

"I perceive that you are a contrarian. Everyone else is looking for heat and sunshine."

"Heat is overrated," Stone replied. "I enjoy a cool day."

"And sunshine?"

"Is most appreciated when rare. Now it's your turn. Where is your second home?"

"In the Hamptons," she said, "in Sag Harbor."

"But you despise the Hamptons!"

"Yes, but I despise Sag Harbor somewhat less than the other towns. Besides, I didn't choose it; my husband already owned the house when we married. And anyway, it's on the market. In fact, I was hoping to sell it to you."

"Don't point that thing at me," Stone said. "My real estate portfolio is threatening to explode as it is."

And then, before they could continue, Dr. Johnny Hon appeared and pulled up a chair.

"May I pick you up at seven tomorrow evening?" Stone asked, before the man could get started.

"I have something a little earlier; may we meet somewhere?"

"Do you know Patroon?"

"I do, but not well."

He gave her the address, then ceded her company to Dr. Hon.

37

EDITH BERESFORD WAS TWENTY minutes late for dinner. Stone was about to order his second bourbon when she turned up, all apologies. Her hair was down, and it fell below her shoulders.

"I am so sorry," she said. "I'd give you my excuse, but it wouldn't be good enough. It would get our evening off to a poor start, and I wouldn't want that."

"Then I forgive you all your sins, so we won't have to work through them. What would you like to drink?"

"What are you having?"

"Knob Creek bourbon."

"Never heard of it. I'll have some of that."

He ordered two, and they arrived quickly. They clinked glasses and drank.

"I feel so clean," she said.

"How's that?"

"I haven't had all my sins forgiven since I was in high

school, during my last confession. I stopped going after that."

"What was your sin?" he asked.

"It would be too embarrassing to tell you."

"Then what was your penance?"

"Ten Hail Marys and swearing never to put my hand in a boy's pants again."

"Did you keep your oath?"

"Why do you think I stopped going to confession? I couldn't face that priest again!"

Stone laughed.

"Are you Catholic?" she asked.

"I'm not a joiner, generally speaking. I think I agree with my late friend Frank Muir, who described himself as a lapsed agnostic."

She laughed. "Good choice. If you were Catholic and I were your confessor, what would you confess?"

"Impure thoughts."

"Oh, good. And what penance would you think appropriate?"

"Forty lashes with your hair."

She looked appreciative. "I should get it cut, shouldn't I?"

"No, at least not until I've done my penance."

Then Stone realized someone was standing at their table.

"Oh," Edie said, "Dr. Hon!"

"You've been following us, haven't you?" Stone asked.

"Of course not, but may I join you?"

"Not unless you have the ecclesiastical authority to do so," Stone replied.

"I fear my degrees are in science, not divinity."

"Then we will not require your services," Stone said. "Now, if you will excuse us." He made a shooing motion with the back of his hand.

Dr. Hon looked sheepish. "Well, it was worth a try."

"Good evening," Stone said with finality.

"That was rude," Edie said when he had gone.

"It was, wasn't it? I'd like to have been ruder, but it was the best I could do without taking a swing at him."

"I thought you did very well. After all, he kept us apart for one evening already. He's nothing if not persistent; I hope he doesn't come back."

"Don't worry, I'm armed."

She looked at him in mock alarm. "With what?"

"A little Colt .380 semiautomatic." He patted his chest under his arm.

"And for what reason?"

"A jealous husband."

"I can't say that surprises me."

"That is a slur on my character. I do not dally with married women. She came to me as a client, sort of, and her husband misunderstood."

"What does 'sort of' a client mean?"

"Well, I met her in a luggage store, when she broke a heel and fell into my lap. I offered her a lift home, got her to her apartment in a wheelchair, and arranged a house call from a doctor. While we were waiting for him to show up, she learned that I was an attorney, and she asked me to suggest someone to represent her in a divorce. She also asked me to recommend a Realtor, as she was looking to buy an apartment and to sell her old one."

"And what was the upshot of all that?"

"Her ankle is better, she is divorced, and she has just moved into a new apartment. And sold her old one."

"My, you do give good advice, don't you?"

"I endeavor to—it doesn't always work that quickly."

"I'm beginning to think I should have opted for the professional relationship with you."

"Oh, no, it would have ended badly."

"Why?"

"Because I would still have wanted the personal relationship. If you had taken advice from me under those circumstances my judgment would have been clouded, and you'd have dismissed me and ended up married to a man who was interested only in your money and, because of that, broke."

"You've been listening to Swifty Whitehorn, haven't you?"

"If I had not, we wouldn't be sitting here about to order the chateaubriand and an excellent cabernet."

"Is that what we're having?"

"Unless you are not a carnivore."

"I am, order it."

THEY HAD FINISHED their dinner and were on coffee.

"Are you really armed?" she asked.

"Really."

"Do you always go armed?"

"Only when there's a jealous husband about."

"Does that happen often?"

"I try to avoid the circumstance."

"Doesn't it feel unnatural to have a weapon concealed on your person?"

"It does not. I was once a police officer and, thus, always armed. One becomes accustomed to it."

"*You* were a police officer?"

"A homicide detective, for most of my career."

"How long did your career last?"

"Fourteen years, then they asked for their badge and gun back."

"Why?"

"They attributed my exit to a knee wound, suffered in the line of duty, but that was just an excuse. The truth is: I was a pain in the ass, and they were sick of me."

"Then it is their loss," she said, leaning over and kissing him. "Enough of this chitchat," she said. "Why don't you show me where you live? I'm still looking for clues to your character."

Stone waved at a passing waiter. "Check!"

38

EDIE BERESFORD STOOD in the middle of Stone's living room and turned 360 degrees, slowly. "I like the pictures," she said, "they show good judgment."

"I'm afraid they say nothing at all about my judgment," Stone replied. "They were painted by my mother, so all they demonstrate is maternal loyalty. However, I like them, too."

"Who was your mother?"

"Matilda Stone."

"I remember that name. She has some work in the American Collection at the Met, doesn't she?"

"She does."

"Is the piano in tune, or is it there just as an objet d'art?"

"Both," Stone replied.

"Then play me something."

Stone sat down, opened the keyboard, and played some Gershwin.

"Very nice. Tell me about the rest of the house."

"My study is over there. Would you like a brandy?"

"Yes, please."

He took her into the room, seated her, lit the fire, and poured them both a Rémy Martin. "This room is very much you," she said, looking around. "Who was your decorator?"

"I was."

"Tell me about the rest of the house."

"There are six bedrooms upstairs, on three floors, and seven baths."

"Why more baths than bedrooms?"

"There are two in the master suite."

"Very wise."

"Downstairs are my offices—in what used to be a dentist's office—a small gym, and a kitchen that opens onto the common gardens out back. There's also a garage."

"How did you find the house?"

"It found me. It belonged to my great-aunt, my grandmother's sister, and she left it to me. I did the renovation, except for the plumbing and electrical work."

"You mean you did the actual work?"

"I couldn't afford to hire a builder on a cop's salary."

"How did you become a lawer?"

"By studying at NYU Law, before I was a cop. When I wasn't a cop anymore, Bill Eggers offered me a job at Woodman & Weld, if I could pass the bar. After a two-week cram course, I did."

"And the rest is history?"

"History in the making. It occurs to me that you have me at a disadvantage. You know nearly everything about me, and I know nearly nothing about you."

"Pretty straightforward: born and raised in an antebellum

house in northwest Atlanta; Daddy a judge; Mother a college professor; educated at Agnes Scott College, in Atlanta; came to New York looking for adventure, found it, married young— big mistake; married a second time—another big mistake, but he had the grace to die and leave me his fortune. Met a nice man at a dinner party, and that brings us up-to-date."

"I'm sure a lot fell through the cracks in that account," Stone said.

"Then you can explore the cracks for the rest."

Stone's phone rang and he checked the ID. "Please excuse me, I have to take this." He walked across the room. "Hello?"

"It's Faith."

"How are you feeling?"

"More and more human. I'm receiving visitors tomorrow morning."

"I'll be there."

"Night, night." She hung up, and Stone returned to the couch and his brandy.

"Not bad news, I hope," Edie said.

"Good news. An employee of mine is in the hospital with extensive injuries; but she's getting better, and I can see her tomorrow."

"How was she injured?"

"She was attacked, but her attackers are in jail, awaiting sentencing."

"What does she do for you?"

"She's my chief pilot—sorry, my only pilot. I bought a new airplane, and it requires two pilots; I'm the other one."

"Will she come back to work when she recovers?"

"I certainly hope so. She's a very good pilot."

Edie glanced at her watch. "Goodness, is it that late?"

"I suppose it is."

"Then I have to go home; I have an early day tomorrow."

"Fred will drive you," Stone said. "Dinner next week?"

"Of course, call me."

He walked her downstairs, kissed her, and put her in the car.

As he reached his bedroom his cell rang. "Hello?"

"It's Dino. You alone?"

"I just put her into the car."

"Who?"

"You don't know this one. Her name is Edith Beresford."

"You're right. Sounds old."

"It only sounds that way. I have *good* news. Your guys can question Faith tomorrow."

"I'm afraid she's old news," Dino said. "Her assailants have already pled out."

"I heard that."

"Still, we ought to have her on the record, so I'll send somebody around."

"You do that."

"Dinner tomorrow night?"

"I've got plans: Cilla is cooking for me."

"Later, then."

They hung up, and Stone went to bed.

THE FOLLOWING MORNING, TV news caught up to events and reported the guilty plea from the two perpetrators at the hotel. They also reported that Mike Adams had been released.

Stone had just finished breakfast when his phone rang. "Hello?"

"It's Swifty," a deep voice said.

"Good morning. I must thank you for introducing me to Edith Beresford. We had a very pleasant dinner last evening."

"Are you going to represent her?"

"She's far too beautiful for a business relationship. I'm going to turn her over to Bill Eggers."

"That should be fine," Swifty said. "I want to thank you, too."

"For what?"

"My son-in-law, my grandson, and I had lunch together yesterday, and it went well. We went back to Howard's office and went over the plans for the renovation of the hotel, and young Mike had some good suggestions to make. He's now the project manager on the hotel for Adams & Adams, his father's firm."

"That's very good news, Swifty."

"Not as good as the news that he's a free man."

"For that you can thank Herb Fisher."

"I have, and I will be in touch with him about more work."

"I don't think you need to worry about Edie. She has a good head on her shoulders."

"I always knew that, I was just playing matchmaker."

"Nice job," Stone said, and they said goodbye.

39

STONE'S CELL PHONE buzzed while he was being driven to Bellevue by Fred. "Hello?"

"It's Cilla, good morning."

"Good morning."

"Are we still on for tonight?"

"We are."

"Good. My intercom is broken. When you arrive, the desk man will have your name and send you straight up to the twelfth floor. I'll leave the door cracked, so just let yourself in. The bar is in the living room so you can make yourself a bourbon and me a vodka on the rocks, then find the kitchen, where I'll be up to my elbows in osso buco."

"My favorite. See you at seven." They hung up.

STONE ARRIVED OUTSIDE Faith's hospital room and looked in to find two men in suits seated at her bedside, so he leaned against the jamb and listened.

"Is there anything else you can remember, Ms. Barnacle?" one of the men asked. "Anything at all?"

"No. I'm sorry to be of so little help."

"If you remember anything else, please call me. I'll leave my card on your bedside table. Good day."

Stone heard the scraping of chairs on the floor, then Faith said, "Wait, I remember something."

The two men sat down again. "What do you remember?"

"Music."

"What kind of music?"

"Classical. On a radio, I think. There was a voice introducing the next piece."

"Could you see the radio?"

"No, I just heard it. After that, I found my way to the window."

The two men thanked her again, then left.

Stone went into the room and found Faith halfway sitting up in her bed, with the sheets pulled up to her neck. He kissed her on the forehead and pulled up a chair. "Feeling any better?"

"I am. The cuts still hurt, but the morphine is taking care of that. I pulled the sheets up because I don't want anybody to see the cuts, which are unbandaged. I was told I have something like one hundred and fifty stitches."

"Then just try to relax. Is there anything I can bring you? Books? Magazines?"

"The morphine makes it hard to concentrate on reading," she said, "but the TV remote is taped to my hand, and I can watch."

"What are your doctors telling you?"

"As soon as my cuts are less painful, I can get out of here; I hope I'm not addicted to morphine by then. The middle of the week, maybe. I won't have to come back to get the stitches out; they'll dissolve by themselves. The cuts are covered by green, transparent tape, which looks like bruising."

"The airplane is waiting for you, when you're ready."

"Thank you, Stone. I'm going to have to take a nap now, so will you excuse me?"

"Sure." He kissed her on the forehead again and left.

THAT EVENING, Stone chose a good bottle of red from his cellar, and on the way to Cilla's apartment he stopped at a bodega and picked up a bouquet of flowers. "Take the rest of the evening off, Fred," he said as he got out in front of Cilla's building. "I'll get a cab home."

"Yes, sir," Fred replied and drove away to his own dinner.

Stone was inspected by the doorman and admitted to the lobby, where he found an empty front desk. Oh, well, he thought, desk men have to go to the john like everyone else. There was a log of visitors on the desk, and he signed in at seven o'clock, then he took the elevator to the twelfth floor and got out. The upstairs foyer smelled deliciously of Italian cooking, and he could hear jazz playing through the door, which was ajar.

He went into the apartment, found the bar, located a vase, put water into it, and fluffed up the flowers, then he poured himself a drink from a new, sealed bottle of Knob Creek and did the same with a bottle of Belvedere vodka. The music was coming from a built-in system and traveled with him as he walked toward the kitchen.

The dining room held a handsome table for twelve, but the walls there, as in the living room, were missing pictures, which were, no doubt, on Cilla's shopping list. "Hello!" he called out as he entered the kitchen.

There were pots simmering on the stove, but no Cilla in sight. "Cilla?" Powder room, he figured. He set the two drinks on the kitchen island, where there were barstools, took one and settled in, glancing at his watch. Five past seven. He sipped his drink, waiting patiently, then it was seven-fifteen. He got up and looked for a powder room. As he turned back, he saw a pair of legs protruding from behind the kitchen island. One ankle was bandaged and the shoe was missing.

He ran to her and found her lying on her back, a large chef's knife protruding from her chest. He knelt beside her, avoiding a pool of blood, and felt for an artery in her neck. Nothing, and her body was cool. He stood up, walked back to his barstool, sat down, and took a big swig of his drink. Then he got out his cell phone and called Dino.

"Bacchetti."

"It's Stone," he said.

Dino must have caught something in his voice because he immediately asked, "What's wrong?"

"I've just arrived at Cilla's apartment for dinner and found her dead in the kitchen, with a knife in her chest."

"Oh, Christ," Dino said. "Are you all right?"

"I am. Will you send your people over here, please?"

"No. You call nine-one-one, like everybody else, and they'll send the people. It's better if I don't get entangled in this since I know both the victim and the prime suspect."

"'Prime suspect'? Are you kidding?"

"I kid you not. That's how the detectives are going to treat you when they arrive, and rightly so. You know as well as I do that the person finding the victim is always a prime suspect. I hope I don't have to tell you not to touch anything and to be completely honest with the detectives."

"No, you don't have to tell me that, so stop telling me that, please."

"Let me know how it goes, pal," Dino said, "but not until you're cleared." He hung up.

"Thanks so much," Stone said to the dead telephone. Then it occurred to him that he might not be alone in the apartment. He set down his drink, pulled his weapon from its shoulder holster, and slipped out of his shoes. Room by room, he searched the place, checking every closet and hiding place, then he went back to the kitchen and did the same there. Nothing. He switched off the burners on the stove.

His mind more at ease, he picked up a wall phone in the kitchen, called 911, and went through their drill. Then he hung up the phone, recovered his drink, went back into the living room, placed his gun and badge on the bar, and sat down to wait for the law to arrive.

40

IRST STONE HEARD the siren coming down Fifth Avenue, then it stopped outside. Another couple of minutes and he heard the elevator door open.

"In here," he called out. "The door is open."

The door opened the rest of the way, and a young man in a dark suit peered around it.

"I'm alone and unarmed," Stone said. "Come in."

The cop came in, gun out in front of him, followed by his partner.

"I've cleared the place," Stone said. "There's no one else here."

"Are you a cop?" the detective asked.

"Retired. My gun and badge are on the bar, next to the flowers and the bottle of wine."

The cop was still pointing his gun. "Stand up," he said.

Stone stood, holding his arms away from his body.

"Hands on top of your head, fingers interlocked."

Stone followed instructions and allowed himself to be

handcuffed and thoroughly searched. The cop kept his wallet.

"A gun and a badge are over here," the other cop said from the bar. "Detective First Grade."

"Clear the place," the first cop said.

"Will you uncuff me now?" Stone asked.

"You just stand right there. I'll decide when to uncuff you."

The other detective came back. "There's a woman in the kitchen with a knife in her chest," he said. "I called for the ME and a team. Otherwise, all clear."

"Okay," the younger man said, "you can sit down now."

"Uncuff me first," Stone said.

"I'm not concerned with your comfort, I just want answers."

"Well, you're not getting any until you've uncuffed me," Stone said.

The older cop uncuffed him. "Have a seat, Mr. . . ."

"Barrington," Stone said, sitting down and picking up his drink from the side table. "And you?"

"He's Detective Calabrese. I'm Muldoon."

"I didn't know there was a Muldoon left on the NYPD," Stone said.

"We're a rare breed," Muldoon said.

Calabrese went to take a look at the corpse for himself, then came back. "Did you touch anything?"

"The phone on the wall. And I turned off two burners on the stove. Dinner was cooking."

"Do you always walk around barefoot?"

"I took off my shoes when I was clearing the apartment. They're in the kitchen."

"I'll get them for you," Calabrese said.

"Why are you here?" Muldoon asked. Calabrese came back and tossed Stone's shoes on the floor, and he put them on.

"I was invited to dinner," Stone said. "I arrived at seven. She told me the intercom was broken, and she'd leave the door open for me. The desk man was absent, so I came upstairs. I put the flowers in some water and poured us both a drink, as she had asked me to. Then I went into the kitchen, and didn't see her. I sat on a stool for a while, then I went to look for her and saw her legs sticking out."

"One of them has an Ace bandage on the ankle," Calabrese said.

"A sprain." Stone told them how he and Cilla had met.

"You got a guess on a suspect?" Muldoon asked.

"The ex-husband, one Donald Trask. They've been divorced for two weeks. She gave him a lot of money to get out of the marriage, but maybe not as much as he would have liked."

"You look pretty calm for somebody who's found a corpse with a knife in it," Calabrese said.

"I've seen more corpses than you have," Stone replied.

"Maybe," Calabrese said.

"Certainly," Muldoon offered. "You got an address for this Trask?"

Stone checked his phone and gave him the address. "He moved in there a week ago Friday. He owns several guns, but his carry license may have been revoked. He failed to list a new purchase."

"Was there any animosity between them?"

"Plenty, all on his part. He beat her up a couple of times,

put her in the hospital once. You might want to talk to the attorney who represented her: Herbert Fisher, at this number." He gave Muldoon his own card. "He's my law partner."

"If Trask has guns, why would he knife her?" Calabrese asked.

"No ballistics on a knife," Stone said, rolling his eyes. "And you might check with the desk man to see if Trask announced himself. He may have come in while the man was away from his post, as I did, then left down the stairs to the garage."

"You've got this all figured out, have you?" Calabrese asked.

"I had time to think about it while I was waiting for you to show up," Stone replied.

"What time did you say you arrived?"

"Seven o'clock. You can check the log downstairs; I signed in."

"Trask is a good lead," Muldoon said. "We'll follow it all the way."

"If it doesn't pan out," Stone said, "then I haven't got a clue. She never mentioned anybody else to me. They didn't have any kids, and he wasn't the sort to make fast friendships."

"Do you know him personally?"

"He showed up at my office once, thinking I was her lawyer. I straightened him out, and he left. He called on another occasion; he was very angry. He was hanging around my block, but a friend of mine discouraged him, and I don't think he came back. He did behave himself at the divorce hearing, I'm told. He'll have a gun safe in his apartment."

Then a parade of technicians began to enter the apartment and were directed to the kitchen. The detectives' lieutenant arrived and listened to Stone's story all over again, then told the detectives to go detain Trask. As they were leaving, the ME came out of the kitchen.

"The knife wasn't the cause of death," he said.

"I would have thought that would do it," Muldoon said.

"She was shot first," he said, "then stabbed, probably to cover up the gunshot wound."

"Did you dig out a bullet?"

"We'll do that in the lab. I'll let you know. Oh, I'd put time of death at between six-thirty and seven PM." The ME went back to the kitchen.

Muldoon shook Stone's hand and left with Calabrese in tow. Stone recovered his gun and badge, tied his shoes, and followed them.

Downstairs, the desk man was back at his post.

"I logged in while you were away," Stone said, turning the logbook around. "Did a man named Trask arrive to see Ms. Scott?"

"Nobody arrived," the desk man said. "I saw your name in the log. She had said she was expecting you."

"Tell it all to the cops when they get around to you," Stone said, "and don't leave anything out."

He went outside, where it had begun to drizzle. The doorman managed to get him a cab.

"You a friend of Ms. Scott?" he asked as he opened the door for Stone.

"Yes," Stone replied.

"We hardly got to know her," the man said, then closed the cab door.

Stone rode home depressed. He needed another drink.

41

STONE WENT TO HIS STUDY, poured himself a drink, and called Dino.

"Bacchetti."

"Okay, I'm clear, no thanks to you."

"Who did they send?"

"An old pro named Muldoon and a kid called Calabrese."

"Yeah, I know them both. How'd they do?"

"Muldoon did just fine. The kid could barely keep up and was, in general, a pain in the ass."

"It figures. You weren't such a hotshot, either, when you were a green detective."

"Neither were you," Stone said.

"I got a report on the interview with Faith Barnacle," Dino said. "That's new about the music. She may come up with more later."

"Let's hope so," Stone said.

"What are you worried about? The killers have pled out."

"Yeah, you're right. I'll stop worrying."

"Have you eaten anything?" Dino asked.

"No, but I'll see what's in the fridge."

"Later."

"Sure." Stone hung up and went down to the kitchen. He found half a roast chicken and some peas in the fridge and nuked them, then opened half a bottle of a cabernet and sat down in the kitchen booth, eating slowly and watching the rain run down the windows. The Turtle Bay gardens looked bleak.

He rinsed his dishes and put them in the dishwasher, then went upstairs, undressed, and got into bed. He tried NY1, the local news channel. Cilla's murder had already filled the Breaking News slot; there was no mention of Donald Trask.

SEAN MULDOON AND DANTE CALABRESE got out of their car and went into Donald Trask's building.

"I can't wait to talk to this guy," Calabrese said.

"You shut up, and I'll do the talking this time. You'll learn more by listening." Muldoon flashed his badge at the man on the front desk. "Is Donald Trask at home?"

"Yes, he is." The man reached for his phone, but Muldoon stopped him. "What time did he come in?"

"I came on at six. I guess he walked in closer to six-thirty."

"How much closer? It's important."

"Okay, between six-twenty-five and six-thirty-five. That do?"

"We'll see; what's his apartment number?"

"Seven D, to your left out of the elevator."

"Don't announce us," Muldoon said.

"I'm supposed . . ."

"Do you want to be arrested for interfering with a police investigation?"

"No, sir."

"Then stay off the phone. We'll surprise Mr. Trask."

"All right, sir."

The two detectives got onto the elevator and pressed the button. "Remember," Muldoon said, "I'll take the lead. We're going to be real polite, put the fella at ease, you understand?"

"Whatever you say, Sean."

"That's good. I like that. Remember it."

"I did okay with Barrington, didn't I?"

"No, you didn't. You were up against a man with more experience than you. You'd have gotten along better if you'd treated him as a senior colleague, instead of a perp."

The door opened, and they rang the bell for D. Muldoon saw some light appear in the peephole, then the door opened but was secured by a chain. Muldoon showed him a badge. "NYPD," he said. "Are you Mr. Trask?"

"Yes. What about it?"

"Please open the door, we'd like to talk to you."

"About what?"

"Mr. Trask, would you rather talk to a SWAT team?"

"Oh, all right." The door closed, the chain rattled, and Trask stood there in his pajamas, a book in his hand—*Oliver Twist*. Muldoon thought that Donald Trask didn't look like the type for Dickens. "Let's go sit down, shall we?" he asked.

Trask stood aside and let them walk down a hall to the living room. The place wasn't in perfect order; there were cardboard boxes stacked in the living room. "Sorry about the mess, I just moved in."

"Not at all." Muldoon tossed a pile of books from a chair onto the floor and sat down.

"What's this about?" Trask asked again.

"First, I'm obliged to tell you that you're not under arrest, and you don't have to talk with us. You can have an attorney present, if you like."

Trask thought about that. "I guess I don't need a lawyer. Ask whatever you like."

"Mr. Trask, what did you do this evening?"

"I had a burger and a beer at P. J. Clarke's."

"What time did you arrive at Clarke's?"

"Around five, I guess. I went straight from my office, about a block from there."

"Did you see anyone you knew at Clarke's?"

"No, I don't think so."

"Do the bartenders know you?"

"I've been there before. But there's no reason for them to know my name."

"Had the waiter served you before?"

"I don't recall that he has."

"What time did you leave Clarke's?"

"After six, I guess. It was raining, and I couldn't find a cab, so I walked home."

"And what time did you arrive?"

"Six-thirtyish. The network news was just coming on when I got upstairs."

"What was the lead story on the news?"

"I wasn't listening all that closely. The flu epidemic, I think. I was making myself a drink."

"Did you have a drink before your burger at Clarke's?"

"No, I was hungry. I ordered a beer and drank that with my burger."

"Did you make any detours on the way home? Anything at all?"

"No, I told you, it was raining. I was getting wet, so I hurried."

"Do you mind if I take a picture of you?" Muldoon asked, producing his iPhone. He snapped one before Trask could reply.

"Okay, before we go any further, I want to know what this is about," Trask said.

"It's about your wife."

"I don't have a wife."

"All right, your ex-wife, Priscilla Scott. When was the last time you saw her?"

"At our divorce hearing. There were plenty of witnesses."

"To your knowledge, did Ms. Scott have a will, and are you mentioned in it?"

"Yes and yes. We both did new wills a couple of years ago. Why are we talking about wills? Has something happened to her?"

"Yes, she's deceased, I'm afraid."

Trask's eyebrows went up; it was the first emotion he'd shown. "Jesus, was she in an accident?"

"No, she was murdered."

"You're kidding me!"

"I am not, sir. She was found by a dinner guest with a knife in her chest."

Trask gulped. "Was her dinner guest named Barrington?"

"Why do you ask?"

"Because if he was there, he's the one who killed her."

"Mr. Trask, do you own any guns?"

"Yes."

"Where are they?"

"In my safe."

"May I see them, please?"

Trask walked over to a bookcase and moved some books aside, revealing a safe. He punched in a code, opened it, and stood back. "There you go."

Muldoon walked over to the safe, removed each weapon, sniffed its barrel, and then set it on the bookshelf. "Mr. Trask, do you have a New York City gun license?"

"I do."

"May I see it, please?"

Trask found his wallet and handed him the license.

Muldoon handed it back. "This Beretta has been fired recently," he said.

"I went to the range at lunchtime today."

Muldoon nodded at Calabrese, meaning, *Note that.*

"Do you mind if I take the Beretta with me?" he asked.

"What for?"

"Just to have it looked at. Don't worry, we'll return it to you in good order."

"Okay, sure, why not?"

Muldoon pocketed the pistol and turned to go. There was a coatrack in the hall with a raincoat hanging from it. He made a point of running his hand over it as they passed. "Thank you and good night, Mr. Trask."

"Don't mention it."

The door closed firmly behind them, and the chain rattled.

"Why didn't you pull his license?" Calabrese asked.

"Because the Beretta has been registered, so we have no excuse. I've got the gun, though. If he's our guy, then he thinks we won't find the bullet. And by the way, his raincoat is a little damp, but not as wet as it would get walking here from Clarke's. Let's run over there and see if anybody recognizes him from his photograph."

They did so, and nobody did.

42

MULDOON AND CALABRESE went downtown to the morgue and found the ME working on Priscilla Scott's cadaver.

"Anything?" he asked.

"I found a bullet," the ME replied. "It's a nine-millimeter round, Federal Personal Defense, Hydra-Shok—a hollow point."

"I'd like to run it over to ballistics," Muldoon said.

The ME handed him a small, zippered plastic bag containing the slug. "Good luck. Hollow points expand, and the tip of the knife blade hit it, too. In short, it's a mess. Don't count on it to seal a conviction."

"You're such a pessimist, Doc," Muldoon said, pocketing the round.

"Sign the chain-of-custody log," the ME said, then went back to his work.

"I'm going over to ballistics," Muldoon said to Calabrese. "I want you to go back to your desk, start googling and making calls to find out if Trask used a car service around six o'clock, and if so, where did it pick him up and drop him off. If the name doesn't register, try his description and if he paid in cash."

"Jesus, there must be two hundred car services," Calabrese moaned.

"That's why you're doing it instead of me," Muldoon replied. "Now get on it."

MULDOON FOUND A WOMAN still working in the ballistics lab and showed her the squashed bullet. "It's a Federal Hydra-Shok," he said, and explained the circumstances of the shooting.

"I can fire one into the tank, purely for comparison, but it's not going to come out looking anything like that. I'd have to fire it into a side of beef with the same floor material under it, and even then, it would just be hoping for the best. I'll put your slug under my scope, though, and see what we come up with."

Muldoon handed her Trask's 9mm. "Try firing it from this. I'll wait."

MULDOON WAS NEARLY finished with the *Post* when the tech came back and handed him the two slugs, each tagged, and the Beretta. "The best I can tell you is that your weapon could have fired the murder slug, but any identifying marks have been obliterated by the slug's expansion. The knife point didn't help, either. Sorry about that."

"You can only do what you can do," Muldoon said, sighing. He went back to the precinct and found Calabrese asleep with his head on his desk. Muldoon drew a cup of cold water from the cooler, drank half of it, then poured the rest into Calabrese's ear.

"What the fuck?" Calabrese yelled, raising a laugh or two in the squad room.

"I trust you have succeeded in your task," Muldoon said.

"As a matter of fact, I have, sort of," Calabrese said, sticking a tissue into his ear.

"Really? Let's hear it."

"Well, Trask has an account with Carey Limousine, but he didn't use them. He went halfway down the list and found a service, then ordered a pickup in front of Bloomingdale's, half a dozen blocks from Clarke's. He was dropped off at the Château Madison hotel on Madison Avenue and went inside. The car waited there for twenty minutes before he came back, then dropped him two blocks from his apartment. The driver says he never got a good enough look at his fare to describe him."

"Right," Muldoon said. "Of course, the Château has a side-street entrance on Sixty-eighth, so he could have walked straight from the front door and out of there, walked the two and a half blocks to Scott's apartment building, committed the murder, then walked back to the Château and out the front door, then to the drop-off."

Calabrese beamed at him. "We got him, right?"

"We got him, wrong!" Muldoon said. "That's too thin for a prosecutor to get a conviction."

"How about the ballistics?"

"All they could tell me is that the bullet could have come from Trask's Beretta. The round was a hollow point, which spreads out on contact, so there were no identifying marks good enough."

"Which leaves us where?"

"Outside, in the cold," Muldoon said. "All our evidence is circumstantial. If you could call it evidence. Trask coulda hired the car, he coulda taken the route we think he did, he coulda shot the woman, then knifed her. Coulda doesn't cut it."

"You explain it to the lieutenant," Calabrese said.

"I figured."

STONE AND DINO had dinner at P. J. Clarke's.

"So?" Stone asked.

"So, what?"

"So where is the investigation into Cilla's murder?"

"In a warm, sunny spot called 'nowhere.'"

"Explain, please."

Dino took him through Muldoon's report to his lieutenant.

"None of that is exculpatory," Stone pointed out.

"None of it is incriminating, either," Dino replied. "In fact, young Detective Calabrese thinks you're a better suspect than Trask."

"Swell."

"And he's right."

"So, Donald Trask is going to walk?"

"I didn't say that."

"You may as well have."

"You never know what will turn up. I mean, the guy doesn't have a working alibi. We just need more evidence."

"Didn't your crime scene team come up with anything?"

"Sure they did: your fingerprints on the kitchen counter, the telephone, and, of course, the bar."

"Horseshit," Stone said.

"Listen, if you were investigating this murder, you would be your chief suspect."

"Is this why you didn't want anybody to know I'd called you, instead of nine-one-one?"

"You might say I could see this coming. I didn't want my word to be the only thing clearing you."

"But I'm cleared, anyway."

"Don't count on it. Muldoon and Calabrese are still investigating, and they might come up with more evidence."

"Against me or Donald Trask?"

"Take your pick. You should relax in your personal certainty of your innocence."

"That's not going to carry any weight with Muldoon and, especially, Calabrese, who would love to hang this on me."

"Remember when you were ambitious?" Dino asked. "It's like that. Don't worry, you'll talk your way out of this eventually."

43

MULDOON WOKE UP CALABRESE. "Come on," he said. "Where are we going?"

"To arrest Donald Trask for the murder of Priscilla Scott."

"Have we got some new evidence I don't know about?"

"Nope." They got to the car. "You drive." Muldoon gave him a new address.

"What is that place?"

"Trask's office."

"He actually works? How much did he get from his wife?"

"Eight or nine million, I hear."

"He said she had a will leaving everything to him."

"He may believe that, but it ain't so."

"And you know this, how?"

"I spoke to her attorney in the divorce; he drew a new will for her immediately after she hired him, and he let Trask's attorney know it."

"Then that removes the will as a motive for her murder," Calabrese pointed out.

"Only if he didn't know about the new will. By the way, his attorney's office is in the same building with Trask's. We'll have a word with him."

THEY SHOWED THEIR BADGES at the front desk, and after a phone call, they were escorted to a conference room where a man in his shirtsleeves was working at a table filled with stacks of documents.

"Terry Barnes?" Muldoon asked.

"One and the same. What can I do for you, and make it fast."

"You represented Donald Trask in his divorce?"

"Yes."

"Do you remember Herbert Fisher mentioning to you on a phone call that he was drawing up a new will for Priscilla Scott?"

Barnes screwed up his forehead. "Jesus, I don't know. I've got four hot cases running—just look at this stuff." He waved an arm at the tabletop.

"Try and remember," Muldoon said.

"Oh, yeah, I think he did mention it."

"And did you mention it to your client?"

Barnes thought and took a breath to answer, then stopped himself. "That's privileged information—attorney-client communication, you know?"

"It's a real easy question."

"It's still privileged."

"You know about Priscilla Scott's murder?"

"I own a TV."

"Are you representing Donald Trask in that matter?"

"No, just the divorce and a later real estate transaction."

"Well, the question pertains to the murder, not the divorce, so the communication between you wouldn't be privileged, right?" Muldoon held his breath. He could see Barnes's mind working.

"Nice try," Barnes said finally. "I mean, really nice. A lot of guys would have fallen for that. *I* might have fallen for it, if I had a cold or a hangover. Now, beat it."

They beat it. They got back into the elevator and rode up a couple of floors and found the Trask Fund. They had to back up at the door to let a couple of moving men get a desk into the hallway. The reception desk looked as though it had been pushed to one side, out of the center of the room. Muldoon went through the drill. They were shown into Trask's office, where he was packing files in moving boxes. There were no extra chairs in the room, so Muldoon leaned against the wall.

"What is it?" Trask asked. "As you can see, I'm busy."

"Moving offices?"

"Shutting it down."

"Ah, that's right, with your newfound wealth from your ex-wife's will, you've no need to work anymore, have you?"

Trask shrugged. "So what? If I want to be a gentleman of leisure, that's my business."

"Just out of curiosity, what did her estate amount to? I mean, with the death of her wealthy mother, followed a year later by the death of her wealthy father, her inheritances must have been considerable."

"I guess you could say that."

"How much is her estate worth?"

"Beats me. I haven't seen any paperwork yet. Probate takes time."

"A lot more than you got in the divorce settlement, right? Want to take a stab?"

"No, I don't. I have no idea."

"Fifty million? A hundred million?"

"Could be, who knows?"

"You must have a pretty good idea, or you wouldn't be retiring, would you? I mean, eight or nine million gets knocked down by the purchase of your new apartment; that must be two, three million, and I expect you've got some debt, right? And you have to give your clients their money back from the fund—and the market's way up."

"I'll manage," Trask said smugly.

"Look we can call down to the probate court and get a number; why put us to that bother? Are you trying to annoy us?"

"Nope. I don't give a shit whether you're annoyed or not."

"It looks like you're going to be in a bind pretty soon, doesn't it?"

Trask managed a small smile. "Not much chance of that."

Muldoon stood up straighter. "Then you haven't heard about the will?"

Trask stopped packing files and looked straight at him, something he hadn't done before. "What are you talking about?"

"The new will that Cilla made before the divorce."

Donald Trask's face went slack, but his eyes were still fixed on Muldoon. "What?"

Before Muldoon could respond, the phone on Trask's desk rang and he picked it up. "What? Hey, Terry, what's up? Funny you should mention that, they're here now." Trask listened intently for a minute. "Thanks, Terry," he said. Then he hung up and turned back to Muldoon. "You were saying?"

Muldoon's heart sank. "I was asking if you knew about the new will," he said.

"Oh, sure, I knew about that before the divorce. Her lawyer told my lawyer. Anything else?"

"I got a question," Calabrese said. "Why'd you lie to us?"

"When was that?" Trask asked.

"When you gave us an account of your actions on the night of Cilla's murder. You said you walked home from P. J. Clarke's in the rain, but your coat wasn't very wet. The reason for that is, you hired a car service to pick you up at Bloomingdale's, then you went to Château Madison, and from there you walked over to Cilla's place and shot her, then you knifed her."

"Not me, pal," Trask said. "You can call my car service, Carey, and ask them."

"No," Calabrese said, "you didn't use them. You called Phoenix Limos and paid cash. Your driver recognized your description."

Trask shook his head. "Not me. A case of mistaken identity."

"And no one at Clarke's could put you there for a burger and a beer," Muldoon added. "Not a single person. Imagine that."

"All of which means nothing," Trask said. "Now, I'm all through with this. If you want to speak to me again, call my attorney. Goodbye." He went back to packing his files.

———

BACK IN THE CAR, Muldoon let loose on Calabrese. "Listen, numbnuts, you just blew everything in about a minute. Now Trask knows everything we've got!"

"Did you see his face when you told him about the will? He had no idea. His world just fell apart."

"Yeah, but the look on his face is not admissible evidence that could help us. Now we're back where we started! And that was Terry Barnes on the phone, telling him he forgot to tell him about the will being changed. So we won't get another shot at him on that!"

Calabrese's face was red, and he turned his attention back to his driving. "I like Barrington for it, anyway," he said.

"I'm caring less and less about what you like," Muldoon said. "Until you get a fresh idea, keep it to yourself, and if you get one, tell only me."

"Yes, boss," Calabrese replied acidly.

"You're goddamned right!" Muldoon said.

44

IDWEEK, Stone and Fred went to Bellevue to bring Faith home. A nurse brought a wheelchair, and Faith got herself out of bed, walked the few steps to it, and sat down.

"Not too bad," she said. "They've had me walking for two days."

They wheeled her downstairs and got her into the rear seat of the car with Stone. "Have you . . ." he began.

"No, I haven't—not a thing. Well, one thing: I think the music I heard was high-quality sound, good bass and nice midtones. It wasn't tinny, like from a portable."

"But you didn't see the radio."

"No, I didn't."

"The new information might be helpful," Stone said. "I'll pass it on."

"I'd appreciate that. I got tired of talking to cops very early on."

Back in the garage they got her into the elevator and

upstairs and unlocked her front door. She walked in and looked around. "Wow," she said, "this beats a hospital room every time."

"Make yourself at home," Stone said. "Helene will bring you some lunch. Any requests?"

"Something very unlike hospital food," she replied.

Stone went to his office and asked Joan to pass that on. He called Dino.

"Bacchetti."

"It's Stone. We got Faith home from the hospital; she seems to be doing real well."

"Swell."

"She remembered something else," Stone said.

"What's that?"

"It's not much, but the music she heard was high quality, good bass, very clear midrange. It sounds like one of those small, high-fidelity FM radios you see advertised in the *Times*."

"You're right, it's not much," Dino replied, "but I'll mention it. How does Faith look?"

"Much better. The bruising on her face is pretty much gone, or can be covered with makeup. Her cuts will take a while to heal, but they don't seem to be slowing her down."

"I'm happy for her. Can I go now?"

"Make yourself happy."

Dino hung up.

Stone dealt with his correspondence and phone messages, then Joan buzzed. "Edith Beresford, on one."

Stone picked it up. "Hello, there," he said, with as much cheer as he could manage.

"You don't sound so good," she said. "Is something wrong?"

"It hasn't been a good week so far."

"Don't tell me the jealous ex-husband is still around. Has he hurt you?"

"He murdered his wife," Stone said.

"What? Is he in jail?"

"The police don't have enough to put him away. In fact, there's an opinion in the NYPD that I'm a better candidate."

"Nonsense! You wouldn't hurt a fly!"

"I've hurt many flies in my day and a few criminals, too, but you're right. It's just that I arrived at her apartment for dinner and discovered her body. Homicide detectives tend to consider whoever discovers the body a suspect, and now that they haven't been able to nail the obvious killer, the ex-husband, they're looking at me askance."

"Well, you tell them I said to stop it! I won't have it!"

"I'll be sure to pass that along during my next third degree, right after they employ the rubber hose."

"What you need is to go out to dinner with me. I'll cheer you up."

"I may not be cheerable for a few more days."

"Come to me. I'll cook you dinner."

"I'm sorry, I don't think I could handle that twice in one week."

"Oh, God, I can't believe I said that."

"Let me get through the funeral, which should be later this week. I'll call, I promise."

"If you don't, I'll just come and get you." She hung up.

Stone called Herb Fisher.

"Hey. How you doing?" Herb asked.

"So-so. Who's planning the funeral?"

"A cousin of Cilla's. It'll be Saturday at a little church in Greenwich, you should get a note about it."

"I won't count on that, but if I do, I'll accept."

"Yeah, I heard the cops are looking at you a little too closely."

"I guess they've got to do something with their time," Stone said.

"At least Trask won't get a penny out of her death. I drew her a new will, as you suggested, and I told his attorney."

"I know."

"Let me know if you need a good lawyer."

"You know somebody?" Stone asked.

"Just call. I gotta run."

Joan came in with an envelope. "This was just delivered." He opened it.

Dear Mr. Barrington,

I know that you and Cilla were good friends, and I hope you can join us for her service this weekend. The information and RSVP number are below.

Yours,
Mary Scott Dunham

Stone handed it to Joan. "Please tell them I'll be there."

"Are you sure you want to go?" she asked.

"Yes, I'm sure." He wasn't all that sure, but he was just going to have to tough it out.

———

THE CHURCH WASN'T VERY LARGE, and it was packed. Stone sat a couple of rows behind the family seats and paid close attention to everything that was said.

The service ended, and a woman caught up with him. "Mr. Barrington," she said, "I'm Mary, Cilla's cousin."

Stone shook her hand. "She was a lovely person. I'm very sorry for your loss."

She took his arm and walked out with him. "Did you see Donald?"

"No," Stone said. "He had the nerve to come?"

"He did, though I certainly didn't invite him. He sat in the back row and got out as quickly as he could."

On the front steps, Stone looked around the parking lot.

"That's his car," she said, nodding toward a black Mercedes SUV driving away.

"I'll remember it," Stone said.

45

STONE SAID HIS GOODBYES and got into his car. "Let's go home, Fred," he said, "and keep an eye out for a black Mercedes SUV."

"Anybody we know?" Fred asked.

"Somebody I'd rather not know, who's probably still limping from the last time he met you."

"Ah, that gentleman. I'd love to meet him again."

"If you do, he'll be armed. Remember that."

THE FOLLOWING DAY Stone called Edie Beresford.

"Hello, you. How did the funeral go?"

"Beautifully, except that the murderer turned up and sat in the back row."

"What chutzpah!"

"That's the word for it. Are you free for dinner this evening?"

"I am."

"Then I'll pick you up at seven. Do you mind if some friends join us?"

"Not in the least. Who are they?"

"Dino and Vivian Bacchetti."

"Is he the police commissioner?"

"He is. We were partners back during my cop days."

"Where are we going?"

"Caravaggio, in the Seventies."

"It's around the corner from me; I'll meet you there."

"As you wish." He hung up and invited the Bacchettis.

STONE WAITED OUTSIDE the restaurant, and twice, a black Mercedes SUV circled the block and drove past slowly. The windows were too dark to see the driver, but Stone got the Connecticut plate number.

Dino and Viv showed up a moment later, and Stone told him about the car.

"Black windows? That's against the law." Dino made a call. "It's Bacchetti. I want to report a Mercedes SUV with black windows." He gave them the plate number. "Pick up the driver and be warned, he's probably armed. Take him to the precinct, write him a ticket, and relieve him of his weapon and carry license. Reason? He's a suspect in a murder." He hung up. "Now we can eat."

They were in the middle of their main course when Dino got a call. He listened, said, "Thank you," and hung up. "Donald Trask is in custody, disarmed, and Muldoon and Calabrese will be interrogating him as soon as his attorney arrives."

"Well, at least they're inconveniencing him," Stone replied.

"And making him madder," Dino responded.

EDIE INVITED THEM ALL BACK to her place for a cognac. She had an apartment on Fifth Avenue that reminded Stone all too much of Cilla's in its size, shape, and elevation.

"Tell me," Edie said to Dino, "is Stone still a suspect?"

"That's for the investigating detectives to decide," Dino said. "I can't tell them not to suspect him."

"But surely, you don't share their views?"

"Not really. I just can't get in the way of procedure for a friend. He'll sweat it out okay, don't worry."

Dino got another call and listened, then hung up. "Trask, on advice of his attorney, has declined to answer questions," he said. "Muldoon will make sure somebody at the papers gets the story. That'll turn up the pressure a bit. Also, he has to get a new lawyer. Muldoon heard Terry Barnes tell him not to call him again, and he gave him another lawyer's card."

"Want to guess who he'll call?"

"What's your guess?" Dino asked.

"Alfred Goddard," Stone said.

"Isn't he a mob lawyer?" Edie asked.

"You're very well informed," Dino said. "He used to be a mob attorney, but there's not much of a mob anymore, so he now specializes in representing people who are guilty of major crimes, having had a lot of experience at that. My guy, Muldoon, caught a glimpse of his card."

"That's the last word we'll hear from Donald Trask," Stone said, "until the trial."

"Are you kidding?" Dino replied. "What trial?"

"There isn't going to be a trial?" Edie asked.

"Not until my guys have come up with a lot more evidence than they have now."

"Dino," Stone said, "may I make a suggestion?"

"Sure, as long as you don't expect me to take it seriously."

"Get Muldoon to send another crime scene team to Cilla's apartment and lift every print anywhere in the kitchen."

"That's grasping at straws," Dino said. "Do you know if Trask has ever visited Cilla's apartment?"

"He wouldn't have done so," Stone said. "There was too much anger in the divorce to get him an invitation. If they can find a single print of his, he was there for only one reason."

"All right," Dino said, "I'll make the suggestion to Muldoon."

DINO AND VIV excused themselves and left, but a hand on his arm kept Stone from leaving.

"Stay," Edie breathed into his ear. "Stay the night."

"I've already given Fred the rest of the night off," he replied.

They kissed, and she undid one of his shirt buttons, slipped her hand inside and fondled a nipple.

"Sold," Stone said, and they took the walk to her bedroom, shedding clothes along the way.

They turned back the bed's covers and got into it.

"I'm going to make this good for your morale," she said, reaching for other parts.

"I believe you," Stone said, then gave himself to the moment and the rest of the night.

———

THE FOLLOWING MORNING at the precinct, Muldoon put down the phone. "The commissioner wants the crime scene guys to make another visit to the Scott apartment and go over the kitchen again for prints."

"As long as they're taking another look," Calabrese said, "they might as well get all the prints off Trask's gun. It's in the evidence room."

"Dante," Muldoon said, using his partner's first name for the first time, "I believe you've switched your brain on."

"Yeah, well, we should have printed him last night," Calabrese said.

"Don't worry," Muldoon repled, "he was printed when he applied for his carry license." Muldoon made the calls.

46

STONE, his morale refreshed, slipped out of bed at daybreak, got into his clothes, kissed Edie lightly on the ear, and let himself out of her apartment. Downstairs, he walked briskly through the lobby, nodded at the desk man, and allowed the doorman to get him a cab.

A half hour later he was in his own bed, eating his usual breakfast, when his cell phone rang. "Hello?"

"You sneaked out on me," Edie said, petulantly.

"I didn't know how long you might want to sleep," he replied.

"I was looking forward to waking you," she said.

"My apologies. When next we meet I'll find a way to make it up to you."

"I'll accept that promise," she said, then hung up.

THAT AFTERNOON, Donald Trask sat across the desk from his new attorney, Alfred Goddard.

"Call me Alfie," the lawyer said. "You like to be called Don?"

"I prefer Donald."

"Okay, let me tell you how this is going to go, Don: first of all, you're through talking to the cops." He plucked a few cards from a tray on his desk and shoved them across. "Anybody asks you anything, like, 'Isn't it a nice day?' you give him my card and tell him to call me. Do you clearly understand that?"

"I do."

"If you should find yourself temporarily in a jail cell, especially don't talk to anybody there. The DA is notorious for producing cellmate witnesses who swear the defendant made a full and complete confession, and the prisons are full of people who talked to cellmates."

"I understand," Trask replied.

"I want you to understand something else," Goddard said. "If you went to trial tomorrow, I'd get you off scot-free, based on what they've got now for evidence."

"That's encouraging."

"The thing is not to give them another shred of evidence for free."

"Do you want to know whether I did it?"

"No, and I'll tell you why. If you told me you did it, then I couldn't put you on the stand and allow you to deny it. That would put me in deep shit, as well as you."

"I understand."

"Anything else you say to me is privileged—attorney-client relationship—so, apart from copping to the crime, feel free to talk."

"All right, why couldn't they convict me now with the evidence they have? Can't a jury do anything they like?"

"It's my job to see that they want for you what I want for you, and I'm good at it. I have one client who never confessed to me, but I believe had personally committed at least a dozen murders. He's never served a day in prison."

"Good work," Trask replied.

"Another thing to remember, Don. The cops are not legally required to tell you the truth. They can tell you they've got movies of you killing your wife, if they feel like it. And if you fall for such a lie, you're done. All the more reason not to talk to them, or even listen to them."

"I'll remember," Trask said.

"Donald, have you got a temper?"

Trask shrugged. "Sometimes."

"Not anymore. You can't afford it. If somebody at a cocktail party accuses you of murdering your wife, politely deny it and find somebody else to talk to."

"All right."

"If somebody in a bar takes a swing at you because you were looking at his girlfriend's tits, get up, apologize, pay his bar tab, and get out of there."

"All right."

"From now on, Don, you're going to have to work at being the nicest guy in the world—even to the fucking media. If somebody points a camera at you and sticks a mic in your face, give him a little smile and say, 'I'm sorry, but I'm sure you know that I can't talk about that right now.' Remember, in the unlikely event that this should ever go to trial, there will be future members of your jury watching this on TV."

"All right."

"Help old ladies across the street, and if somebody's dog

bites you, laugh it off, pat him on the head, and get a rabies shot."

Goddard got up and walked him to the door. "Just relax, Don. Keep your mouth shut and everything will be all right."

Trask decided to believe that.

As he walked out of the office building Trask was surprised to see the two detectives, Muldoon and Calabrese, sitting in their car watching him. Muldoon even took a cell phone photo of him. Trask smiled, gave them a little wave, and crossed the street to get a cab.

"He looks awful happy," Calabrese said.

"Don't worry about it," Muldoon said. "He's just had the pep talk from Alfie Goddard, that's all. He's still scared shitless."

47

STONE AND DINO met at their club, known to its members as the Club, and to hardly anyone else. The Club occupied a double-width townhouse in the East Sixties, and also had a garage, which allowed its members to enter the building discreetly.

They had a drink at the bar first and subtly gawked at their fellow members—senators, moguls, athletes, and the occasional movie star, in town to do publicity on his or her new film.

"I've got news," Dino said, taking care not to be overheard.

"I hope it's good news," Stone said.

"It's sorta good news," Dino replied.

"How sorta?"

"About seventy-one percent."

"Seventy-one percent of what?"

"Seventy-one-percent chance of being a hit."

"A hit record?"

"A hit print. The crime scene people went back to Cilla's apartment, which is still an official crime scene, and went over the kitchen with an extremely fine-tooth comb. They came up with a partial print on the wall phone."

"That's fantastic!" Stone enthused.

"Not yet."

"What do you mean?"

"I mean, we don't know yet when he touched it, but the computer that compares prints with our arrest database says the partial has a seventy-one-percent chance of belonging to Donald Trask."

"Couldn't it be encouraged to change that to ninety-nine percent?" Stone asked.

"You don't encourage computers, and they don't have a sense of humor, either."

"Well, seventy-one percent is a lot better than it might be."

"Yeah? Alfie Goddard is going to tell the jury that there's a twenty-nine percent chance that the print belongs to one of the other millions in the national crime database, and that constitutes reasonable doubt."

"Then put an expert on the stand who'll testify that a score of seventy-one percent is a near-certainty, and there's no room for reasonable doubt."

"Then Alfie will put his expert on," Dino said, "and when he gets through, the jury will be so screwed up that their own confusion will constitute reasonable doubt."

"Well, at least it's a hundred-percent certainty that it's not *my* fingerprint," Stone said with some satisfaction.

"Well . . . no, sorta," Dino replied.

"What do you mean?"

"I mean they also found a print on the phone that the computer says is one hundred percent yours."

"But . . ."

Dino raised a hand to stop him. "But you used that phone to call nine-one-one, didn't you?"

Stone slapped his forehead. "I should have used my cell phone."

"No, you did the right thing. Now they have a recording of the call with a time stamp on it, which, along with your fingerprint, backs up your story."

"Well, I suppose that should be a relief," Stone replied.

"Not really," Dino said.

"Why is it not a relief?"

"Because Alfie is going to tell the jury that, while the partial has only a seventy-one-percent chance of belonging to his client, the police have a full print on the phone that has a hundred-percent chance of being yours. How do you think the jury is going to react?"

"They're not going to convict me," Stone said.

"Maybe not, but every defense attorney in a homicide case is looking for an alternative suspect to his client, and even if they won't convict you, they won't convict Donald Trask, either." Dino put down his glass. "Let's get some lunch, you're looking a little pale."

"I am not pale," Stone protested, following Dino to a table where waiters held chairs for both of them.

"Just be glad you're not on the stand testifying right now," Dino said, sitting down and snapping open his heavy linen napkin and then addressing the waiting maître d'. "I'll have the seared foie gras and the strip steak, medium rare." He indicated Stone. "He looks as though he'd like just the clear broth."

"I'll have the bruschetta and the spaghetti carbonara," Stone said quickly.

"If you're sure you can keep it down," Dino responded.

"You know," Stone said, "if you had two detectives on this who were as smart as Muldoon, instead of just one, they would already have cleared this case."

"Well, Calabrese is young, but he's not stupid," Dino said.

"I'll tell you what they need to do," Stone said. "They need to drag Donald Trask downtown and put him in a lineup so the Phoenix driver can point him out."

"That's a big risk because the driver has already said he probably couldn't identify his passenger. If he fails to pick out Trask, then Alfie Goddard will have another point for the jury to consider. Why don't you come up with an idea that helps us instead of Alfie?"

"Okay, how about getting the two bartenders at P. J. Clarke's who were on duty that night at the lineup, too. They'll fail to pick Trask because he wasn't there that night."

"Trask's story is that he sat at a table, not the bar, and ordered his beer from there," Dino said. "And not picking somebody out of a lineup is not incriminating."

"How many waiters were working that night?"

"Twelve, and they were run off their feet that night."

"They could have picked out you or me, if we had been there," Stone said.

"That's because we're in there twice a week and we tip well," Dino pointed out. "Trask says he's there, maybe once a month. You know how many people go in and out of that joint in a month?"

"No, how many?"

"I've no idea," Dino replied, "but Alfie Goddard will find out, and he'll use it against us at trial."

Their first course arrived, and Stone ate only half of his bruschetta.

"What's the matter?" Dino asked, pointing at the other half of the bruschetta.

"I'm on a diet," Stone replied.

Dino speared the remaining piece with his fork and ate it in two bites.

"You're a pig," Stone said.

"Yeah, and I'm a hungry pig," Dino replied.

"You know, Dino, you sound like you're more on Trask's side than mine."

"I'm on the side of the firm of Muldoon and Calabrese," Dino replied, "and every time your name comes up, they look hungrier and hungrier."

48

IT WAS RAINING AGAIN, but Stone didn't have to look for a cab because Dino's official SUV was standing by in the garage. They got into the backseat, the driver opened the garage door with his remote, and they drove into the street. They had driven halfway home, down Second Avenue, when the driver pulled over and stopped.

"Drop Barrington off at his house," Dino said to the driver.

"Sure, Commissioner," the driver said, putting a finger to his ear to listen to the radio. He turned around. "Commissioner, you're wanted at Gracie Mansion ASAP."

As he spoke, Dino's phone buzzed. He answered it. "Yes, sir," he said, then hung up and spoke to his driver. "Okay," he said, "let's get to Gracie Mansion. Hop out, Stone."

"Can't I come?" Stone asked, looking outside at the pouring rain.

"You're not invited," Dino said, reaching across Stone and opening the door on his side. A passing car nearly took off the door. "Beat it, pal."

"Into traffic?" Stone asked. He crawled across Dino and let himself out on that side, stepping into ankle-deep water in the gutter.

"Is that better?" Dino asked.

"Oh, shut up," Stone yelled, but the door had already slammed shut. The SUV was speeding away, its lights on. He ran across the sidewalk and found an awning to stand under while he waited for a cab. He saw one coming, but the shop door behind him burst open, and a woman ran across the sidewalk and threw herself in front of the taxi.

"Hey!" he yelled at the woman as she got in.

"Bye!" she yelled back and slammed the door. The cab's overhead light turned off, and it drove away.

Stone thought about calling Fred, but he knew as soon as he did a cab would arrive. He stood there for another ten minutes before a cruising black town car pulled to the curb, and the window slid down. "Where you headed?" the driver yelled.

"Turtle Bay!" Stone yelled back. "Ten bucks!"

"Thirty!" the driver yelled.

"Twenty!"

"Thirty!" the driver yelled.

Stone ran across the sidewalk and dove into the town car.

"Up front," the driver said, rubbing his fingers together.

Stone dug out his cash. "I've only got a fifty," he said. "You got change?"

"Nope. I just started work. What's it gonna be, pal?"

Stone gave him the fifty. "I'll get change when we get there."

———

AFTER FIFTEEN MINUTES of dangerous driving, the car pulled up to Stone's house. "Hang on," he said, "I'll get some change."

He got out and ran for the office door, then rang the bell. The town car drove away. "Hey!" Stone yelled at him.

Joan opened the door. "Hey, yourself," she said, then pushed a finger into his lapel. "You're soaking wet."

Stone went inside and shook like a dog. Bob, his Labrador retriever, came over, sniffed at him, and backed away. "We went in Dino's car," he said, "so I didn't take a coat or an umbrella, then Dino got a call and abandoned me."

"Hang on," Joan said, "the phone's ringing."

Stone shrugged off his sodden jacket and hung it on a hat rack; his trousers followed.

"It's Dino," Joan said, "on one."

"Tell him to go fuck himself," Stone said.

"I can't tell the police commissioner that. He might have me arrested."

"Okay," Stone said, dumping out his shoes and squishing across the carpet in his stocking feet, "I'll tell him myself." He picked up the phone. "Go fuck yourself," he said.

"I beg your pardon," a woman's voice said.

"Who are you?"

"I'm Deputy Mayor Whitehorn," she said.

"I'm so sorry. I thought you were Dino Bacchetti."

"Do I look like Dino Bacchetti?"

"I can't see you."

Dino came on the line. "Did you really tell Caroline to go fuck herself?"

"I thought it was you, but as long as you're on the line, go fuck yourself."

"The mayor has asked that you join us for a task force meeting on the Scott homicide."

"When?"

"Ten minutes ago."

"First, I'll need to throw away all of my clothes, which have been ruined in the rain."

"Why didn't you take a cab?"

"Don't start. I'll be there in half an hour. If that's not soon enough, you can tell the mayor to go—"

"Yeah, I know," Dino interrupted. "Shake your ass." He hung up.

"Joan!" Stone yelled. "Tell Fred to get the car out, while I change clothes."

"Fred's out."

"Find him fast and get him here!" Stone went up to his bedroom, hung everything up in his bathroom to dry, and toweled off. He got into fresh clothes and went down to his office, where he pulled on a trench coat, jammed a hat on his head, and grabbed an umbrella.

"Fred's waiting at the curb," Joan said. "When will you be back?"

"Who the hell knows?" Stone said. He hit the outside door at a run, opening the umbrella, then he stopped. He was standing in bright sunshine. The only water around was dripping from the trees on the block. He got into the car.

"Where to, sir?" Fred asked.

"Gracie Mansion."

"I'm sorry, sir, I've never been there. What is it?"

"The mayor's residence: Eighty-eighth and East End Avenue, approximately. Go there, and we'll find it together."

Fred headed uptown, splashing through huge puddles left by the rainstorm. They found the mayoral mansion, more or less where Stone had said it would be, and a guard admitted them to the grounds. Stone got out of his coat and left it with his hat and umbrella on the backseat. "I don't know how long I'll be, Fred. Don't get lost."

Someone opened the car door for him, and someone inside the house opened the front door. The inside door opener turned out to be a leggy blonde in a business suit.

"Hi," she said, sticking out a hand. "I'm Caroline Whitehorn. I've recently gone and fucked myself. Right this way."

49

STONE FOLLOWED CAROLINE Whitehorn down a hallway, appreciating the view from the rear, until she opened a door, which turned out to be the mayor's office.

"Have a seat," she said, "they'll be here in a moment."

"Keep me company," Stone said.

"All right," she replied, taking a facing chair. "What are you doing here?"

"I haven't the vaguest idea."

"The task force?"

"That must be it."

"You're not a cop."

"Retired, a long time ago."

"How come you're dry, when everybody else in the group is soaking wet?"

"It's a long and sad story."

"I'll bet."

Another door opened, and the mayor walked in, followed

by Dino, Muldoon, Calabrese, and a uniformed assistant chief Stone didn't know.

The mayor was Dino's predecessor in the commissioner's job and had engineered Dino's rise in the department. He offered his hand. "Thanks for coming all the way uptown, Stone," he said. "How come you're not soaking wet like everybody else?"

"I lead a pure life, Mr. Mayor. God is good to me."

The mayor chuckled and sat down behind his desk. The others were in various states of dampness. Dino looked him up and down, amazed.

"Don't ask," Stone said before he could.

"All right," the mayor said. "What the hell is going on? Don't you even have a suspect?"

"We have two, sir," Muldoon said.

"And who might they be?"

"The ex-husband and Mr. Barrington."

The mayor laughed out loud.

"Mr. Barrington was on the scene and armed," Muldoon said.

"Don't mention Mr. Barrington and the word *suspect* to me again in the same sentence," the mayor said. "Who's the ex-husband?"

"One Donald Trask, former hedge fund operator."

"I know a Donald Trask from the Athletic Club," the mayor said.

"That's the one," Muldoon replied.

"I can see him as the perpetrator," the mayor said. "The man's a bully and an ass."

"That's the one," Stone said.

"So why isn't he vacationing at Riker's?"

"Sir," Dino said, "we've got circumstantial and inconclusive evidence, but nothing that will convict him." He related Trask's story and what they believed to be the truth. "And," Dino added, "Alfred Goddard just came on the case."

"Ah," the mayor said. "If Trask would just shoot Goddard, we could remove two thorns from our flesh."

"I don't think we're going to get that lucky," Dino said.

"So you want me to declare this little group a task force so it will get your detectives off other cases and make more resources available?"

"In short, yes, sir," Dino replied.

"All right," the mayor said, waving his hands like a magician. "*Pfffft!* You're a task force." He looked around at the silent men. "Come on, one of you must know that joke."

Stone raised a hand. "Guy goes into a soda shop and says to the soda jerk, 'Make me a malted.' The soda jerk says, 'Okay, *pfffft!* You're a malted!'"

The mayor roared as if he had never before heard it. Everybody else pretended to laugh.

"Okay, I said you're a task force. Now get out of here and clear this case." He pointed at Muldoon. "And get Barrington out of your thick head!" He shooed them out of his office.

Stone and Dino walked out of the building and stood on the front porch. Rain was pouring again, and a flash of lightning and a clap of thunder greeted them. Caroline Whitehorn was standing on the porch, clutching a folding umbrella. "I don't think this is going to do it," she said, holding up the tiny umbrella, "and the motor pool doesn't have a car available."

"Can I give you a lift?" Stone said.

She looked at him sharply. "Where?"

"Where are you going?"

"The River Café, Brooklyn."

"Of course. You can drop me at my house on the way," Stone said. He looked through the gloom for his car but couldn't see it. He got out his phone and called Fred.

"Yes, sir?"

"Where are you?"

"They made me wait outside the gate, sir."

Stone looked at the gate that was about two hundred feet away.

"I've got this," Caroline said. She took a remote control from her pocket and pressed a button. Down the driveway, the gate rolled open.

"Okay, Fred, gate's open," Stone said, then hung up.

A moment later, the Bentley emerged from the gloom and stopped. Stone got the door for Caroline.

"How about me?" Dino asked.

"I believe the City of New York provides you with transportation," Stone said. He got in and closed the door, while Dino got out his cell phone and started calling his car.

"That was mean," Caroline said, but couldn't suppress a laugh.

"It's an unhappy story," Stone said. "It will save us both a lot of time if you will just accept that he richly deserves it."

"I'll try."

"Fred, please drop me off at the house, so I can get a ham and cheese sandwich on stale bread, then take Ms. White-horn to the glorious River Café, under the Brooklyn Bridge, where she's having a sumptuous dinner."

Fred got the car back on the streets. "Sir, shall I wait while you eat your stale sandwich?"

"No, I'll have it alone in the kitchen and watch the rain roll down the windows."

"Oh, all right!" Caroline said. "Would you like to join me?"

"That depends on who you're joining," Stone said. "He might not fully appreciate my company."

"It's not a he, it's a she."

"In that case, I'd love to join you. Fred, never mind the stale sandwich. We'll both go to the River Café." He turned to Caroline. "Dinner will be on me."

"Are you sure you can afford three meals at the River Café?"

"Fred can sell the Bentley while we're dining."

"Yes, sir!" Fred said. "I'm sure I can get top dollar in Brooklyn!"

50

STONE AND CAROLINE Whitehorn walked into the River Café and were immediately shown to a table, where a brunette version of Caroline sat waiting.

"Stone Barrington, my older sister, Charlotte Whitehorn," Caroline said.

"I'm not that much older," Charlotte said, offering Stone her hand.

"Ages older," Caroline said.

"A year and a half," Charlotte responded.

"Twenty months," Caroline replied.

"Now, now, ladies," Stone said. "Let sleeping dogs lie."

"Are you calling me a sleeping dog?" Charlotte asked.

"No, I'm simply employing a cliché, to no effect whatsoever. I suppose this argument has been going on your whole lives?"

"Ever since Caroline learned to count," Charlotte replied. "How did you two meet?"

"Stone told me to go fuck myself," Caroline replied.

"That always works with Caroline," her sister said.

"Then he weaseled his way into this dinner by giving me a lift and threatening me with a stale sandwich."

"I'm afraid I don't understand."

"Caroline means that I rescued her from a downpour and ferried her all the way from Gracie Mansion to here, and she only invited me to dinner when I said I'd pay for it."

"That's my little sister," Charlotte said.

"She calls me that because she knows it makes me crazy," Caroline said, "and you didn't offer to pay until after I had invited you to join us."

"Tell me," Stone said, "are your parents still living, or are they reposing in an insane asylum somewhere?"

That got a laugh from both of them.

"I suppose we deserved that," Caroline said.

"You must be related to Mikeford Whitehorn?"

"His granddaughters," Charlotte said. "Our dad was Mikeford, Jr."

Stone was jostled when someone passed his chair. He looked up, annoyed, to see the back of Donald Trask being seated two tables away with a much younger woman.

"Wasn't that Donald Trask?" Charlotte asked.

"It was."

"I read about him in the papers this morning. Isn't he one of two suspects in his wife's murder?"

"He is the *only* suspect," Stone said firmly. "The police finally came to their senses about the other, entirely innocent, fellow."

"Stone was the other suspect, until the mayor cleared him today," Caroline said.

"You weren't at that meeting," Stone said.

"I was, sort of," she replied.

"You were eavesdropping?"

"The mayor often asks me to do so. He sometimes likes to have a witness."

"She's just nosy," Charlotte said. "If Donald Trask is the only suspect in his wife's murder, what's he doing dining at the River Café with someone a third of his age?"

"The police didn't have enough evidence to cancel his reservation," Stone replied.

"And women that young are the only ones stupid enough to be seen with him," Caroline added.

"Are we certain about Stone's innocence?" Charlotte asked, archly.

"Sort of certain," Caroline replied.

"If I'm ever on trial for murder," Stone said, "I hope you two are not on the jury."

"Never mind," Charlotte said, picking up a menu. "What are we having?"

A waiter came and took their order, and Stone ordered a bottle of the Far Niente chardonnay.

"Very nice," Caroline said, sipping the wine.

"I ordered it because it has the most beautiful label of any wine," Stone replied.

"So, apart from the aesthetics, you are ignorant of wines?"

"I didn't say that. I'm also fond of the wine."

"I think you're right about the label," Charlotte said, examining it, "and about the wine, too."

"It's good to have my judgment affirmed," Stone said.

They had finished two courses and had ordered dessert when Stone rose. "Will you excuse me? Nature calls."

They nodded. Stone left the table and headed back toward the entrance, where the restrooms were. When the thick door closed behind him, noise from the restaurant ceased. He attended to nature, and as he was zipping his fly, he heard restaurant noise again, then silence, then a voice.

"Turn around," it said, and it was thoroughly unpleasant, as voices go.

Stone turned to find Donald Trask standing, leaning against the door, holding a small semiautomatic pistol in his outstretched hand.

"You're under arrest," Stone said, because he couldn't think of anything else to say.

"Yeah? For what?"

"For carrying a firearm in New York City without a license."

"I have a license," Trask replied.

"Revoked," Stone said.

"Oh, what does it matter?" Trask said, then he fired the pistol.

Stone had already begun to turn away from him and to sweep an arm toward the gun, when he felt a sharp pain in his head and collapsed onto the floor, striking his head on the sink on the way down. He passed out just as he heard the door slam.

STONE CAME TO ON A GURNEY in the entrance hall of the restaurant with an EMT holding a bandage pressed to his head. His neck was wet and sticky where the blood had flowed down. A small crowd had gathered, including the Whitehorn sisters. "Are you all right, Stone?" Caroline asked.

"I'm not sure," he replied. He tried to touch his head but ran into the EMT's hand.

"Did you do this just to get out of buying dinner?" she asked.

The headwaiter was standing next to her.

"Put dinner on my account," Stone said to him, then passed out again.

WHEN STONE WOKE again he appeared to be in someone's beautifully furnished living room, except he was lying in a hospital bed, surrounded by a bank of monitors, and he had a terrific headache. He groped for a call button but hesitated: Who would show up? God or Satan? This had to be the waiting room of one place or the other. He pressed the button. The door opened and a half dozen people entered the room led by a nurse.

She found a switch and sat him up in bed. "How are you feeling?"

"I have a terrible headache," he said. "May I have some aspirin?"

A doctor stepped up beside her. "How about some morphine instead?"

"That will do," Stone replied. Something was injected into a tube in his arm, and a moment later he felt warm, and the pain receded.

"You've been shot in the head," the doctor said, "but not in a serious way. You'll have a scar on the corner of your skull, but a plastic surgeon closed the wound, and it will be invisible under your hair."

"That's very thoughtful of you," Stone said. "I'm hungry."

"I'm told you had a good meal, but you vomited it up in the ambulance. Between the scalp wound, which bled profusely, and the blow to the head, I'm afraid your suit may be a total loss. However, we've sent it to Madame Paulette to see what they can do with it."

"What kind of a place is this," Stone asked, "that it's furnished like the Waldorf and sends bloody clothes to Madame Paulette's?"

"You are in a suite at New York Hospital," the doctor said.

The nurse handed him a menu. "What would you like?"

There was seared foie gras, a rack of lamb, and a soufflé on the menu. "A bacon cheeseburger, medium, and onion rings," Stone replied. "How much does this room cost?"

"You're not to worry about that," the nurse said. "The Whitehorns are paying for it."

"A policeman would like to speak with you," the doctor said. "He has an Italian last name, but I can't remember it."

51

DINO CAME INTO THE ROOM, walked up to the bed and peered closely at him. "Can't you even go to dinner at a nice restaurant without getting into trouble?"

"What happened to me?" Stone asked, feeling his head. "The last thing I remember, I was peeing in the men's room."

"Yeah? That's it?"

"Is this something to do with Donald Trask?" Stone asked. "He was in the restaurant, too."

Dino shook his head. "The maître d' says Trask left the restaurant with a woman ten minutes before somebody found you in the men's room. Who else hates you?"

"Beats me."

Dino looked around. "Did you bring your own decorator?"

"I'm told this is a suite of some sort."

"Listen, a bed in a shared room in this hospital is something like five hundred clams a day. I can only imagine what *this* is costing." He waved an arm for emphasis.

"I didn't book it, believe me."

"What I don't understand," Dino said, "is how somebody could fire a gun at you in a small men's room and miss. Can you shed any light on that?"

"Jesus, I told you I don't remember. Maybe the guy's just a lousy shot."

"He must have had the shakes, too. I mean, it was what, four feet?"

"I remember a voice," Stone said. "Not so much what was said, just the voice."

"What kind of voice?"

"Male. Unpleasant."

"Hey, that's a big help; I'll put out an APB for males with unpleasant voices."

"I remember getting up from the table, and Trask's table was empty. I guess I didn't see him leave."

"Well, you were having dinner with two beautiful women: Who can blame you? It's nice of you to confirm Trask's alibi, though." Dino touched Stone's forehead. "You've got a bump there, and it's going to turn into a bruise. How'd that happen?"

"Are you trying to trick me into remembering?" Stone asked.

There was a knock at the door and a waiter entered, pushing a room service cart.

"What's this?" Dino asked.

"Food," Stone replied, handing him the menu. "You want something?"

"Thanks, I ate."

The waiter whipped off the silver cover and presented the burger. "Would you like it on your table, sir?"

Stone nodded.

The man pushed the table to Stone's bed and positioned it, then served the burger and a glass of water.

"What, no wine?" Dino asked. "And didn't you already eat at the restaurant?"

"The doctor told me I threw up in the ambulance. They've sent my suit to Madame Paulette's." Stone took a bite of the burger. "Perfect," he said, "and so are the onion rings. Listen, I don't know where my cell phone is. Will you call Joan and ask her to bring me a complete change of clothes?"

"Yeah, okay," Dino said.

"Who are you assigning to my case?"

"Muldoon and Calabrese, who else?"

"Who else?" Stone echoed.

"They're probably still at the restaurant."

"Having a good meal, no doubt."

"They'll get around to you, don't worry."

"Have you posted a guard on my door?"

"For what?"

"To protect me. Somebody just tried to shoot me in the head, you know."

"He'd never get to you in this joint. I had to flash my badge three times to make it to the room. Sorry, suite."

The nurse ushered in Muldoon and Calabrese. They pulled up chairs and watched Stone eat his cheeseburger.

"Something I can do for you?" Stone asked between swallows.

"Yeah," Muldoon said, "give us your account of how you got shot."

"I'm sorry, I don't remember being shot."

"He's also had a blow to his forehead," the nurse said, helpfully. "It's no surprise that he can't remember."

"He remembers a voice," Dino said, "male and unpleasant." Muldoon made a note. "What . . ."

"He doesn't remember what the voice said."

"Sorry about that, fellas," Stone said. "Does that make me the chief suspect in my shooting?"

"Very amusing," Muldoon said with a straight face. "We checked your weapon, it hadn't been fired. Did you know that Donald Trask was also in the restaurant?"

"Yes, but his table was empty when I got up to go to the men's room."

"That's what the headwaiter said, too."

Another knock at the door, and the Whitehorn sisters entered the room. "Are we disturbing you?" Caroline asked.

"No, ma'am," Muldoon said. "We were just leaving." They left.

"You've met Dino Bacchetti, haven't you, Charlotte?"

"I haven't," Charlotte said, and Stone introduced them.

Stone pushed his tray table away. "Thank you for coming to see me."

"It's the least we could do," Caroline said. "I mean, if you hadn't been having dinner with us, this wouldn't have happened. Did they catch him?"

"Catch who?" Dino asked.

"Donald Trask. He did this, didn't he?"

"If he did, nobody saw him doing it. Everybody says he left the restaurant ten minutes before this happened."

"Oh." Caroline looked at her watch. "Well, if you'll excuse me, I'd better get back to Gracie Mansion and find out if I still have a job."

"Blame everything on Stone," Dino said. "The mayor will believe you."

The women left.

"You seem to know a lot of Whitehorns," Dino said.

"Only three."

"Four. You're forgetting the grandson."

"Oh, yeah. What's his name?"

"Adams."

"Right."

"They've started ripping out the interior of that hotel already," Dino said.

"It must have been scheduled for a while."

"How's Faith?"

"Recovering very quickly, considering what she's been through."

The nurse came back with the waiter and had him take Stone's dishes away.

"When are they kicking you out of here?"

"I can't leave without a suit," Stone replied.

"We're keeping you overnight," the nurse said. "That's standard with head injuries, and you've had two."

"Now he'll have an excuse to stay," Dino said.

52

WHEN STONE WOKE the following morning, a suit was hanging on the back of his door, along with a white paper bag. The suit was the one he had worn the day before, with a Madame Paulette ticket attached, and the white bag held his freshly laundered shirt, underwear, and socks. His shoes, newly polished, were on the floor, stuffed with tissue paper.

Breakfast arrived, having been ordered from a doorknob menu card, as in a hotel. The waiter swept away the lid to reveal soft scrambled eggs, breakfast sausages, a toasted Wolferman's English muffin, fresh-squeezed orange juice, and a thermos jug of coffee, with Hermesetas sweetener in a dispenser, and a *New York Times* next to the tray. It was all exactly what he would have had at home.

He consumed his breakfast greedily, poured himself a cup of coffee, sweetened and stirred it, then picked up the *Times*. He had not made the front page, for which he was grateful, but he was annoyed not to find a report on the inside pages, either. This was the newpaper of record? He scanned it, then went straight to the crossword puzzle.

The nurse entered. "How's your headache?" she asked.

"What headache?"

"I'm glad to hear it. When you finish the crossword, you can go home."

"It's a Saturday; do I have to finish it?"

"Take it with you. The paper is complimentary."

"I'll bet that's all that's complimentary," he said.

"Your bill has been paid."

The doctor came in and confirmed the nurse's instructions. "Take it easy this weekend," he said. "No strenuous physical activity—and that includes sex."

Stone was instantly horny. The nurse, a plump woman of about sixty, was starting to look good. "When will I be healed?" he asked the doctor.

"If you aren't dead or back in here by Monday morning, you may resume all normal activity, including . . ."

"I know, I know."

Stone shaved with a provided razor, showered, then inspected his suit. "Remarkable," he said aloud to himself. "No blood, no vomit."

His cell phone began ringing, and he finally found it in an envelope, fully charged, inside the laundry bag, along with the contents of his pockets. His shoulder holster was there, but no gun. He answered the phone just before it would have gone to voice mail. "Hello?"

"I forgot to tell Joan to send you clothes," Dino said.

"Yeah, I noticed that. Fortunately, Madame Paulette worked

her wonders and delivered this morning, so I won't have to leave in a hospital gown."

"How'd she do?"

"Wonderfully well. I'm not throwing away the suit."

"How's the headache?"

"What headache? You were right about my forehead, though. I have a bruise."

"I'm sure it's very attractive. What are you doing for the weekend?"

"Nothing, if my doctor has anything to say about it, and that includes no women."

"For a whole weekend? You'll explode."

"Why don't you and Viv come over to my house for dinner?"

"Sold. Seven?"

"See you then."

Stone thanked the nurse and anyone else he could see and left the hospital wing by its private entrance, where a uniformed doorman found him a cab in seconds.

HIS HOUSE WAS EMPTY and disturbingly quiet. Stone sat down in his study, picked up the phone, then hung up. He had been thinking about the Whitehorn sisters, but they constituted a problem. They had both texted him their numbers, but by calling either one of them, he would insult the other. And anyway, how to choose? He decided to play for time: maybe something would happen to direct him to one or the other. He called Caroline.

"Good morning," she said. "When do you get out?"

"Half an hour ago," he replied. "I'd like to invite you and Charlotte to dinner at my house this evening."

"On a Saturday night? You're calling a girl on Saturday morning for a Saturday-night date?"

"Two girls," he said. If one of them was busy, that could be his break.

"Hang on." She covered the receiver for a moment, then returned. "We accept," she said.

"You live together?"

"We can't afford to live apart, at least not in the style to which we've become accustomed."

He gave her the address.

"I know," she said. "I stole your card from your wallet while you were still unconscious."

"I forgive you. Seven o'clock?"

"How are we dressing?"

"Up to you. I'm wearing a suit and a tie, both of which have been restored to me by Madame Paulette, in perfect condition."

"It was a mess the last time I saw it."

"It apologizes. Seven o'clock."

"We'll be there. You couldn't decide, huh?"

He started to reply, but she had already hung up. He called Helene and asked if she and Fred had dinner plans; they did not. He gave her a menu. "Dinner at eight, please, and ask Fred to pick us two bottles of good claret." Fred was as good a judge as he.

DINO GOT THERE FIRST. "Viv's coming from the office. Some sort of flap, so she'll be a little late. Did you manage to get a date?"

"Two," Stone replied.

"Two dates?"

"The Whitehorn sisters."

"You couldn't decide, huh?"

Stone shook his head. "Dangerous to decide."

"So you're hoping one will decide for you?"

"I'm leaving this one in the hands of Providence."

"Maybe one of them will fart during dinner, or some-thing."

"Or something," Stone replied. "I have a terrible feeling it's not going to be as easy as that."

"I hope not," Dino said. "If it were, it wouldn't be any fun to watch."

53

F RED MANNED THE FRONT DOOR, taking coats and directing the Whitehorn sisters to Stone's study. Stone had just poured his and Dino's drinks when the women walked in, wearing equally elegant but distinctly different outfits. Everybody kissed the air. Fred served canapés, then went to help Helene.

The four of them sat down, Dino taking a love seat to leave room for Viv.

"You have a bruise on your forehead," Charlotte said.

"I know, and I can't remember how I got it."

"But your hair covers the bullet wound," Caroline echoed.

"I'm pleased to hear it," Stone replied.

"Have you killed that awful Trask man yet?" Charlotte asked.

"I can't answer that question in the presence of the police commissioner," Stone said.

"Well, you are going to kill him, aren't you?"

"Ahhh . . ."

Dino interrupted, "What else can you do? The man's been gunning for you for, what, a month? Desperate measures are required."

"So, you're suggesting I kill him before he can kill me?"

"It's less work for my people and the court system if you do. Who could blame you?"

"A court of law," Stone said. "I think a plea of self-defense requires a little more immediacy than finding him and shooting him."

"You never drew your gun while he was shooting you," Dino pointed out.

"You were carrying a gun at the restaurant?" Caroline asked.

"Caroline," Dino said. "In your line of work you're constantly surrounded by people carrying guns."

"But Stone is a civilian."

"Semi-civilian," Dino said. "He's carrying a badge your boss gave him."

"All right," she said. "Why didn't you return fire, Stone? Were you just standing there with your dick in your hand?"

"You've seen *The Godfather* too many times," Stone said. "I can't remember what happened, but like Dino, I wish I'd killed him."

"You're not even sure who shot you," Charlotte said.

"Who else but Trask?" Dino replied.

Viv joined them, having let herself in with her own key. Dino introduced her to the Whitehorns and fixed her a drink. "Okay," she said, "somebody bring me up-to-date."

Dino gave her a graphic rehash of the conversation so far.

"Yes, Stone, you should hunt him down and kill him."

"Then you could hire Alfie Goddard to represent you," Dino said.

"God," Stone replied, "I hope I'm never in *that* much trouble."

A voice came from the doorway. "Excuse me, Stone?"

Stone looked up to find Faith Barnacle standing there, wearing a coat, her bag over her shoulder.

"Faith, this is Caroline Whitehorn and her sister, Charlotte," Stone said, rising.

"How do you do?" Faith said.

"Would you like to join us for dinner?"

"Thank you, Stone, but I've already eaten. I just wanted to let you know that I'm going out for a walk. I no longer need a guard, do I?"

"No, you don't. Have a nightcap with us when you get back."

"Thank you, I may do that." Faith left.

"She's very attractive," Charlotte said. "Who is she?"

"She's my pilot," Stone replied. "She's also the woman who survived an attack by the East Side Murderers."

"Oh, yes, they worked in Mike's hotel," Caroline said. "Grandfather says you were instrumental in clearing him."

"All I did was recommend an attorney, who did the rest."

Fred came in and called them to dinner.

The leaves of the dining table had been removed, and it was now round, seating the five of them comfortably. Fred had decanted two bottles of Chateau Palmer '78, and the table was set with Stone's mother's china and silver. Stone seated himself between the two sisters.

They finished their first course, and Charlotte said, "So,

Stone, do you have some sort of fantasy about sleeping with sisters?"

"Oh, no," Stone said immediately, "not sisters: twins."

Everyone laughed.

"Then I guess we're safe," Caroline said.

"Not necessarily," Stone replied. "I'm not inflexible."

"Neither are we," Charlotte replied.

More laughter.

"I can't wait to see how you get out of this," Dino said.

"I suppose my next move should be to just take them both upstairs," Stone replied.

"We're not indiscriminate, either," Caroline said, "but we've never been able to share anything."

"Then I guess you'll have to take them upstairs one at a time, Stone," Viv said.

"And therein lies the quandary," Stone replied.

"Who first?"

"Exactly. They're both too beautiful," he said.

"That's a graceful answer, Stone," Charlotte said, "but not a solution to the problem."

"Then there can be only one solution," Stone said.

Everybody got quiet.

"What does Stone mean, Caroline?" Charlotte asked her sister.

"I think he means you and I have to decide," Caroline replied. "And we both know what that means, don't we?"

"Yes, we do."

"Come on, ladies," Dino said, "you're leaving us on tenterhooks."

"What my sister means," Charlotte said, "is that we never agree on important decisions."

Stone took a deep breath and heaved a loud sigh. "I'm glad to be off *that* hook," he said.

Fortunately, Fred chose that moment to serve the main course and top off everybody's glass. Somebody, to Stone's eternal gratitude, chose that moment to change the subject.

THEY HAD JUST FINISHED DESSERT and were on to cognac when Stone glanced up to see Faith enter the room. She looked very shaken.

"Faith?" he said. "Is something wrong?"

"I've just shot somebody," she replied.

54

STONE TOOK FAITH'S COAT, sat her down, and got her a cognac. She sipped it gratefully.

"Did you call the police?" Dino asked.

"I left my cell phone," she said. "It's in my apartment."

"Did you tell the nearest cop?"

"Dino," she said, "you're the nearest cop."

"Then tell me what happened."

"Wait a minute," Stone said. "Faith, this may not be the best time to speak to the police. You've reported the shooting, and now you need to be represented by an attorney before you speak to them again."

"Stone, you're the nearest attorney," Faith said. "I'd like you to represent me."

"All right," Stone said.

Dino spoke up. "Caroline, Charlotte, Viv, will you leave us, please? Have a seat in the living room, and close the door behind you."

"You mean we don't get to find out what happened?" Caroline asked.

"Not just yet," Stone said, herding them toward the living room and closing the door. He sat down again. "All right, Dino, do you want to go off the record here?"

"I don't see how I can do that," Dino said.

"Then please go and join Caroline, Charlotte, and Viv in the living room, while I speak to my client."

Dino shot him a dirty look. "Lives may be at stake here," he said, closing the door behind him.

"All right, Faith," Stone said. "Tell me what happened."

Faith took a deep breath. "I walked up Park Avenue for a while," she said, "then I started home. I was walking down Lexington Avenue, and I passed the hotel where I used to overnight in New York. Somebody opened a door and walked away, and as the door slowly closed itself I heard something familiar."

"And what was that?"

"Classical music," she said.

"What kind of classical music?"

"Like chamber music. I'm not sure if it was exactly the music I heard after I was kidnapped, but it was a lot like that. I got to the door before it closed and stepped inside. The lobby has been gutted, but it was clear of debris and appeared to have been swept. There was one work light standing in the middle of the room; the front desk was gone, but I could see a light coming from where the manager's office was. The music was full and rich, like before, and it was pretty loud."

"What did you do then?"

"I started walking slowly toward the manager's doorway. I wanted to see who was in there. My gun was in my bag, and I took it out and worked the action as quietly as I could, then I put the safety on."

"Is the gun still in your bag?" Stone asked.

"Yes."

"Please take it out, pop the magazine, and eject the round in the chamber, then put them on the coffee table."

She followed his instructions.

"Now show me how you were holding the gun."

"Like this," she said, holding out the weapon in her right hand and cradling it in her left.

"Your finger is outside the trigger guard," Stone said. "Was it like that when you were approaching the manager's office?"

"Yes. It's how I was trained. You never touch the trigger, unless you intend to fire."

"All right, now set the gun on the coffee table."

She did so.

"Continue, please."

"I could see part of the office, and it seemed to be intact—I mean I could see a corner of the desk and a lamp. I halfway tripped over something, and as I regained my balance, my heel struck the floor, which is marble, and it made a noise. Immediately, the music was turned off."

"Completely off? Not just turned down?"

"Off or down so low I couldn't hear it anymore. I was right outside the door by then, and I heard something move inside the office. I stuck my head inside, and there was a man standing behind the desk."

"Did you recognize him?"

"No, he was wearing black coveralls, like a jumpsuit, and he had a hood over his head, with holes cut out for the eyes."

"Was he armed?"

"He had his right hand inside the coveralls at his chest, so I assumed he was about to draw a weapon. I stepped forward into the office and yelled 'Freeze!' the way I was taught during training."

"Where was your trigger finger at this time?"

"I moved it from the trigger guard to the trigger. Then it was like slow motion. His hand started to come out of his coveralls, and I fired once, at his chest, then the lights went off, and I felt him brush past me, knocking me off balance. I reached for something to steady myself, but I fell to one knee, which hurt, because I still have stitches in that leg."

"Which leg?"

"My left. I reached out ahead of me and felt the desk, and I used that to support myself while I got my leg under me again, then I ran to the door and looked into the lobby."

"Did you see the man?"

"No. The work light had gone off, and the only light in the room came from the lights on Lexington, coming through the glass front doors. I ran out into the street and looked both ways. Some cars passed, but I didn't see anyone on foot."

"Where was your gun then?"

"Still in my hand but pointed down at the ground. I kept it in my hand but turned the safety on and put the weapon in my coat pocket."

"Did you go back inside to look for the man?"

"No, I was afraid to. I looked in my bag for my cell phone, then remembered that I had left it charging in my apartment.

There were no pedestrians in sight and I didn't see a police car. I started to walk downtown, half running, really, but that hurt, so I slowed down and walked as fast as I could without causing pain. Next thing I knew, I was back here."

"All right," Stone said, "I'm going to ask Dino to come back, and I want you to tell him everything you've just told me."

"All right."

Stone went to the door and opened it. "Dino," he said, "Faith would like to speak to you now."

Dino came into the room, sat down, and saw the gun on the coffee table. "Is that the gun you used to shoot the man?" he asked.

"She doesn't know if she shot him," Stone said. "She only knows that she fired, once."

"Okay, let's hear it all from Faith," Dino said.

Faith began again, and when she had finished, Dino started asking her questions.

55

SEAN MULDOON'S CELL PHONE rang, and he answered it.

"Sean, this is Bacchetti."

"Good evening, sir."

"Where are you?"

"Just finishing dinner at P. J. Clarke's," Muldoon replied. He asked for the bill.

"Good. I know this isn't task force work, but I want you and your partner to go over to the Lexington hotel and check out a report of gunshots fired."

"Has a patrol car checked it out?"

"I want this checked out by detectives, and report to me."

"Yes, sir."

Dino told him Faith's story. "I want you to get into the building, go into that office, and see if anybody's there, and if there is, see if he has any bullet holes in him."

"Yes, sir, we're on our way." Muldoon put some cash on

the table, took the receipt, and stood up. "Let's go," he said to Calabrese. "I'll brief you on the way."

CALABRESE PARKED THE CAR outside the hotel and pulled down the driver's sun visor, to show the police ID on the back. They went to the front doors of the hotel and tried each one; the last one was unlocked, and they went inside, weapons drawn. A single work light cast its glow over the gutted room.

They moved toward the light coming from another room, presumably the manager's office.

"Hello?" a voice called out.

"Hello, yourself. This is the police. Come to the door and keep your hands in sight."

A man appeared in the doorway, his hands up. "Don't shoot," he said.

"Who are you?"

"My name is Michael Adams. I'm the project manager on the remodel of this hotel."

They frisked him, found nothing. "All right, relax," Muldoon said. "What are you doing in here on a Saturday night?"

"I worked this morning. I left my wallet in my desk, and I came to get it." He reached into an inside pocket and withdrew a wallet, then put it back into the pocket.

"How long have you been here?"

"Less than ten minutes," Adams replied. "I was going out to dinner and realized my wallet wasn't in my pocket."

"Have a seat," Muldoon said. "We need to look around your office, do you mind?"

"Not at all," Adams replied. "Something I can help you with?"

"We're looking for bullet holes," Muldoon said.

Adams laughed. "In here?"

The two detectives searched the room for signs of gunfire and found nothing. "Smell anything?" Muldoon asked his partner.

"Demo," he replied.

"Are there any bullet holes in you?" Muldoon asked Adams.

Adams laughed again. "I think I would have noticed," he said, pulling back his jacket to reveal a shirt, unblemished by gunfire.

Muldoon pointed at a radio at one end of the desk. "Have you been playing music?"

"It's always on when I'm working."

"What station is it tuned to?"

"WNYC, public radio."

"Mr. Adams, do you own a set of black coveralls?"

"I do not," Adams replied. "I have a set of white coveralls in the closet over there that I used when demo was under way to keep my suit clean."

Calabrese checked the closet. "They're here," he said, "and they're white. No black ones. Some other stuff—a raincoat and some dry cleaning, still in the bags."

"Mr. Adams," Muldoon said, "to your knowledge, is there anyone else in the hotel right now?"

"No, there is not."

"Have you heard any movement, any footsteps?"

"No, I have not."

"How did you get into the building?"

"I have a master key," Adams replied.

"When you arrived, was there an unlocked door?"

"I opened the one on the uptown side of the front. I didn't try any of the other doors, as I locked them on Friday evening when I closed up."

"How long ago did you unlock it?"

"Ten minutes, I guess."

"Where did you have dinner?"

"I haven't had dinner yet. I thought I'd go to an Italian place around the corner and eat at the bar."

Muldoon looked at Calabrese. "I think we're done here. Sorry to disturb you, Mr. Adams."

"Not at all. I'll walk you out."

The three men left by the unlocked door, and Adams locked it. "Good night," he said. He walked to the corner, turned it, and disappeared.

The detectives got back into the car, and Muldoon called the commissioner.

"Bacchetti."

Muldoon gave him a complete report. "That's it," he said finally.

"What was your impression of Michael Adams?"

"Straightforward, not nervous, truthful."

DINO THANKED THE DETECTIVES and hung up. "Well, you heard it. What do you think?"

Stone shrugged. "I think there are two possibilities," he said. "One: there was a third killer and he's still at large. Two: the third killer was Mike Adams."

"Kind of a coincidence that he was there, isn't it?" Dino asked. "But is there a third killer?"

"There sort of has to be, doesn't there?" Stone asked.

"I guess."

"Why else would a man be at or near the murder scene, wearing black coveralls and a mask?"

Dino picked up Faith's gun from the table, pulled back the slide, and sniffed it. "It's been fired," he said.

Faith spoke for the first time in a while. "I didn't fire it at a ghost or a mirror."

"I think you need to put Mike Adams under surveillance," Stone said. "The building, too."

"We've disbanded that task force," Dino replied. "I'm short on manpower."

"Do you have an alternative?" Stone asked.

"No," Dino replied.

56

STONE REASSEMBLED THE DINNER party in his study, just in time for it to break up. The Whitehorn sisters had been waiting for nearly an hour, consoled only by the cognac bottle.

"I'm going to send you home with my driver," Stone said to the sisters. He saw them to the garage and attempted to kiss them both on the cheek, but Caroline, at the last moment, turned her head and kissed him on the lips.

"No fair!" her sister said, then they got into the Bentley, arguing.

Chalk up a point for Caroline, Stone thought.

Dino and Viv were still in the study with Faith. Dino was finishing his brandy. "I think you'd better reinstate Faith's security," he said.

"Oh, no," Faith said wearily.

"There's still a killer, or at the very least a conspirator, on the loose," Dino said, "and he's seen you and knows you're armed. And we don't have any evidence to support arresting Mike Adams."

"What about the radio?"

"There are thousands of radios like that in this city," Dino said. "Possessing one is not a crime, and neither is listening to public radio."

"Dino's right," Stone said. "Viv, will you take care of the security?"

Viv picked up her cell phone. "I'll call the duty officer." She spoke briefly, then hung up. "They'll be here at eight AM tomorrow," she said.

"Here we go again," Faith said.

"Tell you what," Stone said. "Why don't you call Pat Frank in the morning and ask her for a copilot, then go fly for a while? That'll get you off the streets, and you need some left-seat time after your hospital stay."

Faith brightened. "That sounds good." She stood up. "I'm turning in." She reassembled her gun and slipped it into her coat pocket, then left the room.

"That kid has been through a lot," Dino said.

Nobody disagreed with him.

AS DINO LEFT STONE'S HOUSE he looked across the street and saw a street-sweeping machine coming down the block, which was empty of cars due to the alternate-side parking rules. Then, right behind the sweeper, a black SUV turned onto the block and stopped at the curb, several houses up from Stone's.

Dino got into the front passenger seat of his official car and picked up the radio.

"Yes, sir?"

Dino gave them the address. "There's a black SUV parked on the opposite side of the street. I want a patrol car to block the street above it and another to block the street at the corner of Second Avenue."

"Yes, sir."

"Wait here a minute," Dino said to his driver, then he called Stone.

"Forget something?"

"You might want to come out and get into the rear seat of my car, and come armed. There's what looks like a black Mercedes SUV parked across your street and up a little."

"Be right down," Stone said. He ran downstairs, opened his safe, and retrieved a Terry Tussey custom .45, then grabbed two magazines, hurried out the front door, and got into Dino's car.

"Okay," Stone said, shoving in a magazine, slapping it home, and racking the slide.

Dino picked up the radio. "Is everyone in place?"

"Affirmative, sir."

"All right, Tim," Dino said, "drive down the block and stop sideways. Leave no clearance for a car to get past, and turn off your lights."

Tim put the car in gear and pulled out, watching his rearview mirror. "He's still there," he said. "No, he's pulling out, no lights."

"Good," Dino said. "Okay, everybody, the driver of that car

should be considered armed and dangerous. Go ahead and light up everything."

Stone saw flashing lights coming on at the corner of Second Avenue, then looked back and saw the car at Third light up. Tim drove up onto the downtown sidewalk, turned left, and stopped in the middle of the street.

Dino grabbed the front-seat shotgun. "Stone, you stay inside for backup; I don't want you in a firefight unless we need you."

"Shit," Stone said, disappointed. He looked back and saw the black SUV suddenly drive onto the sidewalk, stop, see his way blocked, then execute a U-turn and accelerate toward Third Avenue. Flashing lights were in his way. He pulled onto the sidewalk to avoid the patrol car, but the cop did the same, blocking his way.

"Here we go," Dino said into the radio, then opened his door and jumped out, shotgun at the ready.

Stone saw Donald Trask get out of his car, his hands up. He was immediately overwhelmed by cops from both ends of the street.

Five minutes later, the block was restored to normalcy.

"I'll call you in the morning," Dino said, then he and Viv drove away.

Stone went upstairs and to bed.

HE WAS AWAKENED by the phone just after six AM.

"Bad news," Dino said.

"Give it to me."

"Trask was unarmed. The most we could charge him with was an illegal U-turn and driving the wrong way on a one-way street."

"Thanks, Dino, that was a great way to start the day."

He hung up.

STONE WAS AT HIS DESK LATER when Faith walked in. "I just wanted you to know, I'm going to Bloomingdale's. I've alerted my forces, and Fred is out front."

"I'll go with you," Stone said. "The elastic on my boxer shorts is giving out, and I need some new ones."

"Suit yourself," she said. "Oh, and I'm flying this afternoon."

Stone got up and joined her.

Fred pulled up at the Third Avenue Bloomie's entrance, and Stone and Faith got out. "How long will you be?" Stone asked her.

"I don't know, hours maybe."

"I'll get a cab home. See you." Stone went inside the store, to the ground-floor haberdashery department, found the boxer shorts, picked out a dozen, paid for them, and got them stuffed into a shopping bag.

He was just leaving the store when someone shouted his name.

57

STONE DIDN'T KNOW where the voice was coming from and looked around.

"Mr. Barrington!" came the call again.

Stone finally realized that it was coming from the uniformed doorman, who walked over with his hand out.

"It's Eddie," the man said. "Remember me?"

"The face is familiar, but you're in the wrong uniform," Stone replied.

"Ah, yes, it should be the Carlyle uniform. I helped you get Ms. Scott up to her apartment in a wheelchair, remember?"

"Of course, Eddie, the uniform confused me."

"I moonlight over here a couple days a week." Eddie looked sad. "I want to offer my sympathy over the loss of your friend," he said. "Ms. Scott was a very nice lady, always good to me."

"Yes, she was," Stone replied, "and thank you, Eddie."

"Her husband, though, he was a different kettle of fish, an asshole, if you'll excuse my Irish."

"I can't disagree," Stone said.

"You know, when I read about Ms. Scott in the papers, the first thing I thought of was that Trask."

"Funny, I had the same idea. So did the police, for that matter, after they stopped thinking I was their chief suspect."

"I saw him that very night," Eddie said.

"Which very night?" Stone asked.

"The night she died."

"Where did you see Donald Trask that night?"

"Well, right here," Eddie replied, pointing at the ground.

"I saw him walk up here from the downtown side. I was about to ask him if he needed a cab, when I saw his face, it just stopped me dead. I needn't have worried; he got into a town car and drove off."

"You said a town car?"

"One of them from the Phoenix service," Eddie replied. "They run a shabbier fleet than some others, but they're cheaper."

"How do you know it was a Phoenix car?"

"Because they have a tag on the trunk lids of all their cars," Eddie replied. "I know my car service cars. It was Phoenix car thirty-one. They number their vehicles."

Stone gulped. "What time was it, Eddie?"

"About six-fifteen," Eddie replied. "I had just come on duty."

"Eddie," Stone said. "If we weren't right out in the open here, I'd kiss you!"

"Well, now, Mr. Barrington, I'm not that way inclined," Eddie replied, taking a step back.

"Listen, don't go anywhere," Stone said. "I've got to make a call." He got out his cell phone and called Dino's cell number. Busy. He called the detective squad at the 19th Precinct and asked for Muldoon.

"Off duty," a detective said.

"Give me his cell number," Stone replied.

"Sorry, we don't give that out."

"Then call him and tell him to call Stone Barrington right back. I'll give you the number."

"Barrington? Did you used to be stationed here?"

"Before you were born," Stone said.

"Oh, hell, I'll get the number for you. Hang on." He came back a minute later and read Stone the number.

"Thanks very much," Stone said.

"Don't mention it. I heard you was always a pain in the ass, and I like that." The detective hung up.

Stone called Muldoon, and it went straight to voice mail.

"Sean," Stone said, "it's Stone Barrington. Call me, if you want to break the Donald Trask case. We've got a witness—Eddie, the doorman—who can put Trask at Bloomingdale's, getting into a Phoenix town car, number thirty-one, at six-fifteen on the night Cilla was murdered." He hung up and called Dino again. Still busy. Eddie had left his side, and Stone looked around for him.

Eddie was standing in the middle of the street, blowing his whistle for a cab, while a woman with a lot of shopping bags waited.

"Eddie!" Stone shouted. Eddie looked toward him, and at that moment a passing car struck him and sent him flying into the woman with the shopping bags.

Stone ran toward the heap. The woman was sitting up and

looking around, but Eddie was out cold, and there was blood coming from where his head had struck the pavement.

Stone's phone rang. "Hello?"

"It's Dino. You called three times?"

"I'll call you back," Stone said. He hung up and rushed to Eddie's side. "Are you all right?" Stone asked the woman.

"I think so," she replied.

Stone felt for a pulse in Eddie's neck and thought it was weak and thready. He called 911 and demanded an ambulance.

"You help him," the woman said. "I'll get my own cab." She began gathering up shopping bags.

The ambulance took only a couple of minutes. An EMT took Eddie's vitals, and got out a stretcher.

"How is he?" Stone asked.

"Not dead yet," the EMT replied, locking the stretcher in place, "but he's trying. He's got a serious head injury."

"I'm coming with you," Stone said, flashing his badge at the EMT and crowding to the rear. "Which ER?"

"Lenox Hill," the man replied.

Stone called Dino.

"Bacchetti."

"It's Stone."

"What the fuck is the matter? Why did you call me three times?"

"Because you were blabbing on your phone for all that time."

"That's what it's for," Dino explained. "What are you all hot about?"

"We've got Donald Trask cold."

"You mean he's dead?"

"No, I mean he's on ice, or will be when Eddie wakes up."

"Eddie who?"

"Eddie, the doorman at the Carlyle. He's got a head injury."

"As I recall, you've had a couple of head injuries lately, too, and that could be the problem."

"What problem?"

"The problem that you're not making any sense."

"All right, shut up and listen."

"I'm listening."

"Eddie, the doorman at the Carlyle, moonlights at Bloomingdale's."

"I thought you were going to start making sense."

"Shut up. On the night that Cilla Scott was murdered, Eddie was working Bloomingdale's and saw Donald Trask getting into a Phoenix town car. Number thirty-one."

"You mean this guy Eddie can put Donald Trask at Bloomingdale's?"

"Now you're starting to listen."

"At what time?"

"Six-fifteen."

"Holy shit. Yeah. You get this Eddie to the Nineteenth right away, and let Muldoon know you're coming."

"Muldoon's phone goes to voice mail, and Eddie is in an ambulance headed for the Lenox Hill ER. I'm with him."

"What's the matter with Eddie?"

"He was hit by a car outside Bloomingdale's while getting a customer a cab."

"How bad?"

"Not good. He struck his head on the pavement. I saw it bounce."

"I'll meet you at Lenox Hill," Dino said and hung up.

Stone hung up, too. He had a look at Eddie, who was now plugged into an IV and sucking oxygen. He didn't look good.

Stone looked around for his shopping bag and couldn't find it. "Well," he said aloud, "I hope the lady's husband or boyfriend wears size thirty-four boxers."

"What?" the EMT shouted, unplugging an ear from his stethoscope.

"Size thirty-four!" Stone shouted back.

58

D INO CALLED MULDOON, and the detective answered. "It's Bacchetti."

"I got Barrington's message," Muldoon said. "I called Calabrese, where should we meet you?"

"Lenox Hill, the ER entrance," Dino said and then hung up.

DONALD TRASK TOOK the call on his cell. "Yes?"

"You know who this is?"

"Yes."

"There's a guy named Eddie, a doorman, who's in the ER at Lenox Hill Hospital."

"From the Carlyle?"

"From Bloomingdale's. He can put you there on the night. I thought you'd like to know."

"I'll leave something for you at the drop," Trask said. Then he got into his coat and took a gun from his safe. A minute later, he was on his way to Lenox Hill, which wasn't far from his apartment.

THE AMBULANCE had some traffic problems—a wreck on Third Avenue—and took longer to get to the ER than Stone had hoped. Eddie seemed to be getting sicker. Finally, the rear door of the ambulance burst open and the EMT was handing over the truck's gurney, while he held the IV bag over his patient.

Stone clipped his badge to his coat pocket and walked rapidly along behind the gurney. Eddie was wheeled into an area marked EXAM 4, and a nurse pulled the curtain closed in Stone's face. "Take a seat!" she yelled. "You can't help here."

Stone took a seat. Muldoon was the next arrival and sat down next to him. "Tell me," he said.

Stone ran down the story for him, and by the time he had finished, Dino had arrived, followed shortly by Calabrese, wearing a new suit. Stone noticed, because he had just seen one like it on a dummy at Bloomingdale's: it was made by Ermenegildo Zegna, an Italian company, and it cost more than three thousand dollars.

Dino noticed it, too. "What's with the suit?" he asked Muldoon quietly.

"He dresses better off duty, I guess," replied the detective, who was wearing a tracksuit and sneakers. "I think he must have a rich girlfriend."

A doctor came out of the exam room and looked at the

group. "Is the guy on my table a cop? He was wearing a door-man's uniform. Was he undercover?"

"He's a doorman," Stone said.

"One we need to speak to," Dino added.

"He's not conscious and is obviously concussed. We're sending him downstairs for scans to make sure there's no brain injury."

"When can we talk to him?" Muldoon asked.

"When he wakes up," the doctor replied, "and I can't guess when that will be. I'll know more when I see his scans."

"Okay," Dino said to his group, "there's no point in all of us hanging around here. Calabrese, you're low man on the to-tem pole, so you do the hanging and call me the moment he seems to be coming to."

"Yes, boss," Calabrese replied.

"Let's go get some coffee," Dino said to Stone and Mul-doon. They found the doctors' lounge, made themselves at home, and took advantage of the free coffee and donuts.

A moment later, a woman who looked familiar to Stone entered the room and looked around. "Ah, there you are," she said, walking over to Stone and handing him a Bloomie's shopping bag. "You dropped these. I had my cab follow the ambulance."

"Thank you," Stone said.

"I'd have kept them, but my husband is a size forty-four," she said, then walked out.

"What was that?" Dino asked.

"Boxer shorts," Stone replied.

"You have them delivered wherever you are?"

"I dropped them when Eddie got hit by the car while trying to get her a cab, and they got mixed up with her packages."

"A likely story."

DONALD TRASK ENTERED the hospital by the main entrance, walked through a door marked STAFF ONLY, and found himself in a locker room. He grabbed a green coat with an ID pinned to it and put it on over his jacket, then he started looking for the ER. His cell phone rang. "Yes?"

"He's downstairs from the ER where they do the MRIs and CT scans. I'm there, and it's very quiet."

"Then you take care of him," Trask said. "There's twenty-five thousand, cash, in it for you."

"Nope, I'm not that greedy." He hung up.

Trask walked back into the hallway and checked the signs, then he took an elevator down two floors and got off. The quiet was broken only by occasional hums. He walked from door to door looking through the windows, until he found a room where a man on a stretcher was being buckled in and readied for entering a large machine. Outside the door a cart held an ornate uniform coat. He had found Eddie.

Trask waited for a moment while the medical personnel cleared the room, then walked in, drawing his weapon. A voice behind him shouted, "Freeze! Turn around" He raised his hands, still holding the gun, and turned around.

Calabrese fired two shots: One caught Trask in the neck and the other hit above an eye. He collapsed in a heap. "One case cleared," Calabrese muttered to himself. He walked over to Trask, still pointing his gun, and checked him for signs of life. The man was dead. Then the detective heard another voice.

"That's not how we clear cases," Dino said. "Drop your weapon or join your pal."

Calabrese turned to find the commissioner and Muldoon facing him with drawn weapons, while Barrington looked on. Calabrese dropped his weapon.

STONE, DINO, and Muldoon walked into Eddie's hospital room an hour later to find him sitting up in bed drinking soup through a glass straw.

"Hi, Mr. Barrington," he said, "who are your friends?"

Stone introduced Dino and Muldoon. "They'd like to hear your story, Eddie," he said, "if you're feeling up to it."

"My story?" Eddie asked. "What story?"

"The one you told me a couple of hours ago at Bloomingdale's."

"I wasn't working Bloomie's today," Eddie said. "I was at the Carlyle." He furrowed his brow. "I think. What am I doing here? Nobody will tell me anything."

"You were hit by a car," Stone said, "and you have a concussion."

The doctor entered the room. "I've seen your scans," he said, "and you have no serious brain injury. We'll keep you overnight, which is policy in these cases, and you'll be back at work in a day or two."

Eddie looked at Stone. "Does this make any sense to you?"

"Eddie," Dino said, "I think we'll wait a day or two, then talk again." The three men wished him well, then left.

"That's the second guy in a week I've talked to who had no memory," Dino said.

"I guess we're not going to need Eddie, anyway," Muldoon observed.

"Can I give you a lift?" Dino asked Stone.

"Sure," Stone replied.

59

THEY GOT INTO DINO'S car and headed downtown on Lexington Avenue. Stone looked at his watch. "You want some leftovers for dinner at my house?"

"Sure," Dino replied.

"It's weird, but I have a strange feeling of letdown."

"Yeah, I get that sometimes," Dino replied, "when a case is cleared."

"Are you having any luck from your surveillance of Mike Adams?"

Dino shrugged. "Well, we were a little slow off the mark on that one," he said. "But now that we've got Donald Trask off our hands, we can make some manpower available."

"What's going to happen to Calabrese?"

"That's up to the DA, but if he's charged with murder, he'll probably get off."

"You think?"

"The union will weigh in and get him a hotshot attorney.

He'll claim he was making an arrest of an armed suspect, who drew a weapon. Which is true, except that Muldoon and I saw how he handled it."

"I, as well."

"You don't count."

"Thanks a lot."

"Calabrese will be off the force soon, though. You can count on that. Muldoon found an envelope in his partner's pocket with Trask's old Greenwich address on it, containing eighteen hundred dollars and change. He's been tipping Trask along the way. That's why Donald-boy was so hard to nail."

"So Calabrese nailed him for you."

"As a way of covering his ass. Should I be grateful?"

"Well, you cleared a case, and you'll have a bad cop off the force. That's not a bad day."

"I guess not," Dino said, brightening.

Suddenly Stone said, "Driver, pull over!"

"What for?" Dino asked.

"We just passed the hotel," Stone said, "and there was a light on at the back of the lobby. Why don't we check it out?"

"Oh, what the hell," Dino said. "Back it up, Tim."

Tim reversed and set them down in front of the hotel.

"No work light in the lobby," Dino said, peering through a door.

"Looks like it's coming from the manager's office," Stone said.

Dino started trying doors and found one unlocked. He opened it and stood back. "After you," he said, drawing his weapon.

Stone drew his own. "With your permission, Commissioner."

"Granted," Dino said.

They moved quietly into the lobby and toward the rear, from which chamber music was coming. They stopped on either side of the manager's office door, and Dino pointed to himself.

Stone nodded and made an ushering motion with his free hand.

Dino peered around the doorjamb, then looked back at Stone and grinned.

Stone made the ushering motion again.

Dino stepped inside the office, weapon pointed, and said, "Freeze!"

Stone stepped inside behind Dino and peered over his shoulder at the figure behind the desk: black coveralls and a hood with holes for the eyes.

"How nice to see you," Stone said to the figure.

"In fact," Dino said, "let's see some more of you. Take off the hood."

The figure didn't move.

"Stone," Dino said, "you do the honors while I cover you."

"I'd be delighted," Stone said.

"I hope he twitches," Dino said, "because I'd rather shoot him than arrest him."

"I know the feeling," Stone replied. He walked clear of Dino and stayed near the wall, out of reach of the black figure, until he was behind the man. Stone frisked him thoroughly and found a small 9mm pistol tucked into a holster at the small of his back. He also found a flat, plastic box in the man's right hip pocket and he laid it on the desk, then stuck his gun in a pocket. He took hold of a wrist and brought it up between the man's shoulder blades and bent him over the desk. Finally, he reached up and placed a palm on top of the hooded head, grabbed a handful of fabric, and yanked.

"Well," Dino said, "look who we have here." He handed Stone his handcuffs and Stone applied them, the first time in years he had cuffed somebody. He stood the man up and looked at his face. "Good evening, Mike," he said.

Mike remained quiet.

Stone opened the plastic box he had removed and found a syringe and a vial of clear fluid inside, set into a foam rubber bed. "What's this, Mike?"

Mike still said nothing.

"Dino," Stone said, "I think the perp is choosing to remain silent, as is his constitutional right."

Dino read him his rights anyway, then he made the call for a patrol car.

Stone had a look around the office and opened the closet door. Behind a few hanging garments he could see an exposed corner of a sheet of drywall. He gave it a tug, and it came free. "Dino," he said, "closet behind a closet. That's where the costume was."

"Oh, good," Dino said.

A siren could be heard approaching, and a minute later a voice from the lobby yelled, "Commissioner?"

"Back here," Dino yelled back, and two uniforms appeared in the doorway. "Take him in and book him on one count of first-degree murder."

"Only one count?" Stone asked.

"We'll let the DA sort that out."

The cops escorted Mike out of the office and the building.

"Well," Stone said, "I think that somewhere in this building is probably a forgotten room that Mike has equipped for his purposes."

"So, we'll charge him with bad interior decorating?"

"It's better than finding a corpse in a garbage bag on Lexington Avenue," Stone said.

"I'll grant you that," Dino said, taking out his phone. "We'd better get a search started." He started issuing orders.

A few minutes later they were back in Dino's car. "I'll drop you at home," Dino said, "but I won't stay for the leftovers. I'm tired."

Stone realized that he was tired, too.

60

STONE WOKE the following morning and checked the news shows for something on the arrest of Mike Adams, but there was nothing. He was able to hold his curiosity until after lunch, then he called Dino.

"Bacchetti."

"It's Stone. Why is there nothing on the news about Mike Adams?"

"You want the whole story?"

"Please."

"Okay," Dino said, "young Mike called Herbie Fisher at the first opportunity, and Herbie arrived as if he'd been shot out of a cannon, clutching a copy of the DA's offer of immunity on all charges, in return for Mike's testifying against the other two. You'll recall that, faced with Mike's testimony and his logbook of their movements, they both bought a deal of life in prison without the possibility of parole. So, the DA declined to prosecute, and Mike walked."

"Shit."

"No, really. We have no evidence that Mike has committed a crime, unless you consider dressing up like a killer a crime. His gun was licensed, and the chemical in the hypo kit was insulin. Herbie produced a note from his doctor confirming that he's a diabetic. Also, I had twenty men searching that hotel and the adjacent building, and they found absolutely nothing to indicate that Mike planned to commit a crime there. Finally, no corpses have turned up in trash cans."

"There's nothing you can do, then?" Stone asked. "That black costume, combined with the fact that he didn't report being shot at by Faith, indicates he's not quite as innocent as we all thought."

"For all practical purposes, yes, there's nothing more we can do. What we *think* doesn't matter."

"I'm still surprised his recent arrest wasn't on the news."

"Herbie managed to get a gag order for that, pointing out that if the news story ran, large numbers of people would believe that Mike is guilty, when there is no evidence to support that contention. Mike's life would probably be ruined. It wouldn't surprise me to learn that a member of the older generation may have made a phone call or two, as well. Also, if the story ran we'd get our asses sued for false arrest and defamation, and that includes you, too."

"It makes a neat package, doesn't it."

"Look at it this way," Dino said. "The fucking case is cleared."

Joan stuck her head in Stone's door. "Caroline Whitehorn is on line two."

"I gotta run," Stone said.

Dino hung up.

Stone steeled himself for the blast from Caroline about having Mike arrested. "Hello?"

"Hi, it's Caroline."

"How are you?"

"Very well, thanks. I called to thank you."

Stone was mystified. "For what?"

"Oh, I know you're being shy and all that, but your man Herb Fisher saved our cousin Mike from a fate worse than death."

"I did hear about that."

"Would you like to have dinner with Charlotte and me this week?"

"Caroline," Stone said, "I regret that I don't have the emotional capacity or the moral fiber to deal with the two of you, and if I made a choice, it would probably be the wrong one, so I'm just going to have to take a pass."

"I understand," Caroline said. "We can be a little hard to take."

"Thank you for your understanding." He said goodbye and hung up.

Joan buzzed him again. "Edith Beresford on one," she said.

Stone picked up the phone. "Edie?"

"That's me."

"I can't tell you how glad I am to hear from you. Let's have dinner."

"Sold," she said.

AUTHOR'S NOTE

I AM HAPPY to hear from readers, but you should know that if you write to me in care of my publisher, three to six months will pass before I receive your letter, and when it finally arrives it will be one among many, and I will not be able to reply.

However, if you have access to the Internet, you may visit my website at www.stuartwoods.com, where there is a button for sending me e-mail. So far, I have been able to reply to all of my e-mail, and I will continue to try to do so.

If you send me an e-mail and do not receive a reply, it is probably because you are among an alarming number of people who have entered their e-mail address incorrectly in their mail software. I have many of my replies returned as undeliverable.

Remember: e-mail, reply; snail mail, no reply.

When you e-mail, please do not send attachments, as I *never* open these. They can take twenty minutes to download, and they often contain viruses.

Please do not place me on your mailing lists for funny stories, prayers, political causes, charitable fund-raising, petitions, or sentimental claptrap. I get enough of that from people I already know. Generally speaking, when I get e-mail addressed to a large number of people, I immediately delete it without reading it.

Please do not send me your ideas for a book, as I have a policy of writing only what I myself invent. If you send me story ideas, I will immediately delete them without reading them. If you have a good idea for a book, write it yourself, but I will not be able to advise you on how to get it published. Buy a copy of *Writer's Market* at any bookstore; that will tell you how.

Anyone with a request concerning events or appearances may e-mail it to me or send it to: Publicity Department, Penguin Random House LLC, 375 Hudson Street, New York, New York 10014.

Those ambitious folk who wish to buy film, dramatic, or television rights to my books should contact Matthew Snyder, Creative Artists Agency, 9830 Wilshire Boulevard, Beverly Hills, California 98212-1825.

Those who wish to make offers for rights of a literary nature should contact Anne Sibbald, Janklow & Nesbit, 445 Park Avenue, New York, New York 10022. (Note: This is not an invitation for you to send her your manuscript or to solicit her to be your agent.)

If you want to know if I will be signing books in your city, please visit my website, www.stuartwoods.com, where the tour schedule will be published a month or so in advance. If you wish me to do a book signing in your locality, ask your favorite bookseller to contact his Penguin representative or the Penguin publicity department with the request.

If you find typographical or editorial errors in my book and feel an irresistible urge to tell someone, please write to Sara Minnich at Penguin's address above. Do not e-mail your discoveries to me, as I will already have learned about them from others.

A list of my published works appears in the front of this book and on my website. All the novels are still in print in paperback and can be found at or ordered from any bookstore. If you wish to obtain hardcover copies of earlier novels or of the two nonfiction books, a good used-book store or one of the online bookstores can help you find them. Otherwise, you will have to go to a great many garage sales.